ISBN-13: 978-1500238636
ISBN-10: 1500238635

Other titles:
Work. Rest. Repeat.
A Post-Apocalyptic Detective Novel

Strike A Match
1. Serious Crimes
2. Counterfeit Conspiracy

Surviving The Evacuation
Zombies vs The Living Dead
1: London
2: Wasteland
3: Family
4: Unsafe Haven
5: Reunion
6: Harvest
7: Home

Here We Stand 1: Infected
Here We Stand 2: Divided

To join the mailing list, and be amongst the first to know about new titles,
or for more information visit:
http://blog.franktayell.com
http://twitter.com/FrankTayell
www.facebook.com/TheEvacuation

Contents

Zombies

vs

The Living Dead

Waverly-Price Retirement Home
England

5th - 11th March

5th March

George Tull glared at the television. On the screen, the Foreign Secretary, Sir Michael Quigley, was pontificating on the need for... George wasn't sure. He'd turned the set on hoping to hear the news, but expecting to hear nothing more than the oft-repeated phrase, "There are no major outbreaks in the UK or Ireland". Instead he'd had to endure yet another rambling speech from the ageing politician.

"What's happened to the PM?" George asked himself quietly. "Haven't heard from him in, what, a week?"

The Prime Minister had appeared on television on the evening of the 20th February, as the world was reeling from the news of the outbreak in New York, but George couldn't recall having seen or heard of him since. Not when the curfew was announced. Not when the Army started patrolling the streets shooting anyone they found out at night. Not when the supermarkets were closed and the rationing began. Not even after the BBC broadcast the video of that plane the RAF shot down over the Channel. Now he thought about it, all the government announcements had been made either by the Foreign Secretary or, since the establishment of the cross-party emergency coalition, Jennifer Masterton. George had always thought she seemed trustworthy, honest even, at least for a politician. Now though, he wasn't so sure.

A small part of him – the part George liked to think of as his internal optimist – had been surprised at how quickly Britain had been turned into an armed camp. The cynical part, which had grown much larger since his wife died and he'd had to move into the home, was surprised they'd waited until the undead walked the streets before they'd abolished the rule of law.

"The Super-Rabies Pandemic is a challenge to us all..." Sir Michael Quigley continued.

"Bloody liar," George muttered as loudly as he dared. "Call it what it is. They're zombies. Even I know that."

He'd only learned what a zombie was after he'd persuaded Mr McGuffrey, the home's manager, to allow him to have a television in his room. That was about a month after his arrival, two years ago. The rule forbidding them in a resident's room was bent for George on the strict understanding that this would keep him out of the Sun Room and away from the other residents. Watching the plethora of late night films was one of the few new pleasures he'd discovered since his wife's death. Before, when he'd had a house of his own, he hadn't watched horror movies. His wife hadn't liked them. Even old Hitchcock films had her leaving the room.

"Poor Dora," he murmured.

His wife had died four years earlier, when he was sixty-three and she fifty-nine. He'd lost his job a few months later when the company he'd worked for went under. It was just one more victim of the recession whose demise rated no more fanfare than a few lines on the local news. Most of their savings had been spent on every unapproved procedure, foreign specialist, and overpriced herbal remedy the internet could discover. He'd even, unbeknownst to his wife, re-mortgaged the house. When it was repossessed, he'd sold almost everything they had owned, scraping together just enough to cover the road tax, petrol and the monthly payments for his private health insurance.

His former secretary had let him live in her summerhouse for most of that year, but when illness had forced her mother to move into the three-bedroom semi, George had moved out. He didn't want to be a burden, not to anyone. He'd left in the middle of the night and drifted south. He'd travelled slowly, revisiting old haunts he'd once been to with his wife, and sleeping in his car at grubby lay-bys until, on his sixty-fourth birthday, he'd arrived at Dover. It was only the sturdy construction of the barriers that had stopped him driving his car over the cliffs.

George had taken it as a sign. Of what and from whom, even now he wasn't sure. He'd spent that year living in his car, stretching the little that he had, waiting for his sixty-fifth birthday. His insurance policy, the one he'd maintained even when he didn't have enough to eat, guaranteed him a place in a retirement home at the age of sixty-five, subject to a medical exam. After a year of little food and virtually no sleep he'd failed the physical with flying colours.

"Liars!" George muttered as the picture changed to a segment on a former supermarket, now part of the nationalised chain of Food Distribution Centres. "That's the same one as yesterday. Same people too. That one there, that woman with the scars and the streak in her hair, I remember her. Yesterday you said it was Crewe, and today you say it's Bournemouth. Liars," he muttered again.

He hated muttering. He wanted to shout. He loved to shout at the TV. That used to be one of the few pleasures he'd allow himself. Always make sure your desires are attainable, his old man had told him. It was almost the last thing he'd said before dropping dead from a heart attack aged forty-one. George had lived his life by that aphorism, eschewing dreams of sun-kissed islands for less lofty, but more easily attainable homely comforts.

Whenever he'd start ranting at the weatherman or some hapless presenter, Dora would head off into the kitchen. She knew it was a sign of a bad day at work needing to be vented away, but the sight of his blustering tirades always made her laugh, and whenever she'd start laughing, so would he. That had been the secret of their happy marriage, knowing when to laugh together, and when to do it alone. Thirty happy years, he thought, and two thoroughly miserable ones as he helplessly watched her waste away.

He checked the time, 11:30. Lunch was served at 12:10 sharp. You weren't allowed to be early, that was frowned upon. Over the last few days, though, if you turned up after quarter past, you'd probably find the staff had disappeared back to their lounge, leaving those residents who were there to freely help themselves to food meant for the latecomers.

"Bloody thieves. Carrion, that's what they are, picking over the carcass while it's still warm," he muttered, but more quietly than before. He wasn't sure if they could kick him out now there was a travel ban, but he wasn't going to risk it. He knew for certain that there was enough food in the home to last everyone for weeks. He'd seen the storeroom.

"We've got to prepare, Mr Tull," McGuffrey had said. "We don't know how long it will have to last. This crisis could go on for weeks. Months even, and what will we do then, eh?"

Except that George had seen McGuffrey load a tray of tinned sweetcorn and another of broad beans into a suitcase, and wheel it down the drive and up the path towards the grace-and-favour cottage he had at the top of the cliffs. George tried to remember when that had been. The twenty-fourth, he thought. Time was so hard to keep track of in the home, where weeks merged into one another and months weren't as important as seasons. He'd watched McGuffrey go back and forth three times that day, and twice the next. On the twenty-seventh, George had confronted him.

"Just keeping it safe, Mr Tull. Besides," McGuffrey had added with a wink, "it's not like the old dears need all these calories, is it, eh?"

Then he'd smiled and walked off. That evening there had been a knock at George's door.

"Your medicine Mr Tull," the nurse had said. Thanks to a private exam, courtesy of his insurance plan, George had ensured he was prescribed nothing stronger than vitamin tablets, which he got from the chemists at the shopping centre in Lower Wentley. He didn't have medicine, certainly none in the evening when all they doled out were sleeping pills to keep the residents quiet. The nurse had walked in carrying a tray covered with a metal warming dish.

"Mr McGuffrey says you're to take this, as required, before bed." She'd lifted the cover, as if she was a magician doing a trick, and there on the tray was a half bottle of Scotch. He didn't drink, not since the week after he'd arrived at the home and began to work out a plan of escape. He'd given the bottle to Mrs O'Leary instead.

George changed the channel again. ITV was showing a match. He bent forward and peered at the top left hand corner of the screen. Arsenal, one. West Ham, two. The elapsed time read 56:18. He leaned back in his chair and tried to lose himself in the rest of the game. It was hard. His mind kept turning to the world beyond the Channel and across the Atlantic. There wasn't much news coming in from overseas any more, but reading between the lines it seemed as if Britain was one of the few functioning societies left.

It was a week since McGuffrey and the nurse had tried to bribe him, as if a cheap bottle of whisky was going to keep his silence. He'd tried to complain. He'd waited until he was sure the staff had either gone home, or retreated to their break room for the evening, and then he'd called the hospital. He'd called his MP, the police, the local paper and the BBC. At least he'd tried to. None of the numbers worked.

He checked his watch again. He'd never been one for eating lunch, preferring to work through and leave work early to spend more time with his wife. He didn't want to be late, though, because the food wasn't for him, it was for Mrs O'Leary.

She'd gone in for an operation in January. The week she was away was the loneliest of George's new life. He'd visited her twice, the first time he'd got a lift from the vicar, the second time he'd taken the bus. Or, to be precise, three buses and a long wait in the rain. When he'd arrived, he'd been soaked. The nurses had made such a fuss, he wasn't sure they were going to let him leave. In the end one of them drove him back to the home when her shift was over. Mrs O'Leary had found the whole thing hilarious, and not a day went by since then that she hadn't reminded him of it.

Since her return from the hospital, she'd been confined to bed except on the days when the physio visited. After he left, and before having to suffer through the indignity of the hoist to return her to bed, George would take her for a walk in one of the home's wheelchairs. She could manage pushing herself a short distance, but after a couple of circuits of the one-storey complex, George would have to take over. The visits by the physio and their promenades outside had stopped after the petrol stations had been closed. Since then, only the staff who lived in the village came into work. He'd asked them to move her out of the bed but, hiding behind some non-existent health and safety regulation, they'd refused.

He'd been hoping that perhaps someone would come and collect her. She had a grandson in Ireland, Donald, who'd visited just before Christmas. He'd stayed for a week at the pub in the village, hired a car and taken them both out every day. George had tried calling him, too, but to no avail. Not that there was anything Donald would have been able to do, now that the airports and ferry terminals had been closed.

George had tried, on his own, to lift her into the wheelchair and he thought he could manage it, but; "If you can barely lift me down, how on Earth are you going to get me back up to the bed?" she'd asked, in her soft Irish brogue.

Arsenal scored an equaliser. He checked the time again. 11:47. Still too early.

There were seventeen residents left in the home. The living dead, he'd called them up until a few weeks ago, but only within Mrs O'Leary's hearing. That didn't seem quite so funny now.

She was sixty-nine years old, and the only resident confined to a bed. George, at sixty-seven was the youngest. The others were old enough to remember the War, but young enough that none of them had had an active part in it. To them it was a time of rose-tinted rationing and halcyon summers where adults had far more to concern themselves with than truant delinquents. They'd grown up in a time when it was more than acceptable for places like the home to display signs reading "No dogs, no blacks, no Irish". By the disdainful way that he and Mrs O'Leary were treated it was clear that they wished they were still living in them. George didn't mind so much, not since he'd come up with his plan.

On Mondays, Tuesdays, Fridays, and Saturdays, George worked for four hours a day in the back room of Mr Singh's electrical shop in the village, learning how to fix computers and home appliances. He didn't get paid because that would have invalidated his insurance, but he got fed. They were proper meals too, not like the textureless, tasteless mush the home served up three times a day. It had taken months, but he'd finally learned enough to get an interview lined up at the refurbishment company in the business park at Lower Wentley. If he got the job he would earn enough to rent a place of his own. It would only be something small, nothing like the house he and Dora had had, probably one of the pokey little studio flats they were building out by the train station. It would be small, but it would be his.

Then there had been New York. The 20ᵗʰ February. Dora's birthday. He'd been in the shop, and watched the television with Mr Singh and his wife as the unbelievable events unfolded. Everyone in the country had watched that, everyone except the residents of the home. They'd not even known about it until he'd got back. He'd told them or, rather, he'd tried to.

The only television in the home, other than his, was in the Sun Room, a dreary den of easy-clean sofas and Formica tables. He'd raced in and turned the set on. Old Mr Roberts had turned it off after a few minutes, saying scenes like that "were an unwarranted disturbance". But it had been on long enough for everyone there to see a blood stained creature, its back broken, its legs twisted, tear a woman apart outside a shopping centre.

When George had started to protest at Roberts turning it off, McGuffrey had said, "What does it matter? That's far away. Not our concern, is it?" So George had retreated back to his room and watched the reports as they came in. He stayed up all night, sitting bare inches from the screen the volume on low, pausing only to walk down the corridor to keep Mrs O'Leary informed.

That night, he'd not slept. Early on the 21ˢᵗ February he'd opened his box and taken out the remains of his life savings. He'd gone to the reception area and waited anxiously for the doors to be unlocked. Then he'd walked down the drive to the footpath that led through the woods and down to the village. He'd been waiting outside when Pauline Fellows came to open the organic grocers. He'd spent £150 on tins and packets of food. She wouldn't sell him any more.

It had taken him five trips to carry the food the hundred yards to the flat Mr and Mrs Singh had over their shop. By the time he had collected his last few bags, Pauline had thrown the closed sign over the door and was emptying the shelves into the back of her car.

He got back from his seventh trip to town at half past five, just as the dinner bell was sounding. Exhausted, and with the doors to the home about to close for the day, he'd deposited his haul in his room and gone to the dining hall. He'd toyed dispiritedly with his lacklustre shepherd's pie, then visited with Mrs O'Leary for half an hour before heading back to his room and collapsing in front of the television. He was just in time to hear the news that there were zombies in Paris and that France was being torn apart by riots. They had nationalised the press soon after that.

West Ham scored. It was a marvellous goal. The striker tackled a mid-fielder just outside the West Ham goal, ran with the ball all the way up to the half way line and then kicked it all the way down the pitch. The goalie didn't see it coming until too late. He dived. George wasn't sure that the ball was going in, but, with less than an inch to spare, it slammed into the bottom left corner of the net. That should have had supporters from both sides leaping to their feet. It was the sort of thing you paid the astronomical price of a season ticket for. But there was no crowd. The stands were empty. The matches were played, but no one was there to watch. He didn't even know who the players were, it certainly wasn't the team they'd been fielding a month before.

He checked the time. 11:51. Stiffly, he got out of his chair and turned the set off. He'd like to see the final score, but the match would be replayed later. He could watch it then. Or he could watch a different game. Who won, who lost or even who played the game didn't matter, not any more.

The dining hall wasn't empty. Mr Pappadopolis, Mrs Ackroyd, Mr Carter, and Miss Conner were there. They were always the first in the queue because they spent most of their waking hours playing an eternal game of bridge at the long table by the never-opened French doors. As long as they vacated the room just long enough for Janice to slop a mop around the floor, their cards were never disturbed. By some unfair rule of possession, they now got that table for breakfast, lunch, and dinner. They always started queuing as soon as they heard the clatter of serving trays and the laying out of the plates.

George nodded a polite greeting, even managing a slight smile, but they ignored him. They always did. That infuriated him. Was he the only one who realised that the world had changed? Maybe they did realise, maybe that was why they were clinging to their routine. George checked his watch 12:05, almost feeding time. It was odd though. He couldn't hear any sounds from the kitchen.

The food in the storeroom was now supplemented by a ration from their Local Food Distribution Centre, or, as he knew it better, the two-storey supermarket in the shopping centre at Lower Wentley, ten miles away. Everyone got a ration, and according to Mrs Singh it wasn't very much.

On the afternoon of the 24th, planning on collecting the rest of his tins and packets from the Singhs', he'd gone down to the village. He'd had to sneak out of the home as McGuffrey had issued a stern warning, unnecessary for all bar George, that no one should stray further than the plinth at the bottom of the drive. When he'd arrived, he'd found the couple sharing a meal with the vicar.

For a meagre ration of two hundred grams of rice, a jar of bolognese sauce and two vitamin tablets, the Singhs had stood in line for four hours. According to the vicar they had been the lucky ones. She'd gone to collect her ration after an extended morning service and hadn't arrived at the supermarket until midday. By two o'clock, when she'd been halfway along the queue, the food had run out. She'd said there would have been a riot if the soldiers hadn't been there.

12:10. He shook his watch and glanced towards the door.

The vicar was notorious in the village for her inability to cook, and the Singhs didn't keep much food in the flat, using most of the space as an annex for their repair business, but they'd not touched his stack of tins. He'd gruffly told them to take what they needed. They'd tried to demure, but not for long. Mr Singh told him that they were thinking of leaving, all three of them, regardless of the travel restrictions. He had a brother, a government scientist, who owned a house in north Wales which he rarely used as he spent most of his time living and working at a lab. Mr Singh said the three of them were going there. He'd asked if George wanted to go with them.

On his way back up the hill, George had been so focused on an internal debate over whether or not he should take them up on their offer that he'd almost been shot. He'd been stunned to see that the group he had first taken to be from the Army was being led by Police Constable Elkombe, dressed in camouflage and carrying a rifle as if he was a soldier. George had not gone down to the village since.

He looked at his watch. 12:15. The kitchen should now be filled with the sounds of slapdash washing up. He glanced over his shoulder, another five of the home's residents stood patiently waiting behind him.

"Bit late, aren't they?" he said, just loudly enough for the other residents to hear, but not so loudly that they'd be forced to acknowledge his existence.

"Hmm," Miss Conner muttered. The others stayed silent.

"Janice been around this morning?" he asked. This time there was no reply.

"Then perhaps one of us should go and check," George muttered acidly. He stepped behind the counter and through the swing doors beyond. The kitchen was empty, save for the unwashed breakfast dishes stacked haphazardly by the sink. He checked the ovens. They were cold.

Priorities, he thought. His biggest had to be Mrs O'Leary. Every morning over the past week he'd taken breakfast to her, helped her use the bedpan and given her as much of a wash as her rigid values would allow. Then he would let her sleep until he brought her lunch. Usually he found she was already awake, waiting for him. He didn't want her to panic, that wouldn't be fair. Nor did he want her to go hungry.

The fridge was locked, so were most of the cupboards. The ones that weren't held little more than tea, sugar, and flour. He had a couple of tins of rice pudding in his box and half a pack of digestives. That would do, at least for now. When he left the kitchen, the residents waiting outside looked at him expectantly.

"No sign of anyone," he said tersely. "Haven't even done the washing up. I think they've gone." Then he turned and walked back to his room.

His box was an ancient, pitted, wooden trunk, three feet wide, by two feet tall by and one and a half feet deep. He'd seen it in a junk shop on the weekend in Truro he and Dora had had in lieu of a honeymoon. It had once belonged to a Napoleonic naval captain who'd stored his souvenirs of war in it. At least that's what the shopkeeper had claimed while Dora was haggling over the price. Other than a few carrier bags, it was the only piece of luggage George had brought with him when he'd arrived at the home.

All that he'd owned which had any real worth had been sold during that bleak year he'd been counting down until his sixty-fifth birthday. He had kept a few items, though, keepsakes and mementos of value only to himself. There were a few tarnished Roman coins he'd bought when they were trying out retirement hobbies during the period when it looked like Dora would recover. There was the wedding photograph of the two of them with her aunt and his uncle, the only family who would acknowledge them after they'd announced their engagement. Then there were Dora's journals, carefully wrapped in the silk scarf he'd bought on the holiday they'd taken after they found out they would never have children. He'd never read them, never opened them, not even during his darkest of times.

When he'd arrived at the home he'd undergone a humiliating examination of his personal effects. Each item, including the journals, had been intrusively inspected out of a need "to maintain the safety and comfort of all our residents." But McGuffrey hadn't discovered that the box had a secret compartment, hidden by a false bottom.

The box was now filled with the food he'd bought from the village. He took out a tin of rice pudding, the half pack of digestives, and two decently sized metal spoons he'd stolen from the cafe in the shopping centre. It wasn't much, he knew, but it was better than nothing.

"Rice pudding for lunch. Very decadent, Mr Tull," Mrs O'Leary said, after he'd explained the situation. "So what are we to do, now?"

"I'm not sure," he replied. She let her spoon clink meaningfully on the side of the tin and gave him a look that had silenced even the most unruly of classrooms during her nearly fifty years of teaching. "I suppose I should look for the staff," he said.

"Or try McGuffrey up at his cottage," she suggested. "Then you're to report back here with what you've found."

"Yes ma'am," he said with a smile.

He checked the Sun Room first, and then the conservatory. Then he wandered along the corridors that led to the bedrooms, and re-checked the dining hall and the kitchen. Some of the residents were still queuing for lunch, but most were now walking the corridors on a similar quest to his own. Of the staff there was no sign. Finally he went to the reception area at the front of the building.

He baulked at the idea of crossing the invisible line behind the desk that led to the staff area, a place residents were not allowed, ostensibly due to the presence of the pharmacy. Instead he walked over to the front doors and pushed. They were unlocked. He stepped outside.

It was cold, with a thin fog blowing in off the sea. He thought about going back inside for his coat, but stopped when his eyes caught sight of McGuffrey's cottage on top of the cliffs.

"The man must be there, where else is he going to go?" George muttered, slightly louder than he'd normally have dared. "And if he's not, then, well… then…" He thought for a moment. "Then I'll just go into town and report the lot of them!"

It was only a short distance, but the hill was steep, the paving stones oddly spaced and slippery from the wintry coastal mist. He was breathing heavily as he climbed the path.

"McGuffrey!" he half yelled, half wheezed when he reached the door. "McGuffrey!"

There was no answer. He thought he saw a curtain twitch, but he couldn't be sure. He walked a few metres back down the path to the small plinth by the road side and sat down. His joints ached. He used not get so tired so quickly. It had been creeping up on him over the past few months. He had found it taking him longer to get down to the village and even longer to get back up. He hadn't wanted to admit it to himself, since it would have ended his dream of one day leaving this place, but he was starting to feel old.

He glanced back at the cottage and again he thought he saw a shadow pass across the window. He got up and walked back to the house and banged on the door until his knuckles were red and the paintwork was scuffed. There was no answer. He was certain now that he could hear an odd thumping and shuffling sound from inside. Slowly, stiffly, he walked around the property looking for an open window, but they were all closed, the net curtains drawn.

As frustration replaced anger, he became aware of how truly quiet the world was. There were no tractors in the fields, no vehicles on the roads, no planes overhead or even ships out at sea. As he turned around on the spot, looking for any small sign of life, he was gripped by a strange fear that he and those in the home were now alone in the world.

He wanted to get away from this place. He wanted to go back to his room, he wanted to close the door, lie down, sleep, and wake up to find the world was back the way it should be. But that would never happen, could never happen, not now. And there was Mrs O'Leary to think of, and what she'd think of him if he went back with more questions and no answers.

He turned to look down the hill to the picture-postcard hamlet that straddled the river. It was an odd little place. The same steep hills on either side that had kept away the property developers had also kept away the tourists. It was only in the last decade when the single-track road had finally been replaced with a two-lane carriageway that the village had bucked the recessionary trend and begun to prosper.

He carefully walked back along the icy path. On the other side of the road lay the woods, through which a footpath ran, leading down to the vicarage and the ancient church that marked the beginning of the village. He knew he could get down there, but getting back up would be difficult.

15

Even if there was anyone with any petrol left still living there, he knew they wouldn't waste it on him. To his knowledge, the only local who ever came up to the home, other than those who worked there, was the vicar.

He hadn't approved of the whole women-vicars business though, as he was never more than a weddings and funerals type of churchgoer, he now wasn't sure why. He liked the Reverend Stevens. She'd made a point of visiting the home once a month despite the frosty reception she received from most of the residents. Even Mrs O'Leary liked the company, since the last diocesan merger meant her priest only made house calls for the last rites. From where George was standing he could just see the vicar's driveway. It was empty, her Land Rover gone. The car could be parked somewhere else, of course, and he couldn't quite see the electrical shop from where he stood, but George was sure that she and the Singhs had left.

He looked back at the cottage. Perhaps he could break down the door, drag McGuffrey out and force him to come back to work. A bitter chuckle escaped from his lips. If he was getting out of breath walking a few hundred yards up the hill, then breaking down doors was beyond him. Besides, as Mrs O'Leary had loudly pointed out when the roads were closed during the heavy snow the previous year and McGuffrey had been forced into the kitchen, "The man could burn water and sour toast". Dispirited by how little he'd accomplished, he walked back to the home.

He stopped in the reception hall. There were rigorous strictures against residents straying across into the staff area, but what did they matter if McGuffrey wasn't going to come out of his house? He stepped around the reception desk and through the door to the nurses' station. The room contained a desk against the long wall, filing cabinets along the short, a few chairs and little else except the closed door that he assumed led to the offices, pharmacy, and the staff break room. He turned the handle and pushed the door open.

Conscious of the rules he was breaking, he walked slowly down the corridor, opening each door in turn. The staff bathrooms were clean, smelling faintly of a more aromatic disinfectant than the cheaper brand George was familiar with from the residents' side of the building. The staff break room was a mess, but in such a way that he thought it might always have looked that way.

The pharmacy had been ransacked. He could find no painkillers or sleeping tablets. As to what else the staff had taken when they left, he was unsure. They had been selective, taking just over half of the medication stored in the large glass-fronted cabinets. He methodically went through those that remained, but could find none of the pills that Mrs O'Leary was prescribed.

The last room in the corridor had a brass plaque on the door, 'Mr RJ McGuffrey BA, BSc, Director of Care'. Inside, on an otherwise spotless desk he found a map and the letter.

"Due to its relative isolation and low population density, it has been decided to evacuate this area. Leaving no earlier than six a.m. on the 7th March and arriving no later than nine a.m. on the 8th March all residents within this zone should make their way to The Benwick Hill Outdoor Sports and Activity Centre, one mile west of Longfield Junction."

The letter was printed except for the place names. Those were handwritten.

"At this muster point, evacuees will be given a physical examination, assessed for suitability for vaccination and then transported to the enclave being established in Cornwall."

Again the name was handwritten.

"Due to the need to keep roads clear for evacuation traffic, evacuees must depart on foot or by bicycle. You may bring with you as much as you can carry, but this should include any medicines you require, and enough food and water for at least two days. In addition, you should bring blankets, sleeping bags, or other warm bedding as well as spare clothing. These items will not be provided during resettlement. Further advice and details of what to expect at the enclave will be provided on the Emergency Broadcasts, to which you are strongly advised to watch or listen.

"A limited bus service will be provided to the muster point for those unable to make the journey themselves due to age, ill health, or other significant factors. This service is available only if those factors were registered with the local authorities before the crisis and with your designated Resettlement Officer prior to the 4th March.

"If you are a Designated Carer for one or more persons, then you must inform the Resettlement Officer on or prior to the 4th March as to how many dependants will require transportation. Please note that for the purposes of the evacuation, an individual is deemed a Designated Carer if, and only if, they have been licensed by the local civil authority to claim the ration on another's behalf.

"If you are unsure whether your property lies within the evacuation zone or if you have any further questions you should address them to your Resettlement Officer who will be located at your local Food Distribution Centre until the 5th March.

Signed…"

George couldn't read the signature. Not that he tried too hard, his eyes were drawn to the date. It was dated the 2nd March, three days ago. He glanced at the map. It was a photocopy of a road map with a crudely drawn circle about ten miles in diameter that took in the home, the village, a dozen farms and a good portion of the sea. He looked at the envelope. There was no stamp. It must have been hand delivered.

"They knew," he said. "They bloody well knew!" He shouted this time. "They left us. They cooked breakfast and went, stealing our pills on the way. Well I'll… I'll…" What? What would he do? What could he do?

He picked up the phone on the desk and dialled 9 for an outside line and then 999. There was no answer. He dialled 9125, the number for the speaking clock. Nothing. He tried dialling his old office number at work, the customer service number printed on the box of bandages, the mobile phone number written down on a yellow post it note with a poorly drawn heart next to it. Nothing, not even a dial tone.

"You don't think he's arranged for us to be evacuated?" George asked half an hour later, when he was drinking tea with Mrs O'Leary in her room.

"Do you?" she asked.

"No," George admitted. "That's why the other staff have gone. They don't want to be the ones left holding the baby. Probably they reckoned someone would show up here, some patrol or, well, someone, and whoever was would be delegated in charge of us. So they all scarpered."

"It's McGuffrey," Mrs O'Leary said flatly. "He's the one responsible, not all these part-timers who never bothered to learn our names." She took another sip of tea "I bet he doesn't fancy the idea of swapping his cottage for a cot in some warehouse."

"Doesn't want to go with us, can't go without us, and can't show his face around here, neither, not now the pills are gone."

"Nonsense," she tutted. "Of course he could. He could have been open and honest about it all from the start. We'd not have judged him any the worse for it. Not that that's saying much. All that can be expected of anyone is that they do the job that's in front of them. No more than that. Now drink your tea. It's getting cold. And then make me another cup. I'm enjoying the indulgence."

George stood up and walked over to the kettle. He'd liberated it from the staff break room, a far more salubrious place than the Sun Room. It was filled with comfortable armchairs, a well-stocked fridge, and a mountain of biscuits and slightly stale cakes that he suspected had been donated for the residents' consumption.

He was feeling calmer than he had after first reading the letter. It was the tea, not the drink itself, but being able to have as much of it as he wanted, when he wanted. It was a type of freedom, he supposed, one he'd given up when he'd chosen an existence in the home over a lonely suicide.

"Yesterday was the fourth," George said, after handing Mrs O'Leary a fresh cup.

"You're thinking of going down to Lower Wentley? Yesterday was the deadline. Besides, how would you get there? You said even the vicar's gone."

"Probably gone. Anyway, it's only ten miles. I could walk it," he said stubbornly.

"Really?" she asked, taking a pointedly slow sip of tea. They sat in silence for a while.

"If I went down to the village, maybe I could find a car," George said.

"And then you'd hotwire it, would you? Or would you just break into the houses until you found a key? And," she said raising an admonitory finger, "what then? They said no cars on the evacuation, didn't they?"

"But if they stopped us, I'd explain," George said.

"Us, is it? And what about the others?" Mrs O'Leary asked. "Our companions in misfortune?"

"Who? The living dead? What of them?" George asked without thinking. Mrs O'Leary said nothing. She just gave him a stern look.

"Right. Sorry. That was in bad taste," George said.

"The way I see it," Mrs O'Leary said, after setting the cup down with studied deliberation, "the government people know we're here. They know McGuffrey was collecting our ration, even if he was squirrelling it away for himself. If they know we're here, then they'll send someone. Now," she added, forestalling his objection, "they may not, I agree, but there's a greater chance of that, than of you making it all the way to Lower Wentley on foot or, for that matter, of stealing someone's car without getting shot by one of the patrols. No, we stay here. And as for our compatriots, well, you can't let them starve, now, can you?"

"I…" George was about to say he could, but then he saw the look on her face. "Fine. I'll see what I can do."

"Good lad. Nothing fancy. They don't deserve pheasant, just warm up a few cans. And," she added as he got up to leave, "be a dear and make sure the doors and windows are all properly closed. Just in case."

"Well this isn't much," Mrs Kennedy sniffed.

"It's what I could find," George said. "It was either stew or a fry up."

"I'd have liked a fry up," Mr Pappadopolis said. "Haven't had one in years."

"Well, you'll like breakfast tomorrow then," George said as equably as he could manage.

"But it's lasagne on Tuesdays," Miss Conner said, staring with suspicion at the inexpertly chopped beef and carrots swimming in thick gravy.

"Today isn't Tuesday, and tonight it's stew. Beef, carrots, onions, some peppers and tomatoes. More than enough to keep you going."

"Probably all night long," Mr Grayson snickered, and the others, some with a furtive glance to make really sure that there were no staff present, laughed too.

"Come on," Mr Parker said, pushing his way to the front of the crowd. "Out the way. Some of us are hungry."

They didn't say 'thank you', but George did get a nod or two of acknowledgement. In the rarefied atmosphere of the home that was as good as an honour from the Queen. George went back into the kitchen to finish the washing up, leaving them to serve themselves. When he returned to the cafeteria everyone was sitting down, eating, and making occasional small talk.

"Look," he began. He wasn't sure what he was going to say, but all eyes were on him now "The thing is… um…"

"Spit it out, man," Mr Grayson said.

"They've gone. The staff. You've realised that, I suppose. There's an evacuation. You might have heard about that on the news." He remembered to whom he was speaking. "No. Okay. They're emptying the cities and the towns inland, pulling everyone back to the coast. London, Birmingham, Glasgow, here as well."

"But we're on the coast," Mr Roberts said in a tone that suggested that this should settle the matter.

"So's Glasgow," Mr Carter chimed in. "Or it's on the Clyde, which is—"

"The letter," George interrupted loudly, before they began one of their pointless debates, "said they were evacuating the village, the area is indefensible. That's what it said. The evacuation is meant to start on the seventh, but the staff have left early, taking about half your medication with them." There was an uncomfortable stirring among the group at this revelation. "McGuffrey is meant to have told a resettlement bod in Lower Wentley that we're here, and then they're meant to send a bus for us. *If* he told them." George paused for a moment to gather his thoughts. "The evacuation muster point, that's where we have to get to, is in Benwick, at that big sports centre there, the one with the go-kart track. There'll be no buses, no cabs, no help. If you want to go, then that's where you have to get to. It's about thirty miles. I'll leave the letter here. You can look at it yourselves. Make up your own mind as to what you want to do."

"Well that's just terrible!" Miss Conner cried. "I'm going to complain. I'm going to write to my MP!" It was said with a finality indicating there was no greater threat or sanction.

"Well, yes, you could do that," George said as patiently as he could manage, "but there's no post anymore, no phone lines either. And even if you could get through, this is a government plan. Your MP knows. They've signed off on it."

"What about our rights?" Mr Pappadopolis said.

"What about them?" George replied. "Look, there's food for now, and I'll cook it up for you, but it won't last forever. You need to decide if you can make it to Benwick. Maybe if you head out someone will help you. There'll be other people, all heading the same way. Or you can stay here, but the food will run out."

"What about you? What are you going to do?" Mr Grayson asked.

"I don't know," George replied, and, dispirited once more, he left the dining room.

6th March

The next day, after the promised fried breakfast, the residents split themselves into two groups. Half embedded themselves in the Sun Room, staring avidly at the television trying to extract any and all information that they'd disregarded over the past two weeks. The other half stayed in the dining hall, playing bridge or patience, or just talking loudly and desperately about anything other than the absence of staff, the outbreak or the undead.

"You missed the announcement today," Mrs O'Leary said when he brought her dinner that evening. He'd moved his television into her room so that she'd have something to do during her long hours of solitude. "Made by that young MP you fancy."

"Masterton?" He said the name too quickly and she laughed. "I never said I fancied her," he went on. "I said it's nice to see an attractive young woman in Parliament."

"That might have been what you said, but it's not what you meant!"

"So what did she say?" he asked, trying to move the conversation onto less treacherous ground.

"They're evacuating the cities. Starting tomorrow. All the inland ones. London too, All to be emptied in twenty-four hours."

"Oh," he said, "so it is actually happening?"

"Seems so."

"You think it'll work?" he asked.

"I think," Mrs O'Leary said after a moment's consideration, "that what they're telling us is the tip of an iceberg so big it could sink the world. And you know what they say, you can't stop an iceberg, you can only ride it until it melts."

George smiled. "That's a good one. You come up with that this afternoon?"

"There wasn't much else to do," she admitted. "After your girl gave that speech they stopped all other programming. It's just the same stuff on what you should take with you. Reminders to wear two pairs of socks, take a spare pair of shoes. Bring bedding, stay with your family, bring water and food for at least two nights. And on and on for about half an hour, and then it repeats."

"And the radio?"

"The same thing. Just the audio of course, but it's the same programme."

"Nothing about us?"

"Nothing about anywhere specific. Any sign of McGuffrey today?" she asked.

"No."

"He might have told them, you know. Someone might come to get us," she said, but without much conviction.

"You want to watch a film or something?" he asked after a while.

"Would you mind?"

He leafed through the meagre collection of DVDs he'd bought second hand from the charity shop. "Brief Encounter?" he suggested.

"Oh, that would be perfect."

7^{th,} to 10th March

On the seventh, the morning of the evacuation, George was woken by the sound of an engine. He hurried outside, just in time to see the small ambulance disappearing down the lane. It wasn't a real ambulance, just a minibus that had been converted to take a stretcher that was only ever used to take residents to the hospital or the funeral home.

He'd thought about loading Mrs O'Leary into the back and just driving them away, but when he'd tried the engine he'd seen the fuel gauge was on empty. He'd fed a piece of wire into the tank, and from the length that was damp when he pulled it out, he thought there was just enough petrol to get over the hills, but it would be free-wheeling down the other side. After that, whichever way you looked at it, it was going to be a very long walk.

At breakfast, a previously prohibited quantity of bacon and eggs, fried bread, and the last of the fresh tomatoes, he'd found four of the residents were missing. None of those who remained had any idea where they had gone or that they'd been planning an escape. After he'd finished the washing up, he went outside to sit on the wall by the gates. He stayed there for most of the day, coming inside only to put together a simple lunch for the residents. He saw no sign of the missing ambulance, and beyond an occasional and oddly shaped shadow at the cottage's window, there was no sign of Mr McGuffrey.

What he was really watching out for, though he wouldn't admit it even to Mrs O'Leary, was a bus or truck or any other vehicle that might have been sent to evacuate the home. None came.

The next three days were consumed with cooking and washing up and caring as best he could for Mrs O'Leary. He checked the doors at night and unlocked them first thing in the morning. Occasionally he'd glance up towards the cottage on the hill, wondering what McGuffrey was up to. He was certain the man was there. The conclusion George had reached was that McGuffrey was waiting for everyone in the home to starve to death. Then he could head off to one of the enclaves, claiming the residents had died, but that he had tried to save them.

At lunch on the ninth, he used up the last of the bread. At dinner on the tenth he used up the last of the beef, and, with the last of the fresh milk gone off, he opened one of the four cases of UHT.

11th March

George had woken after a restless night. He couldn't see what course of action he should take. He couldn't leave the others, nor could they all stay there in the home, not without more food. After breakfast, and after he had deputised Mr Grayson and Miss Conner to do the washing up, he examined the storeroom.

There were now only three and a half cases of milk left. The biscuits and cake he'd found in the staff break room had lasted less than a day. He looked at the rows of packets and cans, trying to estimate how long it would be before they too were gone. Perhaps two weeks, he thought, perhaps less. He decided to go down to the village. He knew that there wouldn't be much there, not if the vicar and the Singhs had been relying on his hand-outs, but he had to at least look.

He took his coat, went down the drive and out to the footpath that led through the woods and down to the village. After half an hour he came round a bend, and caught a glimpse of the river and the houses nestled alongside it. He slowed his pace, with each step nearer his view of the village improved, and his sense of unease grew.

Hesitantly, feeling like he was being watched though he could neither see nor hear anyone, he walked off the path and into the trees. He found a secluded spot a little further down the hill where he could watch the village, hidden from view.

When he'd looked down at the village from the home, he'd been able to make out little more than the rooftops and the patchwork colours delineating flowerbeds from lawns. Now that he was only a few hundred metres from the vicarage, he saw that the windows of the shop, the pub, and the tearoom had been broken. Shattered glass now littered the streets in front of them.

It was a little over a week since Mr Singh had said that they were planning on leaving. George tried to remember how many other people he'd seen on that visit. There had been the armed police patrolling in camouflage gear, but none of them lived in the village, he was sure of that.

Had he seen anyone else? He didn't think so. The village was deserted, that was clear, and going by which windows had been broken he doubted he would find any food there.

"So we're on our own. Can't stay, can't go," he mused. "Or can we?" There were cars in the village, at least a dozen that he could count. None would contain much petrol, but pooled together there would be some. "Enough for one car, at least."

What did he need then? The keys, obviously. Mrs O'Leary had joked about him breaking into a house to look for them, but why not? He'd also need some tubing to siphon the fuel out of the other cars. His eyes were drawn to a small red run-about that belonged to Daphne, the cook from the pub.

In the summers, her disabled sister would visit. A childhood accident had left her in a wheelchair and George remembered being amazed at how the chair and a full load of shopping could fit in the boot of such a small car. He could get that car, drive it back up to the home, get Mrs O'Leary in, and just drive away. Except he knew she wouldn't leave the others behind. Now that he came to it, he wasn't sure he could, either. Which meant he needed drivers. He did a rough calculation in his head. At a pinch they could manage with just three cars, four would be better, but they could manage with just three. He was sure that at least two of the other residents would remember how to drive. And then they would go… go where? He thought for a moment. Cornwall was the obvious choice, that was where the letter said they were eventually going to be sent. His mind made up he turned and headed back up the hill.

"What's *he* up to?" George asked himself when he got to the top of the footpath and saw that the front door to McGuffrey's cottage was wide open. Expecting to see the manager, and preparing himself for at least some kind of confrontation with the man, George walked up the drive to the main doors of the home. There he was stopped in his tracks by a reddish brown stain, splashed across the off-white paintwork.

Gingerly, he pushed open the door and stepped inside. The signs of a struggle were unmistakable. The never-read magazines, usually arrayed neatly on the coffee table, were strewn across the floor. A solitary lilac slipper lay on the floor next to a fire extinguisher that had been pulled down and used, judging by the thin film of foam covering part of the reception desk.

Automatically he bent over to pick up the empty coat stand lying across his path. Then he stopped himself and listened. The home wasn't silent. There was a strange sound, something he couldn't quite place, something he wasn't sure he'd ever heard before. It was coming, he thought, from the dining hall. Slowly, he headed down the corridor, his heart racing faster the closer he got. With each step the noise got louder, until he was only a few feet from the pea-green double doors with their porthole windows. Uncertainly he took a last final step, cautiously twisting his neck so he could peer through the glass window into the dining hall.

The sight froze him to the quick. A trail of blood led from the kitchen to two bodies lying face down near the windows. In the centre of the room lay Mr Pappadopolis, his legs still twitching as McGuffrey, kneeling above him, chewed on the old man's shoulder.

George backed away from the doors. He'd never liked Mr Pappadopolis. There was something about the way that the man with the comic-opera accent was accepted where he wasn't that had created an enmity between them. But no one deserved that fate. The uncertainty that had been gnawing at him since the outbreak evaporated. He knew what had to be done and knew it was he that had to do it.

He returned to his room, closed the door, and wished, not for the first time, that residents were allowed locks. He bent down and pulled out his box.

"Destroy the brain, they said," he muttered, trying to recall all that the news bulletins had said. "Didn't say how or what with, though, did they?"

He pulled out the chain that hung around his neck. On it hung Dora's engagement ring and the key to the box. He unlocked it and, with a grunt of effort, turned it onto its side. The meagre contents spilled out onto the floor. He laid the box down and carefully removed the false bottom. Inside was a bundle almost as long as the box. He took it out and carefully unwrapped the Assegai.

His father had brought it back from the Second World War. He'd taken it from the effects of a blundering captain who'd died during a night offensive that had killed the rest of the squad. It had been in the captain's family for generations, ever since it had been brought back as a macabre souvenir of a massacre in South Africa, and had been taken to this new desert war as an outsized and ultimately ineffective lucky charm.

After the war, George's father, a citizen of Empire and a decorated war hero, had immigrated to Britain. He'd brought the Assegai with him, wrapped in canvas and strapped to the outside of the old kit bag that contained the rest of his worldly possessions. It was hardly hidden, but during the immigration process he received such a thorough examination it would have been discovered regardless. "Family heirloom is it? A spear for a spear-chucker?" the senior immigration officer had said, laughing. "Let 'im keep it."

Dora had thought he'd thrown it out and he would have done had it not been the only thing he had of his fathers. Instead George had replaced the broken shaft, fitted the false bottom to the box, and hidden it there, almost forgetting he had it when he'd moved into the home.

He hefted the spear, tentatively gauging its balance. It was almost like a sword with an elongated handle. He had held it before, but never like this.

He pushed the door open and stepped out into the hallway. His resolve stiffening with each cautious step, he made his way back along the corridor towards the dining hall. Outside the double doors, he paused just long enough to raise his hand briefly to the ring hanging around his neck. Then he shouldered the doors open, levelling the spear in front, as he stepped into the room.

McGuffrey wasn't there. Nervously, his eyes alert for any sign of movement, he moved towards Mr Pappadopolis' body. It lay in a pool of drying blood in the centre of the room. He could tell the man was dead.

There were plenty of small wounds across the body, any of which would have been enough to cause the old man to have a heart attack. Two fingers were missing from his left hand, his face was covered in dozens of deep bloody scratches, and a semi-circular bite mark stood out against the pale flesh visible beneath a ragged tear in his trousers. There was no question as to what had killed him, though. His left arm was unnaturally twisted, white bone exposed where a chunk had been ripped from his shoulder. George forced himself to look at the face, to fix the agonised rictus of confused terror into his memory. After a few seconds, tasting bile in the back of his throat, he had to turn away, back towards the door. Where he saw Mr Parker.

Mr Parker was a bitter man, angry at the world and everyone in it. He'd celebrated his eightieth birthday in November, a dreary affair with a handful of equally sour faced relatives who'd made no secret of their frustration that the old man was still alive. Neither George nor Mrs O'Leary had been invited. To them Parker, and his vocal dislike of everyone and everything, summed up all that was wrong with the lives they had become trapped in. Now, that face was smeared with blood, that expression of universal disgust turned to a snarling grimace.

"Parker. It's me, George," he said, trying desperately to remember the man's first name, and unsure that he'd ever known it. The creature took a falling half step forward, its hand snaking out and clawing at empty air as George took a step back.

"Please!" George cried in desperation as he stared into grey flecked eyes that were absent of all humanity. He took another step backward and his heel touched something soft. The body of Mr Pappadopolis. It wasn't Mr Parker, George told himself, not any more. He took a two-handed grip on his spear, twisting it so that he was holding it like a sword with the blade facing forward.

"I'm sorry," he said, as he raised his arms up until his elbows were level with his ears. "I'm sorry," he said again as he hacked the spear down on its head, cutting through bone and skin, only stopping when the blade was level with the creature's eyebrows.

The body slowly collapsed to the floor taking the spear with it. George bent down and pulled. The blade moved, but only by a few inches.

Grimacing, he put one foot onto the dead man's face, then tugged and stepped down at the same time. The spear came free with a sucking crunch of bone. There was no spray of blood, just a thin trickle of brownish ooze. He wiped the blade on the dead man's coat and looked around.

"Where there's one," he said, speaking only to fill the deathly silence. "McGuffrey. Got to find him. What would Mrs O'Leary—" He'd forgotten about Mrs O'Leary. He almost ran out of the door, not checking the corridor as he turned right, stumbling as he headed past the Sun Room, cursing his legs, cursing his lungs, and above all cursing his age.

He turned the corner and saw two of them. Mrs Kennedy and Mr Carter were both pawing at Mrs O'Leary's door. A door that, like his, had no lock. As soon as one of those hands accidentally found the handle and knocked it downward, the door would swing open and…

"NO!" he shouted. "No," he repeated quietly as they slowly turned toward him. He levelled the spear at eye height, gripping one hand around the butt, ready to push, but also ready to pull it back. "Come on, then. Come on, you greedy eyed, condescending, too-good-for-the-likes-of-us, patronising, self-centred." He aimed the spear between Mr Carter's eyes as he got closer. "Sanctimonious, pompous, self-important, stuck up, arrogant." He thrust out, pushing with one hand. "Bastard!" The spear went in right between the zombie's eyes. This time he kept a firm grip on the spear as it went in, wrenching it out as the body crumpled to the floor.

"I hate you people. All of you!" George screamed as Mrs Kennedy approached. "Had to be the lords and ladies in a little pond. Couldn't be gracious. Couldn't be kind. Couldn't think of what others might feel. What others might want. You're all the same. All worthless. That's why you're here. Not wanted. Not welcome. No use to anyone, not even yourselves." He swung the spear up and overhead. "Well I'm different. Me and Mary, we're different. We're better than you!" he screamed, as he brought the spear down with all the anger he'd kept pent up over the six years since his wife's diagnosis. "We're better than this!" The undead woman collapsed. George breathed out.

"You've been wanting to get that off your chest for some time, I think, Mr Tull." Mrs O'Leary's voice came faintly from her room.

"Aye. Well, you know," he mumbled after a moment.

"I suppose I do. What's going…" she began. "No, I think I can guess. Are you alright?"

"I'm fine. Not a scratch," he added, knowing what she was really asking. "That's three of 'em down, but there's at least one more. McGuffrey."

"I see. Well… you best do what you have to do," she said. "I'll be fine here until you get back. Go on, now."

"Right," he hesitated a moment, but couldn't see any alternative. "I will come back for you."

"You see that you do."

George looked along the corridor, first one way, then the other, unsure which direction to go. What he knew about the undead, at least about these real undead, not the fictional kind he'd become familiar with from the television, was very little. They attacked. They bit, but they didn't eat, not really. They died if you destroyed the brain, and if they got you then you died, then you turned into…

"Mr Pappadopolis. Damn." He realised he should have finished him and the other two dead residents he'd seen before they turned. Once more he headed back to the dining hall.

From the windows, he could see the body of Mr Parker near the door and another one still lying by the window. Of Mr Pappadopolis and the other body that had been by the window, there was no sign. He pushed the door open a few inches and looked through the gap. He could see no one. He paused to listen, but could hear nothing either, though these days that didn't mean as much as it once did. He pushed the door open, his eyes darting left and right as he moved inside.

Mr Pappadopolis was halfway through the door to the kitchen. He must have been in there, George realised, but why? He shook his head, there would be time for questions later.

He glanced around, making sure that the floor was clear, checked over his shoulder, but there was no sign of the other resident. Mr Pappadopolis took another step forward, and George could see past him, and saw the other undead creature behind. Mrs Ackroyd had been in the kitchen as well.

Between him and the two zombies lay the long serving counter. As he watched, they tried to walk through the counter, thumping into it at waist height almost as if they couldn't see that it was there. With each thump and rebound they were being edged slowly along the counter towards the small gap between it and the wall. That would funnel them, George realised. It would force them to come at him one at a time. He raised the spear to waist height, breathed out, and waited.

As the zombie that had been Mr Pappadopolis reached the edge of the counter and lurched forward into the open space of the dining hall, George saw that there was no blood except that which was drying on the man's clothes and face. That same reddish brown ooze he'd seen in Parker's skull dripped from the stubs of his missing fingers onto the once pristine floor.

Drip, drip, drip. George was mesmerised by it, unable to comprehend or understand how such a creature could possibly exist. Drip, drip, drip. Closer and closer. And now it was too close.

George started suddenly, bringing the spear up, swinging it at the creature one-handed. Too low. The tip of the spear grazed along the zombie's throat, scoring a deep line across its neck. It didn't notice, it didn't flinch, it just took another step forward. George swung again, this time aiming at the legs, a long scything blow that knocked it down to the floor.

George changed his grip so he was now holding the spear point downwards and then plunged it into Mr Pappadopolis' skull. The body twitched once and then was still.

He tugged at the Assegai, but the tip was embedded in the floor. He glanced up. The undead Mrs Ackroyd was out past the serving counter and only a few steps away. George looked around for a weapon in vain. The home had strict policies on dangerous objects, going so far as to refuse to serve steak on the grounds that it would require too sharp a knife.

He backed away until his legs banged against something solid. He glanced down. It was a chair. He was at the other side of the room, against the good table with the views of the garden where Mrs Ackroyd had played her interminable game of cards with the other three residents.

He picked up the chair and flung it at the creature. It hit her in the waist, but lacked the force needed to do much more than make it stumble. He looked around for something else to throw, and his eye caught sight of the table's centrepiece – a glass vase containing silk flowers. He grabbed it, turned and saw that it was almost on him. He swung.

It collided with the zombies face, knocking it off balance but not off its feet. He swung again, this time in a windmilling overhand blow that brought the vase down on its head. Both vase and skull shattered. The zombie fell to the floor, unmoving.

George looked down at his hand. There was a cut running the length of his palm where the glass had bitten into his skin. Had he been infected? He wasn't sure. He took out his handkerchief and wrapped it around his hand. He could do nothing more, except hope. Then he retrieved his spear and went into the kitchen.

There was another body in there. He gently pushed at it until he could see the face. It was Mrs Jones. She must have been hiding in there when he'd killed Mr Parker, he realised. It was only a matter of minutes ago, but now that truly was a lifetime. He sighed then brought down the spear onto her head.

He went back into the dining hall, stepped over the corpses and walked over to the last body. It was Miss Conner, he realised, her body now framed by a beam of early afternoon sunlight. He thrust the spear into her skull, then he turned and left the dining hall for the last time.

"You alright in there Mrs O'Leary?" he called through the door.

"I'm fine Mr Tull. Don't you worry about me. How about yourself?"

35

"Well." He took a deep breath. "There were thirteen of us in the home this morning. There's you and me, that's two. I've killed two outside here, and another three in the dining hall. Two more who were murdered. I took care of them, just to be certain, you understand. So that's four residents left. And McGuffrey."

"And yourself?" she asked again.

He looked down at his palm. "I'm fine. Tired, but not too tired. Someone must have gone up to the cottage. Opened the door somehow. McGuffrey must have been infected days ago, gone home and… been trapped, I suppose. Whoever opened the door rushed back here, but they were nowhere near as fast as McGuffrey. That's how he got in."

"I see." There was a pause as they both tried to think of something to say.

"I'm going to continue my rounds, now," George finally said. "You stay safe."

"You too."

George kept the spear at his side as he stalked the corridors of the home. The adrenaline had begun to leave his system and with it, his strength. The question gnawing at the back of his mind was whether any of the residents had made it outside, and whether they had been infected before they left. Though his mind tried to stay focused on the job in front of him, it kept straying to thoughts of that red car in the village, of getting himself and Mrs O'Leary out and away.

He found Mrs Lyndon next. She was stuck in the staff break room, unable to turn the handle to open the door. From the sounds she was making he was sure she had turned inside the room. He stood by the door, trying to work out if there was more than one creature inside. He couldn't be certain but he thought she was on her own.

Holding the spear in his left hand he gripped the handle with his injured right, turned the knob and pushed. The zombie heard the movement, sensed the presence of prey and pushed back. George managed to get his foot in the door, stopping it from closing completely. Then with an almighty heave, he pushed the door open, knocking the undead resident back into the room and down to the ground. He stepped forward, kicking at its arms as it tried to lever itself up. Then, in a move he was becoming experienced at, drove the spear through her eye.

"Some of them might have run," he said to himself, as he wiped the spear on her coat. "Where haven't I checked? McGuffrey's office." Slowly now, he crept up the corridor to the door at the end. He couldn't hear anything except the sound of his own laboured breathing. He threw the door open. The office was empty.

"Three and McGuffrey," he said to himself. "They've got to have run." But could McGuffrey have left the home? These creatures, these zombies, they seemed unable to even open a door. Didn't that mean that if they were inside then they wouldn't be able to get out? Or, if McGuffrey had followed one into the home, then couldn't he just as easily have followed someone out of it? George hoped so. "Where's left?" he muttered. "The bedrooms." He hadn't checked the residents' rooms.

He went back to the main area of the building and, one by one, checked each bedroom. He found only one more resident. Mr Grayson. He was dead, but not murdered by the undead. He'd taken a razor blade and sliced thick gashes along the inside of his wrists.

George checked the last three rooms along that corridor but they were empty. "Then the others have run," he said, and this time he said it with certainty. "You were the last," he said to himself, pulling the door to Mr Grayson's room closed as he passed it. "Just me and Mrs O'Leary left. And we'll be leaving as soon as I've got my breath back."

How though? He wasn't leaving her alone up here while he went down to the village to get the car. What if he couldn't get back up? A chair, that was the answer. He'd get her into a wheelchair. It was downhill to the village. Perhaps he could find two chairs. He'd look, just as soon as he'd rested.

His heart was beating harder, his mouth was dry and he could feel a headache forming behind his eyes. He took a moment to lean up against the wall. All he could hear was the pounding of blood in his ears. He felt nauseous. It was shock, he was reasonably sure of that. He just needed to

37

get back to Mrs O'Leary's room, then he could rest. Just a few hours rest and then they could leave.

At first he didn't notice the pain. Something was tugging at his arm. He pulled it back and saw the blood. And as he turned a dagger of burning ice shot up his arm and into his skull. He twisted, tried to jump back, but he was slow and McGuffrey was fast. Its mouth snapped towards George's face.

He pushed at the zombie, but it was like pushing at a brick wall, there was no give. He swung a punch at the former manager's face. It was a weak blow, but even if he'd had his full strength it wouldn't have been enough to knock the zombie down. It just turned its head slightly, snarled again and lunged. George snarled back. Their faces barely inches apart, George pushed, and managed to get the spear between him and the zombie.

With one hand pushing at McGuffrey, keeping its snapping teeth away from his face, he gripped the spear more tightly with the other. Underhand, he brought the spear up with all the force he could muster. The tip of the blade entered the creature's head just behind its jaw, tearing through skin and flesh to pierce through its tongue, and George could see the tip of the spear through the creature's open mouth.

He gritted his teeth and pulled the Assegai out, then plunged it upwards once more. It went in at a slightly different angle, tearing through the hole he'd just made and up into the roof of McGuffrey's mouth. He jerked the spear out and stabbed up again. The jawbone cracked and skin ripped as the spear went through the mouth and up a further four inches into its skull. The creature's hand spasmed as George twisted the spear free. He thrust it upward one last time. Grunting with the effort he dug it in further, twisting the blade until the creature stopped moving.

He let go of the spear and the body sagged to the ground. George breathed out slowly, bent, and retrieved the Assegai. As he straightened he looked down at his hand. The skin was torn where his knuckles had met McGuffrey's teeth. He pulled up his sleeve and looked at his forearm. There was a trickle of blood running down from a semi-circular bite mark to the bandage on his palm. None of the wounds were deep, nor were they severe, but he knew they didn't have to be. According to report after report he'd watched on the television, even the merest scratch was enough for infection. Sometimes it took minutes, sometimes it took hours, but according to everything he'd seen once you were infected it was only a matter of time.

"I got bit, Mary," he said as he closed the door to her room behind him.

"Oh, George!" And his heart broke at the sound of his name coming from her lips for the first time.

"I've got to go. Got to get out of here. Away from you. I don't know how long I've got," he said, not looking at her.

"Oh, George!" she said again, tears welling up as the enormity of the situation sank in.

"But look. I can't leave you here. Not like this. Someone might come, they might." He tried to imbue the words with all the confidence he didn't feel. "But in that bed, you're not going to stand a chance. I've brought you a chair. It was Mrs Lyndon's," he added. They'd always envied that chair, an expensive model with an electric motor bought by her son. Mrs Lyndon hadn't needed one, she, at least in their opinion, had only used it so as to constantly remind the rest of the inmates of how successful her bank manager son was.

"I got these pills from the pharmacy. There's enough if you wanted —"

"Now, George, that would be a mortal sin. And I think that there's been enough of those recently, don't you?"

"And this is the food. All I had. It's enough for a few days. Well. That's it," he said placing the bag on the foot of the bed. "Come on. Shift yourself up. Sit forward, and we'll swing your legs out first," George said brusquely, wanting it to be done, and done quickly.

"No, wait a moment," she said.

"Oh, come on, Mary, there's no time!" he cried plaintively.

"I know, but I'm not going to die in this." She lifted the hem of the frayed nightgown. "My dress, my good one. And my hat."

He hesitated. He'd no idea how much time he had, but the look in her eye, that same look that had terrified thousands of school children over the years, brooked no argument.

He went to the small closet and took out the solitary ancient dress-bag that smelled faintly of mothballs. It was the one she wore to funerals, the one she wore when she had visitors and the same one she'd worn at their own personal Christmas, eating the cake he'd brought and sharing out the chocolates her grandson had left.

"Now, you'll have to help me, George," she said. "But you'll keep your eyes closed."

"Of course Mary," he said, smiling. He helped her get dressed and then helped her out of the bed and into the wheelchair.

"Alright now, George," she said, firmly.

"Alright, Mary," he replied. They looked at one another for a moment. There was so much that they wanted to say, but now there was no time for it.

"Goodbye George," she said softly.

"Goodbye, Mary." He hesitated a moment. More than anything else he wanted to kiss her, but knew that he might infect her if he did. He turned and walked to the door.

"You know, George, I will see you again," she said.

"I hope not, Mary. Goodbye. Good luck." And he walked through the door, and back into the corridor.

He picked up the Assegai from where he'd left it leaning against the wall and headed towards the exit. He wasn't certain that the last two remaining residents had fled, but there wasn't time to check properly. He had no more time. He had no idea where he should go, just that he should go far enough away so that after it happened he wouldn't go back to the home.

He found his feet taking him up the road towards the cliffs. There was a bench there, overlooking the spit where a U-boat had become stuck during the war. It was a good place, where he'd passed the days when he wasn't working in the electrical shop. He'd take food, a flask, and a book, and he'd sat for hours, regardless of the weather, doing nothing but looking, reading and thinking, but mostly remembering.

There were a couple of fields between him and the bench, owned by a farmer who didn't want anyone using them as a short cut. Especially not George, as had been vocally pointed out to him during a particularly unpleasant conference with McGuffrey last August bank holiday. He'd have to walk down towards the village, then, and take the gate to the footpath half-way up the hill, and...

He laughed. What did any of that matter now? He twisted his Assegai between the strands of barbed wire and tugged it free. Then, humming as he went, he pushed his way through the hedge and walked across the dark damp earth, ready for a crop that would never now be planted.

By the time he had reached the bench it was two hours since he'd been bitten. His time was running out. He sat down, carefully placed the Assegai by his side, and looked out to sea. It was calm. Inland, he could already see plumes of smoke from where fires had taken hold. He thought he heard a scream in the distance, but he couldn't be sure. All he could see was the tranquil blue of the ocean. He concentrated on the sound of waves crashing against rocks. George smiled, and closed his eyes.

The end.

Surviving The Evacuation

Book 3: Family

The Story So Far

The outbreak began in New York on the 20th February. Within weeks, the virus had spread throughout the entire world. Nations fell, law and order gave way to chaos, and anarchy took grip almost everywhere. Here in Britain, Sir Michael Quigley, our Foreign Secretary, took over after the Prime Minister's disappearance. An emergency coalition cabinet was formed that included Jennifer Masterton. Rationing, curfews, martial law, the piratical theft of overseas food-aid, it wasn't enough.

My name is Bill Wright, and the evacuation was my idea. I grew up with Jen Masterton. We were friends and colleagues. Through her, my idea became government policy. My leg was broken on the day of the outbreak so I didn't join those other refugees fleeing the city. I was trapped in my flat, and watched as the evacuees left London. I watched the deserted streets fill up again, this time with the undead.

My supplies dwindling, my leg still not healed, I was forced out into the zombie-infested wasteland. It took weeks, but eventually I managed to escape to the relative security of Brazely Abbey in Hampshire. I took with me what little food and inadequate weapons I could find, and I also brought a laptop and hard drive. On those, I'd stored the files sent to me by a fixer I'd only ever known as Sholto. They detailed the spread of the outbreak and the conspiracy behind it, but without electricity I was unable to view them.

During my escape, I discovered the horrific truth of the evacuation. It had been a lie. The evacuees had all been murdered. The vaccine they'd been given was a poison. In need of more answers, I ventured out in search of the facility that created the virus. On that journey I met Kim, and together we rescued two children, Annette and Daisy. There was barely more than a few hours in which I could relish the triumph of that act before we met five others. Barrett, Chris, Daphne, Liz, and Stewart had been trapped on a farm since the beginning of the outbreak. We returned to Brazely, but the undead followed us. Besieged, we planned our escape. Kim and I were betrayed. Barrett and the others kidnapped the children, leaving us for dead on the banks of the River Thames.

I was unconscious for a time. By the time I woke, Kim had been through the files sent to me by Sholto and she'd discovered the true extent of the nuclear holocaust that had followed the outbreak. She'd also found a potential source of fuel, enough that we could rescue the girls. That source was at Lenham Hill, the facility where the virus was created. It wasn't empty. Sholto was there, and I learned that he was my brother.

He'd tried to stop the outbreak and the nuclear war that followed. He tried to save the world. He failed. Now all we can hope is that we will find the children, and find somewhere, anywhere, on this ruined planet, where they will be safe.

My journal continues…

Part 1:
River, Road
& Railway

River Thames, London
& The Midlands

17th July - 1st August

Day 127, River Thames

"I'll go and see if there are any supplies in the lock-keeper's house," I said as I limped away from the boat.

"Why bother?" Kim asked. "We don't need anything."

"Well, you never know," I muttered. I don't think she heard me.

She was right, though. We've enough food to keep us going until Christmas and enough petrol to get us anywhere in the British Isles. Not just on the mainland but, if we're careful, enough to get us across to Ireland. We worked it out. It's not like there's much else to do.

We've finally got the supplies to get us anywhere we want to go, and finally we know where that is, but for now we're stuck on the River Thames, travelling no faster than driftwood as we let the current drag us back towards London.

We left Lenham Hill yesterday, and made a paltry ten miles before darkness fell. We had to stop. If we'd gone on, we risked passing the boat that Barrett used when she, Stewart, and Daphne kidnapped Annette and Daisy. There was no sign of it yesterday and none so far today.

It was anger, that's why I needed to get away from the boat. It wouldn't be so bad if we could just turn the engine on. We can't. The River Thames is full of locks. At each we have to stop, operate the gate, and wait for the water levels to equalise. It takes an age.

We wasted about a hundred rounds from Sholto's M16 yesterday evening discovering what we all should have realised. If we motor up to a lock with the boat's pitiful engine going at full blast, we find the zombies waiting for us, and the ones we've passed catch up before we can get away. We're now left with two hundred rounds for his assault rifle, eighteen for the sniper rifle, and eleven for the pistol. It'll have to be enough.

What makes it worse, especially for Kim, is that we only went to Lenham Hill in the hope of finding enough fuel to catch up with Barrett and the others. Since we can't use it, all that those wasted days mean is that the children just got further away. I know Kim blames herself for not following Barrett straight down the river. I think she blames me, too.

It's odd that as long as we stay inside this tiny cabin, the smattering of undead along the banks and bridges pay us no heed. There's probably something important in that, something to do with the boat's size and motion that we could use to our advantage, but right now I just don't care. It's been ten days since Barrett took the girls, and if they've left the river they could be anywhere in Britain by now. They might even have found a way past the demolished bridges around central London and be out at sea. I don't know which of those two prospects scares me the most. I try not to think about.

While all of that is frustrating, it's not the cause of my anger. Nor is it the reason I needed to get away from Kim and my brother, if only for a few minutes.

The lock-keeper's cottage was twee. That's the kindest word I can think of to describe a post-war prefab built to last a decade but which perennial local-council austerity meant was never replaced. Ringed with a miniature white picket fence, barely a foot high, the garden was mostly gravel except where it was gnomes. Plastic, ceramic or metal, no two were alike, and each stood guard over a withered plant. Someone had cared deeply for this house. It had been their home, and it must have been a lonely existence, living in a house lost among the towering steel and concrete of the nearby industrial estate. It should have been a poignant sight, that fading echo of someone's dreams, but I was unmoved. I've seen the like too often.

As I picked my way around the side of the house, I was careful not to disturb any of the ornaments. Call it superstition, I've adopted a lot of those in the last few months. At the front of the house lay the river. At the back, beyond the picket fence, lay a road that led to the bridge half a mile downstream. On the other side of the path stood a fence covered in a patchwork of red paint that didn't quite mask the graffiti underneath. Behind that fence were the roofs of warehouses and factories on the industrial estate. They were of no interest to me.

I turned back to the cottage. It appeared deserted, but that didn't mean anything. I looked at the lush canopy of the London Plane trees lining the footpath. There were no birds. I half closed my eyes and listened. I could hear nothing but leaves blowing in the gentle breeze, and the sound of water slowly churning through the sluice gate.

My hand ached. My leg ached. My back ached from sitting on the boat's absurd little bench seat. My stomach ached, rebelling against the unfamiliarity of a high quantity of high calorie food. Even my head ached, from all that Sholto had told us.

I looked at the cottage again, but it was as uninspiring as any of the other dead little houses in the dead little towns on this dead little island. There was nothing to stay for, there, here, or anywhere else in Britain. Nothing. And once we find the children, no reason to linger. We'll leave. On the 2nd August.

I should be happy. I should be grateful. I've spent five months scrabbling about, trying to do more than just staying alive. Then we went to the one place that logically I should have gone to straight from London. We find Sholto, and all of a sudden every idea and plan is cast to the wayside. I suppose I should be happy, but I'm not. Perhaps part of it is that out of all the things he's told us, there's only one piece of news that anyone could call 'good'.

I took one last look around, but it did seem truly deserted. I started walking back to the boat but thought, since I was there, I might as well have a look inside the house. Why not? I'd said I was looking for supplies, after all.

My hand had barely touched the door when it swung inward. I took a step back and levelled the pike. There was no movement from inside and enough light coming through the windows that I could be sure. The cottage was empty. Judging by the dirt, the musky smell, and the pile of discarded belongings from a hasty packing, it had been empty since the evacuation.

There was a sudden, loud, 'caw' from a tree by the road. I spun around. A zombie lurched though a gap in the fence, next to the tree. Its mouth opened and snapped closed. Its arms waved and clawed at nothing as it spasmodically staggered towards me. I stood my ground, waiting and, for once, wishing They weren't so slow.

Its right leg kicked forward, splintering the white picket fence. Then its left leg knocked a gnome from its perch on an ornate toadstool. At that, my simmering anger boiled over into rage. The superstition that had kept me from knocking over those ornaments now meant I couldn't let this creature damage them.

The zombie lurched forward and I swung the blade up. The weight was too much, the balance wrong. Without the two fingers from my left hand I couldn't handle the weapon properly. It slipped and twisted. The flat of the blade hit the creature's cheek, ripping off a chunk of flesh before bouncing down across its body. The tip of the spear-point scored a line across its chest. The zombie was knocked backwards. It was off balance. The problem was, so was I.

I managed to half twist and push the blade. The creature fell sideways a few steps. I fell flat on my back, and I fell hard. Pain shot up every worn and damaged nerve. I saw stars. As they dimmed, I saw the creature getting closer. My good hand still griped the pike. With no real thought, I twirled it round in a long sweeping arc. The zombie stepped forward and the wooden shaft thumped against its leg. I started to roll, trying to find the room to stand up. I was still gripping the pike and as I rolled, the axe-head hooked under the creature's leg, pulling it up. Now it was the zombie's turn to fall down. I scrambled to my feet and managed to thrust the spear-point through the creature's temple before it managed to rise. It died.

I'd killed a zombie. I could still do it. I wasn't useless. I repeated those words a few times, but I didn't feel any better. I'd only managed it by luck so, somehow, it just didn't count. I looked down the path and through the gap in the fence, in the direction from which the zombie had come. There was another creature less than fifty yards away, and another a hundred yards behind it. Behind that one, on the edge of the car park near the warehouse, were three-dozen more. All were heading towards me, all strung out in a line, a good few seconds between each of Them. This was it, then. This would be the proper test. If I could dispatch all of Them, then I would have proved it. I started counting, sizing Them up, gauging the ground, assessing the footing. Everything seemed suddenly quiet. No, everything *was* quiet. The gurgling of water at the lock had ceased.

"Hey, C'mon Bill. The… What the hell are you doing?" Kim snapped. I hadn't heard her approach.

"I was…" I couldn't think of a simple way of explaining it.

"Well let's go," she said tugging at my arm, pulling me backwards. Reluctantly, I let her.

Sholto was standing on the boat, shifting impatiently from foot to foot.

"Zombies," Kim said as we half clambered, half fell on board.

"Right," he muttered, picking up his assault rifle, and aiming it the way we'd just come.

"No," she snapped, pushing the barrel away, "you're as bad as him. Let's just get out of here."

Written like that, this desire to go and find some of the undead seems crazy. It's not, but it's hard to explain why. As a whole, the news that Sholto has brought with him is grim, but even so there's one piece that should have us sighing with relief, if not celebrating out right.

There are other people, they have a boat and they're going to be waiting for him on a beach at a place called Llanncanno, on the west coast of Wales, on the 2nd August. In two weeks, all of this could be over. But it won't be. Even if we find the girls. No, when. When we find the girls, even after that, after we reach this beach it won't be over for me.

"So after you got to the UK, you headed to London, then you went to Lenham Hill?" Kim asked.

"That's the short version," Sholto replied.

"But how did you get across the river?" she asked. "Did you use one of the bridges?"

"Sure, on my way up to Lenham," he said. "On my way down I went through the Tube. I thought, since it was closed at the beginning of the outbreak the tunnels would be empty. I was wrong. It was an undead Underground. I'm not doing that again."

"But you used a bridge, so some of them are intact?"

"This one was. It was somewhere near Richmond. Couldn't tell you where. The city's changed since I knew it."

"Oh." She thought for a moment. "I was thinking about Barrett's plans to go to Scotland." It was the first time she'd mentioned Barrett by name since we'd started our river journey.

"They wouldn't make it," I said. "They didn't have enough fuel."

"Wouldn't matter if they did," Sholto said. "Scotland's gone."

"What do you mean? Gone where?" I asked, knowing the answer even as I spoke.

"Prometheus. Scotland took the brunt of it. Or, it would be more accurate to say that most of the missiles targeted at Scotland were actually launched. Edinburgh, Aberdeen, Strathclyde—"

"Strathclyde? You mean Glasgow," Kim corrected.

"I mean that entire stretch of the west coast," he said. "Faslane, Glasgow, it's all gone."

"What about the Highlands and Islands?" I asked.

"Dounreay took a hit, because of the nuclear power station," he said. "I couldn't tell you about the rest. This was from Captain Mills, and based more on where contact was lost than on any radio signals received."

"Scotland's a big place," Kim said.

"Not big enough," he said.

"England got lucky then," I murmured.

"If you want to call this luck," Sholto replied.

"Let's avoid the editorialising and focus," Kim said. "What are they going to find if they follow the coast up to Scotland? What would we find? A radioactive desert?"

"I've no idea," he said. "They might get lucky. There must have been some survivors, but whether they're still there now, I couldn't say. And as to where's safe in the long term, I couldn't say that either."

"So we just have to hope they didn't get to Scotland. Where else is there?"

"You mean where they might go?" Sholto asked. "You know them better than I do."

"No, I meant in the world," she said. "Places you've seen, the places you've been through. Places we could go after we find the girls."

"Well as I said, there's this village in Ireland, but if I get a vote, it'll be for crossing the Atlantic and going back to America. These islands are too small. Too many nuclear weapons were dropped on them to make anywhere here safe enough for my liking."

"The same has to be true for the U.S., doesn't it?" I asked.

"It's a much bigger country," he said. "You've got to factor in the unpredictability of fallout, but Crossfields Landing was fine when I left."

"That's that village in Maine where you sailed out from?" Kim asked.

"Right. I kept a summerhouse up there. Well, I say summer, they think snow and ice makes for a warm day. Owning a small boat seven hundred miles from DC gave me a legitimate excuse to disappear for a few days at a time. Sometimes I did actually go there. A few times, I even went fishing. Not that I ever caught much. After the outbreak, after Prometheus, that's where I went. There was this kid who'd inherited an old tackle shop the summer before last. He, and a few friends, had dropped out of high school and hitched their way up there. Anyway, by the time I reached the village they'd turned the place into a—"

"Just get to the point," Kim cut in. "How many people were there?"

"About sixty. Give or take."

"And that was months ago. Too long. Too much could have happened. You've no idea if anyone is left at all."

"And no reason to suspect otherwise. That was about a month after the outbreak, and sure that's a long time. But since it all started in New York, that means it was a month after everyone in the world started heading away from that corner of the east coast. I mean, who in their right mind would actually head in that direction?"

"Exactly," Kim muttered caustically. "Yet that's where you want us to go."

"They're good people. Look, it's just one option, and I think it's a better bet, long term, than some village on a rainy island on the wrong side of the Atlantic."

"Maybe," she said dismissively. "That's sixty people. Sixty. And Scotland's gone, England's a wasteland. Where else? I mean, how many people are there left?" Kim asked, again.

"In the whole world? I've no idea. I can only tell you what I saw getting to the Atlantic and then crossing it."

"Then just tell us how many people you know about."

"You want a number? Let's see. There's Captain Mills and his crew on the HMS Vehement. They lost a few when the naval battle kicked off, but there were about ninety left. Then there's the Santa Maria, Sophia Augusto's fishing trawler. They had a crew of twenty-five bolstered by another sixty family, friends and hangers on. Another hundred or so survived from the flotilla. And then there's another hundred in that village on the Irish coast."

"So, in total, as far as you know, that's just four or five hundred people. Out of how many? A billion? More? And that was months ago."

"Exactly," he said, "there's bound to be more by now."

"Or none left at all," she said. "You can't be certain any of them are still alive."

"No more certain than you can be that they are all dead. There's no reason to think they would be. Those guys in Crossfields Landing had more munitions than most medium sized countries, and if they needed to retreat, then there's the sea at their backs. As for the Vehement, exactly who's going to threaten a nuclear powered, nuclear-armed submarine? Anyway, it's Sophia who's going to be waiting for me. Or she'll send someone."

"How can you be certain she will?" I asked.

"I told you. Sophia owes me. She won't let me down."

"You've said that," Kim said. "Half a dozen times, but you've not said why, or why Bill and I should trust her."

"You trust me, don't you?" he retorted.

"Surprisingly, yes. But that's not what I meant. What's your connection with her?"

"I thought I told you? No? Okay, well for that we have to go back a few years."

"Can't you just give us the short version?" she asked.

"Why? What else have you got planned. We've at least another hour before we get to the next lock. As I was saying, we have to go back a bit. Her family's been fishing for years. Father to son to niece to cousin. The surname changed, but someone in that family was hauling cod out of the Atlantic since before Amerigo Vespucci's name was first misspelled. Most recently that was Sophia. She had delusions of acting until her brother drowned, and she realised that living in increasingly smaller apartments, chasing increasingly irregular work was even less appealing than spending the rest of her life knee-deep in fish guts. She returned to Puerto Rico, claimed her inheritance, and discovered it consisted of a boat that leaked more than a five-cent sieve. She'd gone to Hollywood hoping to get rich and didn't see why that should change. She needed a new boat. Ideally she needed more than one. No bank was ever going to front her that kind of cash, so she got her money from a group of unpleasant men with deep pockets and long memories."

"You mean loan sharks?" Kim asked.

"I mean people with a far sharper bite than that. She managed to make her repayments and all was peachy, right up until the hurricane hit. I doubt you'll remember that particular storm. This was back in the dark ages before we had twenty-four hour news. It blacked-out a few hundred miles of coast, destroyed some villages, devastated a few towns and flooded the port. She lost her boats. That didn't stop her getting in a dinghy trying to rescue people stranded by the flooding. And that is how she came to my attention. There was a piece about her on the news. An election was coming up and I thought she'd look good on a stage next to my candidate. By the time I found her, she'd been told that press, fame, and a civics award weren't much use when the interest was due. I say she was 'told', the people she owed the money to had burned down her office, and that was a real feat given the flooding. So I made her an offer."

"What? One she couldn't refuse?" Kim asked sarcastically.

"Of course she could have refused. The alternative was smuggling drugs north and guns south until she was caught or killed. She knew it. I knew it. I offered to pay off her debts, buy her two new boats, and make sure she wasn't bothered again. In return—"

"No, hang on. What do you mean by 'make sure'?"

"I grew up running drugs and guns for an organised crime syndicate in London," he said. "I crossed the Atlantic on a fake passport and bribed, blackmailed, and bludgeoned my way to the top. What do you think I mean? I had the cash, and was looking for a very public good deed to perform. In return she'd—"

"No," Kim cut in again. "I don't buy it. What exactly did you tell her, because I bet you didn't tell her the truth?"

"The truth was that I wanted a way to get across to England without the authorities knowing I'd left. This was back when I was just planning to kill Quigley and old Lord Masterton. My plan was to make a lot of noise about taking my boat out for a week's fishing and hiking, except I'd have been picked up by her trawler somewhere out in international waters. We'd head east, and then her boat would get into trouble and need to be towed to the nearest port for repairs. With a boat that size, and that's why I bought her a boat that size, it would be somewhere in Britain. No one would notice if one of the crew disappeared for a few hours and that was as long as I'd need."

"Seriously? You told her that?" Kim asked.

"Of course not."

"Well, what did you tell her?" she insisted.

"Is it important?"

"Aside from the fact we're likely to meet her? Yes, it's important," she replied. "For all this talk of other people out there somewhere, right here, right now it's just us. We have to trust each other and that means no more secrets, no more sly insinuations or political prevarication. So what did you tell her?"

"Alright, the truth. I told her I was waging my own private war against this mob she'd borrowed the money from. I told her that one day, maybe, I'd have them on the run. When I did, I'd need to follow them across to Europe. Then I showed her a photo, from the front page of the

Washington Post, of me standing next to the President back when he was still the Governor."

"You led her to believe that you were some kind of crusading superhero with West Wing credentials?" she asked, incredulously.

"So what? I wasn't going to tell her the truth. I don't know if she actually believed me or if she just wanted to. I bought her boats legitimately. Two deep-sea trawlers that were state of the art, for their day. All the taxes were paid, and the press was there to film my candidate smashing a bottle of champagne on the Santa Maria's prow. She had what she wanted, and so did I. Until I discovered Prometheus. The more I found out, the plainer it got that I was going to end up with the NSA, the FBI, the CIA, and the rest of that federal alphabet soup on my trail. Sophia and her boat just weren't going to cut it. I had a friend who owned a farm. It was more of a compound really, the kind with its own airstrip. That was how I was planning on getting out of the U.S. When the outbreak hit, that's where I went."

"You'd have been shot down, if you'd flown here," I said.

"Maybe. Maybe not," he said airily. "It didn't matter. By the time I got there the plane was gone. If I was going to cross the Atlantic it was going to be by sea. Except when I managed to reach Sophia, she was already stuck in the middle of that flotilla of refugees all heading for the UK."

"So who brought you to Britain?" I asked.

"I'm getting to that. While the news was still talking about virulent strains, pandemics, and terrorist attacks, Sophia loaded up her two boats with food, fuel, family, friends, and the few lucky strangers who just happened to be passing. She took the boats out, and headed north. They found a secluded bay, and it would have stayed secluded if everything that could float wasn't looking for that exact same thing. Now from what she said—"

"The short version," Kim cut in sharply. Begrudgingly, she added, "Please."

"Alright. A lot of boats sailed into that bay. The Santa Maria was the only ship that sailed out. We're talking about a couple of weeks after the outbreak and she had no idea where to go. She'd lost one boat and a lot of friends. There were thousands of ships out in the Atlantic all in the same... well, I was going to say 'the same boat'. They were all in the same situation, low on food, low on fuel, looking for sanctuary. Most of the ships that set off in those early days had ended up in Greenland. It was inevitable, really. I mean, if you were listening to the radio you heard that the outbreak had spread to nearly everywhere in the world. Then you had a few places like the UK and New Zealand that were warning they'd sink anyone who approached. In the Atlantic, that left Greenland. Not because it was safe, or because there was anything special about it, but because the locals had all headed off into the Arctic instead of hanging around chattering into a radio."

"That's how the virus got there, then?" Kim asked.

"Well technically it's not a virus, but I guess that's close enough. No, that's not how it got there. Those boats had all been at sea for days. The infection came by plane, same as it had everywhere else. By the time those boats arrived, the place was a warzone. You had units from the Scandinavian military who'd been setting up a redoubt in Greenland battling mercenaries, militias, and anyone who could hijack a plane from pretty much everywhere in the hemisphere. Add to that a few locals not quick enough to get out, throw in the undead, and those boats that made it there, well, the few that still had any fuel turned right around. Most didn't. Most people had no choice but to stay and fight, and I guess most died."

"That's not the flotilla that was heading to the UK, though?" I asked.

"No. That was made up of the boats too slow to get to Greenland, and the people who left later on. The Americas, West Africa, even Europe, they came from pretty much everywhere. They'd been drifting out in the Atlantic and the only place left, the one place they could reach that was safe was the UK. And they knew it had to be safe, because they could hear the BBC broadcasting 'there are no reported cases in the UK or Ireland'. That was about the time I called her up asking for a lift. I'd paid for a good communications rig, I mean, there wasn't much point in me planning to use her boat if I couldn't get in touch with her. But like I said, by then she was stuck in the middle of that mass of boats and rafts and everything else. But the radio turned out to help in the end, it's how she managed to get in touch with Captain Mills."

"He's the captain of the submarine?"

"The HMS Vehement, one of the British Trident submarines. He was ordered to launch a missile, and detonate it above the flotilla. He refused in part, I like to think, thanks to me."

"How's that?" I asked.

"Once I'd learned what Prometheus was, I'd tried to come up with a way of stopping it. I'd tried the political route. I'd called in every favour, tried blackmailing every politician I had some dirt on, I even tried just asking nicely. That didn't work. So I tried to get a message to the people who stood between the big red button and the bombs going off. And it looks like that didn't work so well either."

"What?" Kim scoffed. "You sent out a couple of hundred emails titled 'read this and save the world', and this captain actually opened it?"

"No, of course not. It was far more complicated, and a lot simpler, than that. I was very, very good at what I did. But I was desperate. It was my last throw of the dice. That's why I ended up on the run. No, the problem was getting a message to people stuck on a submarine out at sea. The Vehement was in for repairs when the outbreak occurred. It's why I was able to get Captain Mills, and why I couldn't get a message to any of the others."

"And this message from a complete stranger was enough to stop him from launching?"

"No. I said the message was a small part of it. The first order he got when he was underway was a strange one. He was told to open his letter of last resort."

"What's that?" Kim asked.

"The first thing a Prime Minister did on taking office was to write a letter to each of the captains of the nuclear-armed submarines," I said. "The letter told them what they should do if Britain was attacked, and communication with the government was lost. Retaliate, scuttle the boat, seek sanctuary in the U.S. or Australia, or whatever other course suited the whims of the PM."

"Exactly," Sholto said, "so since the letter was only meant to be read when the Prime Minister and the rest of the cabinet were dead, Captain Mills thought being told to open it was odd. When he did, he found the orders weren't for retaliation, but for a pre-emptive strike against oil and gas refineries in Russia. Those were his Prometheus targets, and they matched what I'd sent him. Nevertheless, he cued up the data, waited for the order to launch, and then he sat and thought. When the order to fire came, it was with a new set of targets, the flotilla, and he refused to kill so many civilians."

"But clearly someone else didn't," Kim said. "Otherwise more people would have survived."

"Fortunately there wasn't another sub in the Atlantic. The orders went to some cruisers and destroyers. They launched a conventional attack. Captain Mills decided that if he was going to mutiny he might as well do it properly so he started torpedoing the Navy ships. They retaliated, and..." He noticed Kim's expression. "And after that you had the evacuation, and Prometheus. After a few days, when the dust had settled, the Royal Navy ships had been sunk, but so had most of the flotilla, and the Vehement was damaged. The Santa Maria was still afloat, and Sophia, with Captain Mills, started a rescue operation. They took the people they rescued to Ireland."

"Why Ireland? Because it was closest?"

"Sure. Partly, and partly because it wasn't the UK, but that wasn't the whole reason. You remember that message they were broadcasting? It said there were no threats in the UK and Ireland. So, according to the radio, Britain wasn't the only place that was safe."

"Well, was it?" Kim asked.

"It could have been. Politics." He shook his head. "No one in Whitehall had thought to talk to Dublin about that message. They just broadcast it anyway, and started talking about plans to shift people from the evacuation zones across the Irish Sea. That made Dublin nervous. Of course, the people at the top, Quigley and his ilk, they had no plans to evacuate anyone, but the Irish government wasn't to know that, and Quigley didn't tell them. Worried they were going to be swamped by millions of English refugees, Ireland offered sanctuary to every EU military unit that needed safe harbour. That meant planes, and that meant the virus. When they started pulling refugees out of the water, they'd had a whole stretch of the east coast, south of Dublin. By the time they picked me up they were down to one village."

"Why there?" I asked. "Why not the Atlantic coast? That would have been closer to the flotilla."

"Because" he said with a shrug, "that was where someone had tried to organise a defence. Maybe if they'd set it up somewhere else, more people would have survived. Who knows?"

"One village," Kim said. "A few hundred people left out of all those refugees. It's not much."

"You're focusing on the wrong things," Sholto said. "I'm talking about a few hundred people in a functioning community. Who knows how many other small groups there might be up in the mountains or out on the smaller islands? Maybe I should have said they retreated to one village. From what they said, they've got the seeds of a proper civilisation. Imagine hot water on tap—"

"Wait, hang on," Kim interrupted. "Do you mean you haven't actually seen it? You didn't even go to this village in Ireland?"

"Well, no. Not exactly."

"Not exactly? What does that mean?"

"I'd reached Sophia on the radio I'd bought for her. She passed the message on to Captain Mills, and he and his sub came out to meet me. By that stage, he'd abandoned the rescue operation and was planning a trip around the UK. He wanted to confirm the extent of the nuclear attack, or as much of it as could be seen from a few miles out to sea. He dropped me off, I made my way to London and—"

"So you don't know if there's anyone left in Ireland," Kim cut in, "or that there ever was a village?"

"Why would they lie?"

Kim struggled to find an answer. "Okay," she finally said. "But that doesn't really explain why they'd be waiting for you."

"Because I knew where the virus had been created. The captain saw the importance in destroying that facility, but he wasn't going to launch one of his missiles. He said there was enough radiation loose in the world already. I told him I wanted to look for my brother, but more importantly I said that I'd probably find the scientist responsible for creating the virus at Lenham Hill, and that I'd bring him back along with whatever research I could recover. He was very interested in that. Not interested enough to send anyone with me, but that suited me fine. I'm not a man who likes company."

"So they're expecting you. And if the five of us turn up, and without that scientist, what then?" Kim asked.

"They're not going to turn us away," Sholto said.

"You hope," she muttered. "The address you found for him in Lenham Hill, that's in Wales. Why can't we get to both?"

"If we started off now, we probably could," I said. "But the beach is two thirds of the way up the west coast. The address Sholto found is in the north, about seventy miles east of Anglesey." I drew a rough map. "Here in the middle, that's the Snowdonia mountain range. I don't want to get stuck on a single track road, halfway up a mountain with the undead in front and behind."

"So we go to that scientist's house first, and then we follow the coast around," Kim said. "It would only be a couple of hundred miles. That's just an extra day, two at most."

"We can't," Sholto said. "Anglesey was one of the targets, because of the nuclear power station. We have to assume it was hit."

"Which means," I said, " that whether we go to the beach or go looking for this scientist, we've got to come in from the east. That means backtracking almost into England to get from one to the other."

"Then what if we go to the beach and then get this boat to take us around Wales and we go by sea to this house?" she suggested.

"No," I said, firmly. "We'll find the girls, and then get them to this beach and out to this village or anywhere else that might be safe. I'll go and find the scientist."

As angry as I am at Barrett and the others, at my brother, at Quigley, and anger isn't a strong enough word to describe how I feel about him. As angry as I am at this whole dying world and everyone and everything in it, none of it compares to the anger I feel towards myself.

Sholto tried to stop Prometheus and save the world. He failed, but he tried. That might buy enough goodwill among these people to overlook my involvement in the evacuation plan, but it's not enough for me. That my complicity was unwitting doesn't matter. Neither does the fact that I was no more venal or corrupt than almost anyone else on the planet. If I'd not given into my own fears when I first found out about Lenham Hill, if I'd not buried my head the moment I was stuck in a Ministry of Defence jail for a single night, then perhaps I would have discovered what was going on. I might have been able to expose it. I might have been able to stop it. I could have tried. I know I could have done more. I could have done something. But I didn't. I did nothing, and because of that I won't get on this boat with Kim and the girls.

That's why I went looking for the undead. I needed to prove that I wasn't useless, that I could find the scientist on my own. I needed to prove it to myself, and I needed to do that while it still didn't matter. If I die here, Kim and Sholto will mourn, sure, but that'll be an end to it. If I go off on my own and just never come back, how long before one of them comes looking for me? I can't stand that idea.

We'll find the girls, get them to this beach and then I'll go on. And I won't rest until, at the very least, I know whether the immune are carriers of this virus. Not just for myself, but for everyone among this handful who've survived. It's all I can do, and I just hope it will be enough.

Okay, so I recognise the root of all this lies in the uncertainty around what might have happened to Annette and Daisy, but so what? I have to think about what will happen after we find them. It's far better than thinking about what might have happened to them over the last ten days.

Day 128, River Thames

Another frustrating day. The worst yet. It was around midday and we thought, for a moment, we might have found the girls. We were about fifteen miles past Windsor, when my brother spotted the house.

"That's something you don't expect to see," he said. "Not in England."

"What's that?" I asked, slightly too loudly. The gentle motion of the waves had caused me to drift off into a half-sleep.

"Flags, flying from that house there."

We turned to look. On the north bank was a house with a garden that ran down to the river. At the edge of the lush and overgrown lawn was a flagpole. At the top flew a South African flag with a stylised rugby ball in the centre. Underneath flew the silver fern of the New Zealand All Blacks. Under that was what looked like a plain white sheet.

"It's a flag house," Kim said.

"A what?" Sholto asked.

"Annette said she saw something like this before we found her," she said. "She'd taken refuge in a school, and from the top floor she'd seen a house with smoke coming from the chimney and flags flying in the garden. It was what she was looking for when we found her. She couldn't remember exactly where..." Kim trailed off.

"There's no such thing as a coincidence," Sholto said.

Kim detached the scope from her rifle and peered at the house.

"I can't see any life. No smoke either," she said, as we drifted closer.

"What do you want to do?" Sholto asked. "Whatever it is we need to decide quickly."

"There's no sign of Barrett's boat. No sign of anyone in the house," I said.

"Annette and Daisy could be there," Kim said, her voice taut. "Maybe they escaped and this is a sign. Maybe she hung up the flags just for us to see. We could signal. We should. There's got to be a horn or something on the boat. Or we could fire off a shot. She'd hear that."

"So would the undead," I said.

"So what? We have to do something. We have to stop. We have to see. There's no smoke, but… maybe there's nothing left to burn. It's been nearly two weeks, that could be it."

It was the slimmest of hopes, but Kim was right, we had to check. I'll admit, as we paddled and pulled our way to shore, that hope started to grow in me, too.

The man who lived in this boat had a pitiful little life. He did actually live on the boat, and he'd tried to turn it into a home. That just made his efforts all the more sad. It wasn't a large boat to start with, but he'd partitioned it into little chambers mimicking the rooms he must have had in his house. This cabin, where we spend most of our time, is done out like a living room. The armchair is rotten, the TV is covered in mildew and the arms of the sofa had to be removed just so it would fit in a space little bigger than a prison cell. This cabin, however, is palatial compared to the cupboard-sized bedroom. Ceramic tiles had been stuck to the walls of the cubicle shower room. Judging by the number that had fallen off, he hadn't considered that sticking them on metal bulkheads would require a different type of cement than gluing them to the plaster of a brick wall. He'd even painted the number '17a' on the side where the name should have been, but it was the kitchen that was the most depressing. In the divorce or bankruptcy or whatever had befallen him, the man had been allowed to keep his kitchen appliances. Oven, fridge, dishwasher, all were in a matching charcoal grey. They were too large for such a small boat, and I don't think there was enough power for any of them to actually work. We've been using them as anchors, looping a rope through the handle, throwing one overboard when we need to stop for the night, then pulling the rope free in the morning.

We dropped the oven overboard to arrest the boat's motion, then paddled with a portion of the bench seat, until we were close enough to hook the pike onto the railing around the bank.

It was a large detached house a few square feet short of being called a mansion. Probably built in the 1950s, more recently someone had painted it white and added black mock Tudor beams to the exterior in a stunning display of failed taste.

Sholto leaped off the boat and took the lead with Kim close behind. I limped along at the back, struggling to keep up.

The long lawn leading down to the water's edge was empty. So was the patio along the side of the house. Then we heard that familiar rasping wheeze, coming from the front. Sholto glanced over his shoulder, nodded, and darted forward, around the side of the house and out of sight. I heard the thump of a body collapsing to the ground, followed by a defiant yell. Kim ran forward, her axe raised, and disappeared around the corner. A few seconds later, there was that familiar meaty thud of the axe cleaving through flesh and bone. I limped on as fast as my twisted leg would allow, cursing my infuriatingly slow progress.

When I reached the front garden, I saw the undead. Three were down, but there were another four in the drive and two more by the wide-open gate. Sholto was already moving towards the two by the front door, Kim to another two in the middle of the drive. I headed towards the gate. I swung the pike up, and remembered what had happened yesterday. I let the blade fall, until it was only a few inches above the ground. Gripping as best I could with both hands, I stalked forward as the two creatures lurched at me. Their arms swung, their mouths snapped as I pushed the axe-head forward and out, and hooked it under the first zombie's leg. I pulled. Its leg came up and the creature fell down. I swung the pike to the left, hooked and pulled, and the other zombie was down. I took two paces forward, plunged the spear down, once, twice and They were both still.

I limped over to the gate and pushed it closed. That's when I saw the sign. It had blown over. I opened the gate and went outside to pick it up. It was a blue road sign. Painted over it were the words 'Safe House - Survivors Welcome'.

I turned around to call Kim and my brother over, but they'd already gone inside. I propped the sign up, made sure the gate was closed, and then went to find them. They were in the kitchen.

"There's no one here," Kim said, her voice absent of emotion.

"No one's been here for months," Sholto added.

"There's a sign," I said as I walked around the kitchen and into the open plan living room. "On the road, by the front gate. It says this is a safe house."

"There was a note. Here," Kim said, pointing down at an empty space on the counter. "It's gone."

"Then how do you know it was there?" Sholto asked.

"Because it was taped down," she said, slowly. "The tape and three of the four corners are left. It was a map."

"Of what?" I called out as I bent down to look at the fireplace. Stacked next to it was a mismatched collection of broken furniture and neatly sawn logs. The grate was full of ash.

"No idea," Kim said. "There's an arrow with 'N' at the top, and a few crooked lines underneath, but that's all."

"The cupboards are empty," Sholto said. "They took the map and any food that was here. They didn't leave a note, but then, why would they?"

"Why hang up the flags, then?" Kim murmured, quietly.

"It's two different groups of people," Sholto said. "The first lot set up the sign and left the map. The second lot came along and took it."

"Obviously," Kim snapped. "That's not what I meant."

I wasn't sure what she'd meant, and I don't think she did either.

"Annette would have left a note," I said loudly. "But she wasn't here. I'd say it was two months since anyone was in this house."

"You're getting that from the fireplace?" Sholto asked.

"Hey, don't knock it. I've seen a lot of places like this. Well, places where people have taken refuge for a time. None of them were quite like this, though. The windows are blocked up, but the door was unlocked."

"It was locked, but the key was in the lock," Kim said.

"Same difference," I said. "A safe house, but set up by who? And who for? And who came along and took the map and the food?"

"It doesn't matter," Kim said. "If Annette and Daisy aren't here then we should get moving."

Kim didn't relax until we were all back on the boat and moving, albeit slowly, down the river.

"You think the place Annette saw down in Hampshire was a safe house as well?" Sholto asked, half an hour later.

"It's impossible to tell," I said. "I mean, flying a flag so people know where you are, that's an old trick, isn't it? On the other hand we can't be more than sixty or seventy miles from that house she saw. Perhaps less, but it can't be more than a couple of days on foot, or a day by bike. I think the question, the important one, is if it was the same people, then did that map lead north to the river, or south down to Hampshire."

"And that's one we can't answer, and the more I think about it, the more I think it doesn't really matter," Kim said. "I mean, we've got a boat, right? And we've got the fuel to keep it going all the way around the coast. If that submarine brought you along the south coast, then that's the route we'll take. We'll have to be careful around the Isle of Wight, but even with the radiation that has to be safer than trying to get across Wales by land."

"Take this thing out to sea?" Sholto asked sceptically.

"Alright, no, not this boat. We'll find a different one, a better one. If the river's impassable, then we'll have to. But going by land is unnecessarily dangerous."

"Finding a boat isn't going to be easy," I said.

"It might be," she said. "You don't know. We won't, not if we don't look."

It might be or it might not, but it's all academic. It's something to talk about instead of worrying about the girls. There's been no sign of them today, and no sign of any other living person, no more safe houses, nothing except the occasional zombie on the river bank.

Day 129, Garden View Apartments Kew, London

19:00, 19th July

"There it is!" Kim hissed. "Their boat!"

"What? Where?" We'd set off long before dawn and made good progress as we approached London. The river had swelled and widened as it was fed by tributaries and paved over streams. Cottages and mansions had turned to terraced town houses, then to apartments interspersed with those dismal 1950s tower blocks.

Earlier, I'd been counting the windows, each one a room that Annette and Daisy might be inside of, when we nearly ran into a mostly-submerged police launch. There was a frantic ten minutes of pulling, pushing and fending off, before we were free. After that I kept my eyes glued to the river, watching out for the tell-tale ripples that indicated further obstructions. That was why I'd not seen the boat.

"Which one?" I asked, because now that I was looking, I had no idea which of the fifty or so boats up ahead she was referring to.

We were on that section of the river just south of Richmond, where the river snakes north, before straightening and then flowing west to east through central London. Ahead of us lay Teddington Lock, but between us and it was a huge mass of wrecked ships.

The current had pulled everything that floated downstream. From rubbish to rowing boats to pleasure cruisers, it had collided and crashed into a hundred-passenger tour boat creating a densely packed agglomeration that nearly stretched from bank to bank. It was impossible to make out where one boat ended and another began, let alone which was the one we were looking for.

For me, that race to the river and the fight by the bank is a strange blur. I can remember the faces of the undead, and the strange calm that came over me when I was certain I would die. As I scanned the river ahead, I realised I couldn't remember what that boat looked like.

"Not there," Kim snapped, and pointed at the bank a few hundred yards upstream of the wreckage. "There. The one with the blue stripe. How could you not recognise it?"

I looked and saw and wondered how I could have missed it. The boat was tied to the bank by a single rope attached to the stern. It drifted lazily in the current, a few metres from the shore. Behind it, equally lazily, drifted what looked like three towels, one red, one blue, and one white.

"No prizes for guessing why they stopped then," Sholto said picking up his M16. "You say they just had just the one gun?"

"A double-barrelled shotgun, yes," I replied. "I've no idea how much ammo they had for it, and they might have found some other weapons."

"So, not much of a threat then?"

"Not much of a threat?" Kim scoffed. "They murdered Liz, they were prepared to leave Chris behind before he'd turned, and then they killed an old man working on their farm. And there was his grandaughter. I don't know what they did to her, but whatever it was, they didn't want to talk about it, yet they were happy to talk about murder. No, they're a threat, alright."

"That wasn't what I meant. I'm sorry," he said.

"It doesn't matter," Kim said. She'd detached the scope from the sniper rifle, and was peering carefully at the boat. "No one's on board."

"Why stop on that bank, though?" I muttered. "It's the wrong side of the river for Scotland."

"Why guess?" Sholto said. "If Annette hung those towels over the side, maybe she left you a message."

She hadn't, not exactly, but she had left a clue. On a bench seat in a cabin so cramped and dirty it made our little boat seem luxurious, was a pamphlet for Kew Gardens. On the front was a clear, ink-blue baby's fingerprint. Unfolding the brochure revealed a map of the botanic gardens, and right in the middle, marked out in the same blue fingerprint, was a smiling face.

"Why would they go to Kew?" Kim asked.

"That's the botanical gardens, right?" Sholto asked.

"Yeah, finest rare specimens. Greenhouses, ancient trees, the works," I murmured.

"So why go there?" Kim asked again.

"I don't know," I said. "At one point I was thinking of going there myself. But that was months ago."

"Is there food? Vegetables, fruit, that kind of thing?" Sholto asked.

"Not really," I said. "I mean, there's some but no more than you'd find in the back gardens of any suburban street. There's more exotic stuff in the greenhouses, and when I was thinking of coming here, that's what I was after. For the seeds, you see. But without power, without water, without heat, without constant care and nurturing, everything in those greenhouses must be dead by now."

"So you wouldn't go there?"

"Now? No. It's about four miles from here in a straight line, five or six by road. You could travel the same distance in any direction and have your pick of hospitals, police and fire stations, a university, and more houses and shopping centres than you could loot in a year. Or, if you want somewhere built in a pre-plumbing era, there's Hampton Court Palace a few miles south on the other side of the Thames. No, I wouldn't go to Kew, not now," I said, "but what I'm trying to remember is whether I told Annette that."

"They weren't walking," Kim said abruptly.

"What?"

"They weren't on foot," she said.

"How can you tell?" Sholto asked.

"No fuel cans, for one thing."

"They could have been thrown overboard."

"If they'd been used up," she said. "But if they used the engine to get here, then what about the zombies? Where are They?"

I looked around, properly this time. I'd registered that there weren't any close by, we all must have, but I hadn't considered what that meant. There should have been lots.

Over the last few months, every unsecured boat and piece of drifting wreckage between here and the previous lock had been dragged by the current to become part of that hulking dam. Each bang and scrape should have brought the zombies out to investigate, and they would have stayed, waiting for prey. If the others had used the boat's engine then They would have heard it and headed back up stream towards the noise, making it impossible to get off the boat.

"The fuel tank's empty," Sholto said, straightening up. "And I mean bone dry. It'd be a bit of a coincidence for them to run out right here."

"They took the petrol and drove," Kim said firmly. "The undead followed. It's what they would have done. They wouldn't have split up."

"There's no food either," my brother went on.

"They'd have taken it with them," Kim said.

"No, I meant there are hardly any wrappers. No cans or bottles, nothing."

"They definitely took food," I said. "I loaded it onto the truck back at the Abbey myself."

"Enough detective work," Kim said. "Shall we go to Kew?"

We made sure our little boat was securely tied to the bank a little way upstream. We took our weapons, and enough food and water for a few days. We couldn't carry much else, not on foot, but even so I didn't like the idea of leaving all our supplies unattended. I guess the old-world fear of theft is very deeply engrained. We agreed if we split up, we'd meet back on the boat, and if that wasn't possible then back at the safe house we'd passed upstream.

"London's changed," Sholto said. "Everything seems smaller and bigger at the same time."

"It's bound to, if you left here when you were a kid," I said.

"I've been here since," he said, "but only fleetingly and there wasn't time for sightseeing. There certainly are more apartment blocks, but that wasn't what I meant. Everything seems like it's the wrong size."

I knew what he meant. The roads seemed wider but shorter, the houses more towering but closer together, the shops smaller, their windows darker and now filled with nothing but menace. Where a falling branch had broken a section of fencing I saw a lawn carpeted yellow with daisies and dandelions, but that was the exception. Every other garden we passed was parched, the flowerbeds wilting, the lawns ragged, the trees already beginning to die. Conversely the pavements and walls were beginning to turn green with moss and weeds.

The streets were filled with wind-blown rubbish, yet it would only have taken a few hours work to clear them, a few days more to re-paint the houses, to fix the windows and clean the pavements. It is a city that could be mended and made whole once again. But by the time there are enough people to do that work, if there ever is such a time, nature will have reclaimed what once was hers. The city is lost. We may be the last people ever to see it. For some reason I don't find that at all depressing.

"There. That hat. That's Daisy's," Kim said, running across the road and snatching a bonnet from the top of a rubbish bin. We were in Richmond, about halfway between Kew and where we'd left the boat.

"The bill, it was pointing towards Kew, right?" she asked.

"Why would they have stopped?" I muttered, more to myself than anyone else, as I looked up and down the street.

"Is it pointing to Kew or not?" Kim asked again, more insistently.

"Quiet!" I hissed. The bin was outside one of those generic one-stop-shops selling branded goods at twice the price of the supermarket an inconvenient few blocks further away.

"The window was broken recently," I whispered. "Look at the dirt on the pavement. There's none on the glass."

"They went in there?" she asked.

"They stopped here," I said. "How else would the hat end up on that bin? Just listen."

There was a scratching sound from inside.

"Mice?" Kim asked. It was wishful thinking. We all knew it.

I took a step towards the shop.

"Wait," she hissed, but I couldn't. We had to know.

I stepped over the broken window and into the shop. The aisles were narrow, too close together for the pike. I shifted it to my left hand, and took out the hatchet. The light from outside didn't penetrate far into the shop. It took a moment for my eyes to adjust to the gloom. That was why I almost tripped over the body.

It was male, or it had been, months ago. I couldn't say more than that because a good portion of the head, including the face, was missing. The zombie had been shot at close range.

"Stewart's shotgun," I murmured as I took another step forward. There was a crunch of glass behind me. I whirled round. Kim and Sholto had both stepped into the shop.

I bit my lip, trying to will my suddenly racing heart to quiet down. I breathed out. Listened. There was a long slow scratching coming from the rear of the shop. One foot after another, my back to the shelves, I edged along the aisle, my eyes darting left and right, and forward and back. My right foot came down on a tube of something. The cap flew off, and pinged against a distant metal bracket. The scratching sound, now closer, suddenly became more frenetic.

I'd had enough. I walked as briskly as I could towards the sound, swinging the axe up as I reached the end of the long aisle and turned the corner and saw… just another zombie. Not one of the girls, nor Barrett or Stewart or Daphne. It was just some unknown soul missing an arm and the lower part of both legs. I swung the hatchet down. It died.

I breathed out. Then listened. I couldn't hear anything else. I could make out the shotgun pellets in the wall and floor around where the creature had lain. I turned and walked just as briskly back along the aisle.

"Come on," I said to the other two. "Let's get moving."

"Were they here?" Kim asked.

"They were, but not anymore. They must have gone in looking for food. Stewart or Barrett, probably. Perhaps Annette was told to help with the carrying. Someone fired two shots at that zombie at close range and managed not to kill it. Just blew off its feet and an arm. There was another zombie, but the gun wasn't loaded. They were chased out of the store and it took that long to reload the gun and fire again. That killed the second one. At some point before, during, or after, Annette must have dropped that hat on the bin. It probably was pointing towards Kew. They must have been desperate to have stopped here, especially if they were driving."

"We should hurry," Kim said, already striding off down the street.

No matter how quiet we tried to be, it wasn't quiet enough. Sometimes we'd hear a scurrying from the back of another shop. Sometimes we'd hear a scuffling from behind a closed door or from one of the flats above. Sometimes all we'd hear was the tinkling of glass on the road behind us as undead hands or heads broke through a top-floor window. A few times, that sound of breaking glass would be followed by a bone-cracking thump of a body hitting the pavement. Not every home over those few miles and a few dozen streets has become some zombie's tomb, but enough that it made the whole place seem like a Necropolis.

Three times we turned a corner and found ourselves facing the undead. Once we turned and ran down an alley. Twice we stood our ground, Kim with her axe, Sholto with his machete, and me with my pike. Then we came across three corpses, and they were corpses, not the undead. They were lying in the middle of the road, just short of a pedestrian bridge over the fenced-in railway line. Four crows perched proprietorially on a lamp post above them. Those birds had been busy, turning the bodies into little more than skeletons. Two of the dead lay in the road, one with a carving knife still lodged in its ribcage, the other's skull had been crushed. The third had died sitting with her back leaning against a red post box a few feet from the other two. We paused there long enough to make a hole in the fence, but didn't bother to find out how that third one had died.

"Someone's down there. Someone alive I mean," Kim said.

"But is it Annette and Daisy?" Sholto asked.

As we got closer to Kew, we came across more and more of the undead. I had hoped we could cut through the golf course to the south of the gardens and then just climb over the wall, but we'd given up on that and returned to the side streets. That was how, about two hours after we'd left the boat, we found ourselves lying on the roof of an apartment block overlooking the main entrance to Kew.

"That's the main entrance?" Sholto asked.

"According to this, it's the Victoria Gate," Kim said, looking at the pamphlet we'd brought from their boat. "There's a ticket office, a restaurant and shop."

The gate is a great wrought-iron affair embedded in thick stone. Embedded in the iron gate, and half knocking it over, is a bottle-green SUV. Around it, behind it, and past it, clawing at the building itself, are the undead.

"They drove up, and crashed, but what then?" I muttered, taking the scope.

"Can you see anyone?" Sholto asked.

"No one, but the doors and windows I can see are all blocked up." The building was a relatively new construction, built around a four storey Victorian tower. I quickly played the scope over the rest of the gardens.

The trees were in full leaf, though there were a few fallen branches on a slightly ragged lawn. The fountains weren't running and green was now the predominant colour in the flowerbeds. Otherwise, it can't have looked much different last year. Taking just that section of the view, I could almost believe there had been nothing more calamitous than a great storm. I could even, almost, pretend that the pack of zombies around the front gates were tourists clamouring for tickets. Almost. It was the greenhouse that gave the lie to that fantasy.

The glass had been broken, the frame hewn almost in two. I can only guess at the sequence of events, but without power to keep the interior warm and moist, the soil dried up, the roots lost anything to grip and, one by one or all together, the exotic trees and palms tumbled forward and back, smashing through the glass panes, fracturing the wrought-iron frame. A few panes of glass still hung from a few sections on either side, but otherwise the ground around the greenhouse was littered with dead plants, broken glass, and twisted iron.

Only one tree remains, a majestic giant palm that must have been as tall as the building before the glass had broken. With nothing left to hem it in, it has spread its fronds, each as big as a person, out and up to catch the sun. It's quite a sight.

"There has to be someone in there," Kim said, and I brought the scope back to the building. "Something has to be attracting the undead. Look at Them. They're actually trying to break through the glass. Someone has to be in there!"

"But is it your girls?" Sholto asked. "From what you said and what I've seen, Annette's resourceful. She could have grabbed Daisy when the car crashed. For all we know she could be in one of the apartments below us, watching the street, waiting for us to walk by."

"You think she is?" Kim asked.

"No hang on," Sholto said. "I don't mean we should do a room-by-room search. If we started that—"

"Wait," I said. There was something about the building. Something I'd seen but not registered. "There, the tower. Look at the tower." I handed the scope to Kim.

"A red towel! Hanging from the arch at the top. She's there. See?" She handed it to Sholto.

"She was there," he said, after taking a turn to examine the tower. "We don't know if she's still there now."

"Oh, come on!" she cried. "Look at the zombies around the door. They're trying to get in."

"Someone is in there," he said. "I'm not saying we don't go down there. I'm just saying we need to make sure we know who we're saving. While we're at it, it'd help if they knew we were coming. Does she know Morse code?"

"No," Kim said.

"You didn't set up any kind of signal or anything?" he asked.

"Seriously? What do you think?" she said.

"We'll hang up some sheets," I suggested. "From the roof, here. They'll be visible to anyone down there. That'll give her warning we're coming. No, I'll go and find them. You two keep watch."

Kim's worn out. I haven't known her long, but that's painfully obvious. The last thing I wanted was her charging around from apartment to apartment. A year and a lifetime ago, what had happened to her would have been called slavery and she'd have had decades of therapy to look forward to. What's happened to her since, just keeping alive, keeping me alive, I don't think there's an old world name for it. Now she's at breaking point. As for Sholto, I'm not sure Kim likes him very much. And me? All I know is that the more time I spend with him, the more I'm reminded that he's little more than a stranger who came into my life by blackmailing me.

I took my time going through the apartments. The building was full of noises and I paused at walls and doors, listening for any sounds of life. I heard none. At four I heard the undead. I left Them alone.

The sheets, red ones, came from an equally red apartment, with mirrors above the beds, above the bath and even, inexplicably, on the kitchen ceiling. We hung the sheets over the side of the roof.

That was three hours ago. We're still waiting.

Day 130, Garden View Apartments
Kew, London

03:00, 20th July

Kim woke me around twenty minutes ago. It's too dark to see what colour it is, but another towel has been added next to the red one on top of the tower.

"That's it. They're there. I know they are," Kim said, her tone daring us to suggest differently.

"That's good enough for me," Sholto said. "So what now?"

Day 130, Penlingham Spa & Golf Club
Milton Keynes

20:00, 20ᵗʰ July

"So what now?" Sholto had asked.

"I've been thinking about that," I said. "There are at least two hundred zombies down there. We're not going to be able to kill Them all. We'll have to lure Them away. I'll go back to the boat and bring back some petrol. Then we'll find a car and I'll drive it up to the gates. Kim you stay up here with the rifle—"

"Like hell I will!"

"If you go down there, they'll just start shooting. If Sholto goes down and asks them to hand over the girls, then they just might."

"They won't," she said. "There's nothing in the world that's going to get them to do that."

"The zombies will be gone," I said. "This will be their chance to escape, too. Their only chance, but only if they hand over the girls. That's why you need to be up here with the rifle. If the girls don't come out first, *then* you can shoot them."

"I'm going to shoot them anyway," she said.

"Kim's right," Sholto said. "The time for subtlety has gone. We get the girls out and burn the place down."

"Enough with the posturing!" I snapped. "Six months ago she made coffee and I wrote speeches. Killing people isn't the same as killing the undead. We can't just go in there with guns blazing. I mean for one thing, we've only got a few hundred rounds and most of that is for your M16, which you've admitted yourself isn't exactly accurate."

"No," he said with infuriating patience, "*you* don't understand. I mean we should literally burn the place down. We get the girls out first, and I'll be honest I like the idea of offering Barrett and the others sanctuary. That should get them out in the open, then Kim can shoot them. If that doesn't work, then I want to make sure that, ten years from now, I don't wake up with a knife to my throat. This ends here and now. If we can't shoot them, then we burn them out." He put his hand in his bag and brought out a cylinder. "I brought three of these from Lenham Hill."

"The incendiaries?" They'd been part of the self-destruct system that had failed to go off. "You said they'd detonate on a warm day."

"If the stuff inside comes in contact with the air, otherwise they're harmless."

"When, exactly, were you going to tell us you had them?" I asked sharply. "I thought we agreed, no more secrets."

"No, she said 'no more secrets'. I didn't agree to anything," he said. "Besides, I'm telling you now, aren't I? What is it? You want an inventory of everything I'm carrying? I've got a spool of high tensile fishing wire, half a pack of cinnamon gum, and a set of half decent lock-picks."

Like I said, I don't really know Sholto at all.

"Other people could have taken refuge in there before Barrett arrived," I said. "We can't just blow the place up. There has to be rules. There has to be some kind of justice."

"Exactly," Kim said. "You lure the zombies away and we'll get the girls out."

I didn't miss that she hadn't agreed with me. There was a tense moment before I let it go. After all, they were going to do what they were going to do, and I wasn't going to be in a position to stop them. It's not that I care what happens to Barrett, Stewart, or Daphne, I'm just worried what it might do to Kim.

"The gum," I asked, after a moment, "does that do anything special?"

The tension didn't break, but it fractured slightly.

Perhaps if we'd had more sleep one of us might have come up with a better plan. Then again, Kim and Sholto both seem to think that there's no problem so big it can't be solved with a sledgehammer and a long enough run-up. I really did think that given the opportunity, self-preservation would kick in, and Barrett, Stewart, and Daphne would just run. Perhaps if we'd slept, we might have spotted some of the chasmic holes in the plan. Whatever we did, it was always going to be a gamble. Broadly speaking, it paid off. We did get out of London.

The idea, it was too simple to really be called a plan, had come to me the moment I'd seen how the undead were clustered outside those iron gates. We'd have to use sound to lure Them away, it's all we know that works. Not music, though. With the mess of streets and alleyways that is London, we'd need to have it playing from successive rooftops. We could probably have managed that. The more difficult part would have been in turning one set of speakers off and another on so as to lure the undead further and further away from the gardens. Given time, no doubt Sholto could have rigged something up, he seems to be good at that. But we didn't have time.

It wasn't Annette and Daisy I was particularly worried about on that score. It was Kim. She was so far past breaking point it wasn't going to be long before she decided to try to storm the building. I'd have followed her, and Sholto wouldn't be far behind, and that would have been disastrous for us all. That left my stupidly obvious idea.

"I'll find a bike, go back down to the boat, get some petrol, and cycle back up here. We find a car, one that's close by since we don't want the undead to end up on the roads between here and the boat. I'll drive it up past the gardens and get the undead to follow. I'll head north, for as far as I can. I don't know where that will be, but I reckon I can give you an hour."

"And then?" Kim asked.

"And by then you better be back at the boat. I still say you should stay up here with the rifle, and Sholto goes down there." I raised my hand in surrender. "But I'll leave that up to you."

"Maybe Sholto should drive the car," she suggested.

"I know London," I said. "Besides, I can't run. The car suits me better. And there's another reason it would be better if you stayed up here on the roof."

"Oh?"

"If it works, then cut down these sheets. I'll take the bike with me. When I find a likely spot, somewhere out of sight, I'll ditch the undead. I managed it before. It won't be too hard. I'll cycle back this way to make sure you got away. So if the sheets are gone, I'll know you've made it back to the boat."

"Okay," she said reluctantly. "And then what?"

"You get back to the boat. I'll head down there. If the zombies have followed you, just take the boat back up river. They'll follow the engine, then you just turn it off and let the current carry you back downstream."

"And you'll meet us down by the bank?" she asked.

"Yep. And if I can't, then we'll meet on that beach in Wales."

"I don't know," Sholto said. "It's a bit…"

"Non confrontational?" I suggested. "Getting the girls somewhere safe, that's the important point. I'll be fine. You get them there, get them safe."

By five a.m. we'd found four bikes. The one I claimed for myself was a carbon fibre, long distance touring bike. Judging by the flags and photos pinned to the wall, it had been along The Great Wall, across the Sahara, and up Everest. I'd seen those pictures through the window when we'd been looking for a way into the building. One of the photos had the bike standing next to a barbecue, pedal-deep in snow, the owner clutching tongs in one hand and a burger in the other. I'd seen the owner through that window, too, but even if I hadn't, I'd have known he was in there from the smell. He was sitting against the wall, his legs splayed. He'd written a letter, and then he'd opened an artery on his wrist. The blood had soaked the piece of paper, making it unreadable, his last story forever unknown.

We found bikes for Kim, Sholto, and Annette in the back gardens of a row of terraces a few blocks further east. Their gears were rusty, the tyres perished and the chains loose, but that didn't matter. They'd only be cycling the few miles between Kew and the boat. One even had a child seat at the back.

Then we had to find a vehicle. Anything built in the last fifteen years, with a focus on crumple-zones and limiting damage to pedestrians in a collision, was out. So were the more sturdy looking diesel-powered vans and trucks. It was the wrong kind of neighbourhood. The cars were a mixture of the relatively upmarket and the cheap runabout.

I was about to send Sholto back to keep an eye on Kim, and continue the search on my way down to the river, when we found the Land Rover. It was one of those old Defender models, a battered behemoth that guzzled petrol and belched fumes, built for fields and hills, not the restraints of urban driving. It was perfect. The spare keys were hanging on a hook within easy reach from a broken window so we didn't even have to break into the house.

"I can go with you. To the boat and back," Sholto offered.

"Keep an eye on Kim. Make sure she doesn't… Well, just keep an eye on her, okay?"

"Sure."

"Right." I felt I should say more but didn't know how, let alone what. I got on the bike and cycled south, alone.

Getting back to the boat was far quicker than our journey from it, and not just because I was travelling by bike. I knew which roads to avoid and which were clear. The only delay was when I found a road blocked by a single decker bus driven through the front window of a dry-cleaner's. I could have got the bicycle past, but I didn't like the slow shuffling sound I could hear coming from the other side. I found another route. Considering what I was about to do, stopping to kill the undead would have been a waste of time. Until I got to the boat.

It was inevitable, I suppose. None of us had been as quiet as we should have been when we tied it up and came ashore. Three undead had gathered on the towpath. Two were close to the boat. The third was forty yards further north. Their heads were bobbing this way and that, as They shuffled about in small circles, seeking a sound like a dog seeking a scent. They heard me coming at about the same time I realised I couldn't avoid Them.

I dismounted and looked around. A few bushes rustled in the distance, but otherwise I could see no other zombies and nowhere else for Them to hide. I leaned the bike up against a tree, unslung the pike and started walking slowly towards the first creature.

When I was fifteen yards away I stopped and shifted my grip, angling the pike out so the point was aimed slightly downwards, the shaft held parallel to my body. When the zombie had taken another step forward, as its arms began their clutching grasp at empty air, I scythed the pike around. The blade cut deep into the creature's ankle. It didn't react, not even when it tried to take a step, the bone snapped and it fell face forwards onto the ground. Its hands clawed at the dirt. Its mouth bit down on grass, and I limped forward and plunged the spear-point through the back of its skull.

Then there were two. I edged off the path and onto the grass. I hefted the pike up, angling the point between the eyes of the creature on the left. They were still twenty feet away. I threw a glance over my shoulder. There was nothing behind me. I took a breath and two steps forward, the pike spearing out, my arms fully extended as the point went in between the creature's eyes. The crunch of bone seemed to echo off the buildings. I pulled the pike out, took a hopping skip backward, levelled the weapon and was about to repeat the manoeuvre when I noticed something different about the last zombie.

It was more recently dead, but that alone wasn't it. Its clothing was nearly intact, and again that wasn't what had given me pause. It was that the ends of the coat and bottom of the trousers, both too thick and warm for this weather, had been taped to boots and wrists. The hands were gloved. A solitary strap, perhaps from a mask, dangled from an ear. The woman this zombie had been was someone who had done more than just survive. She'd taken one look at the new world she'd found herself in and realised she needed to adapt. But her preparations hadn't been enough. I was limping backwards now, just as fast as the creature was approaching. It must have looked odd, like some macabre dance, but the more I looked at this creature, the more uncertain I became.

I can't be sure, but I thought I recognised the face. I don't know where from or when. Perhaps it was nothing more than a vague desire for resemblance in a kindred spirit who'd not had my luck. I think it was more than that. I think I once knew her.

My back thumped into a tree and that jarred me back to reality. I swung up and down, and the blade sliced into the face, smashing the skull and forever destroying those almost-familiar features.

I limped back to the bike, wheeled it to the spot where we'd moored the boat, then pulled at the rope until the craft was close enough to climb on board. I grabbed a fuel can, hefted it over the side, and skipped ashore after it. Working out how to carry it took another few minutes I'd not planned for. I settled for tying it to the crossbar. By then the boat had drifted back out into the river. I was tempted to just go. The sun was up, the day was starting to warm, and I wanted to get the next couple of hours over and done with. But I had no real confidence that I was ever going to see the boat again. I tugged at the rope, went back on board, and stuffed my bag with ration packs. Only then did I head back towards Kew.

I tried singing to myself, but I couldn't remember any tunes. I tried to recite poetry, but couldn't recall more than the first few words. I tried making up limericks, but couldn't think of a punch line. No matter how hard I tried to keep my mind away from it, as I cycled back through those deserted streets, I kept seeing London as it had been, as it would have been if not for the outbreak and my evacuation. The thought that I kept returning to was that all of the other cities of the world must be worse. An empty world, crowded with death. That's the legacy we leave the next generation.

I shouldn't have been thinking like that. Here and now, with a fire and in relative safety, it's not helpful. Cycling alone through London it almost got me killed.

I was on just another street, approaching two vans I thought had been parked. It was only when I was level with the rear tyres of the nearest that I registered the broken glass on the road.

Not wanting to get a puncture, I swerved at the same time as a zombie seemed to dive out from underneath the van. It flew head first into the bike's front tyres, knocking me and the bike over. I fell in a tangled heap, the full weight of the petrol can falling on my crippled right leg. The leg brace took most of the impact, but the sudden jarring of metal on those never-healed nerves sent a shooting pain right up my spine.

Something tugged at my left foot. A hand. I kicked out. It was gone. I tried to pull myself upright. The hand was back, gripping my ankle, pulling and tugging and getting tighter. I screamed and kicked, and managed to pull myself free. I staggered upright. I couldn't see straight. I stamped down randomly as I grabbed the bike and limped clear. My hand went to my pocket, my fingers fumbling with the buttons. I pulled out the pistol. The barrel wavered as I tried to focus. As my vision cleared I saw it. Not right in front of me as I'd thought, but still there, on the ground where I'd fallen off the bike. Its legs were missing below the knees.

"No, not missing," I remember saying, as a hysterical laugh escaped my lips. They were both visible, stuck under the front wheel of the van. The zombie must have been between the two vans when they crashed, and it had been stuck there as time had done its work, wearing down the sinews and tendons, until I came along. When it heard me, it leaped, leaving its trapped legs behind.

I kept my mind focused after that.

Kim was waiting by the Land Rover.

"You took your time," she said.

"Zombies. By the boat. Three of Them."

"Oh."

I started filling the tank. "You should be keeping watch. On the roof," I said.

"Sholto's doing that. I…" She trailed off.

I put the cap back on the fuel can, and put it into the back. "Would you give me a hand with this?" I asked, hefting the bike up. Together we got onto the roof and tied it down. Then there was no more reason to delay. "I may not make it back to the boat," I said.

"No, probably not," she said.

"Thanks for the vote of confidence." I tried to grin, to show it was a joke. I don't think it worked. "Get clear of the undead, get the boat across the river, find a car, and keep driving north until you see signs for Wales. Avoid the motorways. Avoid the cities. I'll see you on the beach."

"Will you?"

"I'll do everything I can to—" I began, but she interrupted.

"I can tell when you're lying. You're going to go after that scientist."

I sighed. "Perhaps. If I can. I'd have to, sooner or later."

"Okay," she said, softly as she put her hand on my arm. It was only the briefest of touches. "Okay," she said again, letting her hand fall, her tone now rigid once more. "We'll hang out flags at every house we go to. And we'll leave a note with the date when we were there. You do the same. If you don't make it to the beach, well, we'll be back. I'll be back. On the last day of every month, until you turn up."

"Right. I—"

"Give me thirty minutes to get in position. See you, Bill." She turned and jogged off, before I could finish the sentence.

Words left unspoken are often the most treacherous. You're never sure if what you were going to say is what the other person assumed. I pondered that as I stood by the Land Rover, just waiting for time to pass.

After five minutes I started to feel self-conscious, so I got inside the car. I checked the time. Ten minutes. Fifteen. Twenty-five. Thirty. I turned the key in the ignition. Nothing happened. I tried again. The engine turned over and then turned itself off. I tried again. The engine roared to life, then whimpered to a stop.

I forced my hands away from the dashboard and my feet away from the pedals. I took a breath, then another, and told myself to calm down, wait, count to five, and try again. I'd reached three when I had the metallic banging of something being knocked over. It came from the street to the right. I couldn't see the zombie, but I knew it was there. I muttered "four, five" under my breath as quickly as I could, and tried the key. The engine spluttered.

"Come on, come on," I murmured, coaxing the pedals, my eyes darting around, seeing if, somehow, there might be another car I could take. There was a bang, a cough, and the engine spluttered and gasped into an arrhythmic roar just as an arm windmilled around the edge of the wall. It was followed by a zombie wearing nothing but a pair of lurid blue shorts. It must have been outside during the storms earlier in the year because the dye had run, staining its legs.

I put the car into gear and pulled out. The creature stumbled into the road directly ahead. I'd only reached five miles an hour when I hit it. The creature twisted around as it was shoved backwards, turning a full three hundred and sixty degrees before slapping its arms down on the bonnet. Its bulging uncomprehending eyes met mine. I slammed my foot down, trying to force the car to accelerate as much by willpower as by mechanics. Its face smashed onto the bonnet with a crack of breaking teeth. Fingernails scratched and broke, flecks of paint flew up, and the creature just refused to be dragged under the wheels.

The road was too narrow, too hemmed in by other cars to get up enough speed. After thirty yards, I braked, changed gears, and reversed. It slipped, fell, stumbled back to its feet, and staggered towards me. I pulled out the gun, unwound the window, stuck the barrel out, and fired.

"Sorry," I said, as its body collapsed to the ground.

I wound the window back up and edged the car forward. I took a left, then a right, then right again, trying to pick up some speed. I ignored the zombies that appeared from side roads, and from behind parked cars. I ignored the sound of breaking glass from windows behind and to the sides and out in front. I ignored everything but the road in front as I made my way to Kew.

I took another right and there it was, the wall around the gardens, and the road that led past the main gate. I put my foot down. I wanted to dash past the undead, then stop a few hundred yards up the road until I was sure They were following. The road curved, and I saw the tops of the gates and the undead in the road in front. That's when the plan started to fall apart. They were already heading towards me, and They'd spread out across the road. I wasn't going to be able to drive past Them. I slowed and stopped.

I looked in the mirror. There were only three behind me. I looked up at the buildings. I could see the sheets. I could make out the towels hanging from the tower. I looked back at the road. Pushing and shoving, too many to count, They were getting closer.

I put the car into reverse and did a three point turn. I glanced down at the pistol. How many shots did I have left? It suddenly seemed important.

I edged the car forward, one eye on the three in front, the other on the approaching pack behind. I weaved the car left and right, picking up a bit more speed. Then, with a grimace, I gunned the engine and drove straight at the closest zombie. I swerved at the last moment, hitting it with the right side of the car. The lights smashed, the creature's arms flew up as it was knocked down and under the wheels. The car rocked as I drove over it. I threw the wheel to the left, aiming the car at the next creature. It lurched at the last minute. I missed. I turned the wheel to the right, but I was going too fast. Another miss. I eased my foot off the pedal and let the car coast to a halt, bumping up onto the curb.

I looked in the mirror as I played my foot up and down on the pedal. The engine sounded fine. Behind me, the two creatures were twenty yards away and getting closer. Behind Them, the pack was still approaching. Ahead, the road was clear for two hundred yards up to the next junction where a zombie had just turned onto the main road. I had time.

I leaned over, rolled down the passenger side window, then turned the wheel and edged the car forward so it was at a right angle to the road. The two zombies were now less than ten yards away. They were close enough I could see the grey flecks in their eyes. I picked up the pistol, aimed, fired. Missed. Fired again. One zombie fell, I aimed and fired. The bullet went low, smashing into the zombie's thigh. That was good enough. It collapsed to the ground, its good leg kicking out, its hands scrabbling at concrete as it tried to pull itself towards the car.

The pack was still a few hundred yards away. I edged the car around. There were two zombies on the road in front. Then three, then four. I eased the car forward, waiting until I was less than fifty yards from the nearest one, then I put on some speed, aimed the Land Rover straight at it, hitting it square on in an explosion of guts and gore. I missed the next two, but hit the one bringing up the rear. I looked back. The zombie I'd shot in the leg had disappeared under the mass of shambling feet.

And so it went on. Driving a few dozen yards, slowing, stopping, then darting forward to mow one or two down, then pausing to keep the pack in sight. My pied piper routine seemed to be working. I'd covered less than two miles in just over twenty minutes. The car was battered, but the engine sounded fine. The only problem was that I was heading due south, straight for the boat.

I took the first turning I came to, gunned the engine and ran down two zombies heading down the road towards me. I kept going until I reached an intersection. I braked. I waited, playing with the accelerator, letting the engine roar and bark until I was sure the pack was following, and then I waited some more. Then I picked the road that had the fewest undead on it, drove forward to the next intersection, and the waiting began again.

All my careful planning and thoughts about which roads might be best went out the window as I drove randomly through south London. Despite the undead, and the obstacles and rubbish that blocked the streets, driving was easy. The idea came to me that I could just keep this up, find an empty road and drive on through and out of London. I could go straight to north Wales and be halfway there before I ran out of fuel. In two days, three at the most I could be at the scientist's house. Perhaps I could even make it from there down to the rendezvous before the 2nd August. It was a perilously beguiling idea. Now that we'd our separate ways, it wasn't likely I'd see Kim, Sholto, and the girls before we all reached that beach. Certainly, there was little point in trekking around the country trying to find some sign of them. But what if they stayed on the river, waiting for me? I had to go and check.

I looked down at my watch. Well over an hour had gone by. I looked around trying to work out where I was. The road was bracketed by the same generic mix of fried chicken outlets, mini-marts, and betting shops that could be seen in any British city. I drove on until I saw a sign. I misread it and thought I was half a mile from Clapham Common. I thought if I could get to the Common, I could drive straight across it, leave the car, but take the rest of the petrol with me. Then I could cycle down to the boat, check they weren't waiting, cross the river, find another car and then, next stop, Wales. I put my foot down. The road bent, went under a bridge I was certain shouldn't be there, twisted, and then I saw a sign. Kew, half a mile.

I don't know how I got lost, or how I didn't realise. I suppose without any people, the landmarks looked different. Perhaps I just wasn't paying enough attention. Perhaps it was guilt, or something else. Whatever it was, I couldn't turn around, and I couldn't turn east. I had the river to the west so had no choice but to keep going south, back to Kew.

It wasn't too much of a problem, I told myself. It had been over an hour and a half. They should have got the girls free by then. I decided I'd — I didn't finish the thought. I turned a corner, saw the high wall around the gardens, saw the apartment block, saw the road was clear of the undead, and saw the sheets still hanging from the roof. Then I saw the reason why.

Kim was walking backwards, out of the gates, Sholto's M16 in her hands. I shifted gear, trying to coax another couple of seconds of speed out of the engine, my eyes scanning every which way for any sign of the girls or my brother. Kim paused, shifted her position, and fired. Then I saw Sholto. He darted out past the wall, Daisy under one arm, Annette being half pushed, half carried in the other. I smashed my fist down on the horn.

"In. In!" I yelled. They must have heard me. Sholto, at least, had seen me. He darted into the road angling towards the car, as Kim let loose a burst from the assault rifle. I brought the car to a stop, Sholto and the girls between it and the gates.

They opened the doors at the same time as I opened mine.

"Kim!" I yelled.

There was the far louder explosion of a shotgun. Kim stood her ground and fired again.

"Kim!" I bellowed, but I was already running towards her. I rounded the wall, and staggered to a halt. There seemed to be zombies everywhere. A forest of hands all reaching out, grasping towards us, just feet away. Then I realised that, no, we were safe. They were stuck on the other side of the ticket barrier, but then there was a metallic screech as a bracket gave, and the top of the barrier jerked forward a couple of inches. Kim fired again. She wasn't aiming at the undead. She was shooting into the building.

"It's over. We've won." It was a fatuous thing to say. "Just leave—" There was another shot, a loud percussive blast from a shotgun. I didn't see where the shot went or who had fired it.

"Not now Bill," Kim said, as calm as the eye of a hurricane. "Not yet."

I grabbed her and started pulling her back toward the car. She didn't seem to notice, she just fired again. Annette had already opened the rear door.

"Just get—" There was another shot, this time hitting the gate with a plinking of paint and iron. Kim raised the gun, pulled the trigger. Nothing happened.

"Now, Kim! Let's go!" My voice was hoarse and desperate.

"Stewart's still in there! He's still alive!" she screamed back.

"Kim! Please!" It was Annette. Where nothing I said seemed to be reaching her, that did. Her expression changed ever so subtly, not softening, if anything it became far harder, colder, and deeper than any I'd seen her wear before.

"Okay," she said, taking a step towards the car.

There was another shot. Paint flew from the bonnet. I turned. I saw him. Stewart was standing on one of the ticket kiosks. I don't know how he managed to get up there that fast. He yelled something. I didn't hear what. He half raised the shotgun. It went off before it could bear on us, blowing the scalp off one of the zombies beneath him. He opened the breach, his hand going to a pocket. I raised the pistol. I hesitated, but only for a moment. There wasn't time. We wouldn't get away. That's what I thought. I pulled the trigger.

He stopped moving. He stood there for a moment, motionless. Then he half raised a hand, his head rocking left and right. Then he looked at me and I'll remember that look. It was puzzled confusion. He shook his head slightly, took a step forward. His foot was over the edge of the ticket kiosk. He fell down into the mass of zombies waiting below.

"It's done," I murmured, wishing I could think of something more appropriate. There was another screech of metal, this time accompanied by a cracking of cement as two of the barrier's supports moved under the weight of the undead. I ran back to the car.

"We all in? Everyone okay?" I asked as I got back in the car. "Kim? Annette? How's Daisy."

"Daisy's fine," Sholto said. The engine started.

"Of course she is," Annette said. "She's a fighter. You took your time."

"Sorry about that," I said, as we moved off.

"Kim?" I glanced over at her. She was staring ahead, eyes unblinking. "You all right?"

"Yeah," she said slowly. "Yeah. Seems so."

"What went wrong?" Sholto asked.

"I got lost," I said. "What about you?"

"You saw," Kim said. "The car only got rid of the undead out on the road, and that didn't happen immediately. You remember how fast a zombie walks? And a zombie at the back of a pack can't move until those at the front have cleared off. It took an hour before enough of Them had disappeared that we could go out on the street."

Like I said, it would have been better if we'd slept before coming up with a plan.

It had been less than two hours since I'd started driving around south London. As we headed south, I was trying to work out how much of that time had been spent driving on that same road, between Kew and the boat, and how many zombies might still be in front of us.

"This is going to be tight," I said.

"What does that mean?" Kim asked.

"We might not be able to go straight to the boat."

"What's this about a boat?" Annette asked.

"It's about a mile away. We've got enough food for months, and enough petrol to get us to the coast."

"That's good," she said.

"Yeah, yeah it's just—"

"Up ahead," Sholto interrupted softly. There were seven in the road, heading towards us.

"Hold on," I said, angling the car towards the curb.

"No, behind Them." He pointed.

I took another look. Behind the seven were at least a dozen more. I cursed as I slammed my foot down on the brake. There was a yell of protest from the back.

"Sorry," I muttered, as I threw the car into reverse, backed up fifty yards and turned into a side road.

The undead were everywhere now. Five here, ten there. On every road and every side street and it seemed like arms were stretching down from every window. There was no longer any chance of avoiding Them.

"This isn't going to work, Bill," Kim said. Daisy whimpered as we thumped over another body.

"I know."

Heading north or east into London was no good. All the undead I'd been luring away from Kew were there. We couldn't go south. That left west, and west was the river.

I looked at the fuel gauge. It was still more than half full.

"It was Richmond Bridge, you said you crossed?" I asked. "You think we can get the car over it?"

"Sure, it was pretty empty," Sholto said, with a confidence I'm sure was meant to reassure. It just made me think he couldn't remember.

"Then that's what we'll do. We'll see if we can get away from the undead, then get back to the boat later." I knew we wouldn't as soon as I said it.

The bridge was empty and clear. I don't know why it wasn't demolished, but then I don't know why the other bridges were. It doesn't matter. It's just another one of those questions to which we'll never know the answer. Once we'd crossed the river, the going was easier. Not easy, though. The undead began to fill the road behind us, and often up ahead. The way to drive in the city was to bomb down the roads as fast as the car would allow, stop at each junction, wait and listen, and then pick which turning to take. Even so, we ended up running over at least one of the undead every few hundred yards. The real difficulty lay in finding a route that was clear of obstructions. Every fourth or fifth junction we'd be forced down some road half blocked with a car or van, and we'd have to push our way through with a screech of metal, flecks and sparks flying as the paint was scraped away.

"It's no good," I said.

"What?" Kim asked

"The roads. If we keep doing this we're going to end up in Westminster, back at the river, or completely broken down."

"We can't turn around," she said flatly.

"There's a hotel at Charing Cross," Sholto said. "I stayed there for a couple of days on my way to Lenham. It's a good spot. Doors on each side and easy access to the rooftops."

"No," I said. "We need to get out of London."

"Then stop here," Kim said. "Just for a few minutes. Until you know where you're going."

I did, on a narrow alley with warehouses either side. Daisy started to cry. Not loudly, not that full-blown wail of an infant in torment, but with a persistence that said she wasn't going to stop until her needs had been met.

"We can get out here," Kim suggested. "Continue on foot, find some bikes, get back to the boat, take it up stream, and find another car somewhere else."

"No," I said. I was trying to think. "We're finally across the river. I don't want to go back."

"The food and the fuel are back on that boat," Kim said.

"And it'll be days before the zombies around there go back into that dormant state. Two days, three, four. It doesn't matter. Listen to Daisy, we can't stay in London."

"Well where then?" she asked. "We can't stay here."

"No," I said. "But, I think… I think I know. Yes. The fastest way out, right? Okay. This is going to get bumpy."

"What is?"

I put my foot down, and pulled off once more.

"Bill?" she asked, warningly. "What's going to get bumpy?"

"The train lines. That's the only way. Where are we?" I leaned forward to peer at the meagre patch of skyline visible above the tall warehouses. "Right, it's about a mile."

I turned the corner and angled the car around.

"What is?" Kim asked. "A level crossing?"

"A bridge."

A couple of years ago, Jen had had to do a piece for the news. It was a segment on constituency boundary changes. In that particular constituency, the boundary was being moved from one side of the railway line to the other. Since no one lived on the tracks, no one was being affected. She was giving the interview to make a point out of how much parliamentary time was being wasted.

The bridge was a good spot for the interview. It was also a great spot to get down to the tracks themselves as the only thing separating the railway from the road was a steep slope and a flimsy chain-link fence. I remember it well because, when the journalist asked where we'd like to record the piece, neither of us considered that with a train going by every thirty seconds it would be next to impossible to record a two minute interview.

"Eyes open. We're looking for three tower blocks," I said, as I took turning after turning, trying to get out from that mass of warehouses and side streets and back towards somewhere more familiar. "They're on the east side of the bridge, about half a mile from it."

"Like those ones?" Annette asked, her hand darting forward.

"No. It's three tower blocks, close together," I said after glancing at the skyline.

"Oh. Those ones, then?" she said, pointing of to the left.

"No, not them either."

"Oh. How about those?"

"No."

It took half an hour to find the railway line. It took another fifteen minutes to find the bridge. By then I'd stopped looking in the rear view mirror. The road was packed with the undead, more than I could easily count.

"Seat belts on," I said, eyeing the fence.

"It looks solid," Kim said.

It wasn't.

The front bumper had barely connected before the fence collapsed. The car slid down the embankment, coming to a halt on the tracks. I looked left and right. I could see for a mile in either direction and nothing moved. I looked behind. A zombie appeared at the top of the embankment.

I put the car back into gear, and drove up and over the rails, just as the creature tumbled head first down the slope. The Land Rover slewed left and right as the wheels tried to find purchase on the loose gravel. I glanced behind. The top of the slope was now full of the undead. There were dozens of zombies at the top of the embankment. Dozens more were tumbling down onto the tracks and who knows how many were close behind.

I shifted gears again, got the wheels straight and we drove off. After ten minutes the undead behind us were lost to sight. We left London.

Day 131, Penlingham Spa & Golf Club, Milton Keynes

03:00, 21st July

Thunder. I can't remember the last time I heard that. It's woken Daisy, and it took forever to get her to sleep. At least nothing can hear her over the sound of the storm. Hopefully.

The only illumination, other than the lightning and the embers of our fire, comes from a light from one of the bikes. It's the kind that charges itself up as you cycle. Since we're stationary, we've got to wind the pedals by hand to keep it charged. It's a pain. That's something else to look for as soon as we've found food and water and everything else we're going to need. But we can't do that yet. Not until this storm stops.

Getting out of London was a little more eventful than I just wrote, but not by much. It took half an hour to get into the rhythm of driving along the railway tracks, sometimes in the middle, sometimes alongside them, sometimes jolting along with one set of wheels on the sleepers, the other kicking up a spray of gravel. The tracks often bent or branched in odd directions thanks to the vagaries of the Victorian builders who originally laid them, and that slowed us down, but it was by far the safest way of travelling we've found.

Annette noticed it first.

"We're higher than the houses," she said abruptly.

"That's right," Sholto replied, clearly distracted.

"No," Annette said, her voice dripping with the irritation of the young at the stupidity of the old, "I mean we're much higher."

"Well of course, trains are usually…" I trailed off. I understood. "The embankment."

In most places the railway was built on a rise a few feet higher than the surrounding houses. In some places it was built even higher. There were a few places, like the bridge where we'd come down, where this wasn't the case, but not many. The salient point being that the undead can't climb up a steep slope, not easily, and not before we were already driving off into the distance.

The only real danger came when we had to make our way past abandoned locomotives and cargo wagons, or through stations and level crossings. Even then, the danger was limited. The zombies heard us coming and obligingly stepped into the middle of the tracks where we could see Them from afar.

Even if the journey had been more difficult I don't think we'd have cared. We were together. We were all alive, and we were all, more or less, well.

"What's that?" Kim asked. I glanced in the mirror. Annette had taken a book out of the canvas bag she'd brought from Kew.

"Our book. I've been teaching Daisy to read. It's the story of the plants. I grabbed it from the shop before…" She coughed before continuing with forced brightness and a brittle smile, "I've been teaching her to read."

"Hey, that's a good idea," Sholto said in a cheerfully condescending tone. "Might be a bit advanced for her, though."

"You don't need to patronise me," Annette said. "Who is he?" she added, turning to Kim.

"Oh, right," I said, grinning. "Introductions. Sholto, this is Annette and Daisy. Annette, this is Sholto, my brother."

"Really?" Her eyes widened, and she seemed animated once more. "Cool! How did that happen?"

And for the next twenty miles, he told her. It was a slightly edited version of the story, expurgated as much for our benefit as for hers.

"Do we have a plan?" Kim asked. "I mean, I take it we're not going back to the boat."

"No plan, not really. We'll follow the train line as far as we can. And no, there's no point going back to London. We'll find food somewhere else."

"Will we make it to the beach?" Kim asked.

"Why do we want to go to a beach?" Annette asked.

"There's a boat waiting for Sholto. If we can get there by the 2nd August then we'll be able to get a lift."

"Another boat? Really? You didn't tell me that bit," Annette said.

And the next five miles were spent explaining that.

"Sholto's a silly name," Annette announced, when she was finally satisfied that we'd told her all the details.

"It's as good as any other," he said.

"Not really," she said. "What's your real name?"

"Real name?" he asked.

"Well, he's Bartholomew Wright. So are you a 'Wright'?"

"Ah, I see. Well that's another long story—" he began.

"And one that can wait," Kim interrupted. "Daisy needs feeding. And changing if we can manage that, but food comes first."

"We can't stop here," I said, looking around.

We were driving through a cutting with six-foot-high embankments hemming us in on either side. Above them protruded a mess of steam-stacks, steel chimneys and plastic pipework, as uninviting as it was menacing. I tried to coax a little more speed out of the car, thankful for once that the noise of the engine blocked out any sounds from the nearby undead.

The embankments became lower, and the industrial clutter turned into neat little houses nestled around an old railway station. There was a collective intake of breath as we drove past the platforms. That breath stayed held when we reached the other side and drove through a level crossing. The barrier, a painted wooden pole with a metal grating hanging from underneath, looked absurdly flimsy. It was already moving under the weight of a dozen zombies pushing against it trying to reach our car. Then, as the station became a church, then a cemetery, then fields, the breath was released and turned into a half-laughing sigh as the town disappeared into the rear-view mirror.

About five miles further north, we crossed a twenty-foot long bridge over a river too small to be marked on the road atlas we'd found under the back seat. A field to the left had a forlorn 'sold for development sign' planted firmly in the soil. To the right was an empty patch of concrete about the size of a football pitch, crisscrossed with white painted squares, each neatly numbered. A faded sign facing the railway read 'Farmers Markets Wednesdays & Saturdays. Antiques Fair Sundays'.

"This'll do," I said, pulling the car to a stop. We had a clear view for a couple of miles in every direction. "I can't see anything but birds."

"We made it," I said, as we got out of the car.

"Hmm?" Kim asked, taking Daisy from Annette.

"Out of London," I said.

"That's important is it?" Annette asked.

"Well, perhaps only to me," I replied.

We scavenged wood from the railside, spared a splash of petrol to get the fire going, and then realised what we'd forgotten.

"No saucepan?" Sholto asked.

"It was in the bag, on the bike," Kim said.

"Don't you have anything in there?" Annette asked, pointing at Sholto's bag.

"Just some cylinders. Work stuff."

"Work stuff? What's that supposed to mean?" she asked suspiciously.

"Explosives," I told her. "There's no point trying to hide it from her," I said to Sholto, "she'd only go and look."

"So what *do* we have?" Kim asked, as Annette eyed Sholto with renewed wariness.

We had the food I'd taken from the boat that morning and the little remaining from the day before. It came to about thirteen meals' worth. There was some rope, some matches, my journals, a few pencils, Daisy's book, a few water bottles, and a tin mug I'd liberated from Longshanks Manor. It had belonged to Archibald Greene, the butler there. He'd kept it on a shelf next to a set of fine bone china that he never used. I'd never asked him why he kept it or where it had come from, but I'd always wondered. That's why I took it with me. And we had our weapons, of course, and the clothes we stood up in, but not much else.

The mug was balanced on the edge of the fire, and we stood and watched and tested whether that saying about a watched pot applied to an old tin mug.

"Daisy can eat this stuff, right?" Kim asked peering doubtfully into one of the pouches of dehydrated food.

"Well, it's full of E-numbers and preservatives, but what else is there?" I asked.

"That's what I thought," she said.

"Food and bikes," I said. "That's what we need next."

"And a saucepan," Sholto said.

"And some more mugs," Annette added.

"And some diapers," Sholto added.

"And toilet paper."

"And blankets."

The list grew as, in defiance of folklore, the water came to a boil. It turned out that Daisy could, theoretically, eat the stew once it was rehydrated. She just didn't want to. She took one cautious sniff at the spoon, wrinkled her nose and turned her head away.

"Maybe when it's cooler," Kim suggested.

"Yeah. We should be going anyway," Sholto said, pointing back the way we'd come. An indistinct figure was moving jerkily across the distant bridge towards us. We got back in the Land Rover and continued north.

"What about stopping at a town?" Kim asked. She was pouring over the map, trying to work out where we were. For some reason, no one ever thought that a train driver would need to know which way was which. The few signs we did pass seemed to be in code. Instead we were relying on the names of the stations we drove through. The trouble was that few of those were in our map, and the handful that were didn't tally with the occasional glimpses of signs on the roads the train tracks went over, under, or alongside.

"I don't know. Towns are dangerous," I finally replied.

"Less so than cities, and what's the alternative?" Kim asked.

"We've got petrol," I said. "Enough to get us another hundred miles. Probably a bit more, and if the track ahead is anything like the last twenty or so, we'll do it in a couple of hours. But when it runs out, we're going to be on foot."

"We could find more petrol," Annette suggested.

"Perhaps, but we could spend all day looking for it. Besides, the problem right now is the engine. It's just too loud. We need to find somewhere to ditch the car, and get away from it before the undead start gathering around. Ten miles. Twenty for preference."

"I'm not walking that," Annette said.

"No. We need bikes. Then we can cycle off, find a farm or somewhere like that. Somewhere with some fruit trees and thick walls. Somewhere big enough there's a room we can soundproof so that Daisy won't be heard. Then, tomorrow, we'll do the same. We've nine days and about three hundred miles to cover. If we can manage fifty miles a day, we'll be fine."

"That might be pushing it," Sholto said.

"I know," I said. "But let's take it one day at a time."

After another hour, with the last of the fuel in the tank and the needle hovering around the halfway point, I brought the car to a stop. I checked behind, ahead and to either side. All appeared peaceful.

"It's time to find some bikes," I said.

"We're out of petrol?" Kim asked.

"We will be soon. We've eight miles of straight track behind, two ahead, the nearest town is a mile after that. We've got at least half an hour before the nearest zombie finds us."

"But it's the middle of nowhere," Annette said.

"Not quite. Look down there. Do you see the rugby posts? That means a school, and out here that's got to be a boarding school. Some of the kids and the staff would have had bikes. Since the schools were evacuated by train, they'll have left them behind. It's worth a look. Better odds than going house to house." I opened the door and added, "Kim, if you boil up some water, I'll go and—"

"Woman does cooking, while man goes hunting? I don't think so," she said. "Sholto and I'll go down there. You get a fire started and get ready to get going if we come back at a run." She handed Daisy to me before I could object.

"Don't look at me," Sholto said with a grin, before following her down the embankment and off towards the school.

There were plenty of fallen branches to burn, and we had a nice little fire going by the time we spotted Kim wheeling a bike across the playing fields.

"There are bikes," she called out triumphantly when she'd reached the bottom of the slope.

"Evidently," I said.

"There's a shed half full of them," she said. "They're slightly rusty, and the tyres are very flat, but we found a pump."

"Great," I murmured.

"That's not all," she called out. "There's a minibus with half a tank of petrol. That'll get us another twenty miles."

"Every little helps," I muttered.

"What's in the bag," Annette asked, already halfway down the embankment.

"You can take the bike up to the car. These too," Kim said, pulling some cans out of her pack. "Found them in the refectory, because a place like this can't just have a canteen. I got a saucepan as well. And these." She pulled out a fistful of tea towels. I looked at her quizzically.

"Daisy does need a change," she said.

Kim was already heading back towards the school when Annette, struggling under the combined weight of the bike and the supplies, reached the top of the slope.

"Do you want to change her?" I asked hopefully.

"Oh no, I've done that plenty of times. I wouldn't want you to miss out on the fun."

She set about boiling up some water while I did what I could with the tea towels. Daisy didn't complain. Much.

It was another half an hour before we saw them again. Kim was out in front and definitely hurrying this time. Sholto was thirty feet behind. Both were cycling hard through the long grass of the rugby pitches. There was only one thing that could make them hurry, and that was confirmed a minute later when a zombie stumbled around the corner of one of the red brick buildings. It was followed by a second, then a third.

Annette was halfway down the embankment before I could yell at her to get in the car. I put Daisy in, grabbed the pike, and then stood and waited anxiously. I hated that, standing there, knowing I couldn't help. By the time Annette reached the bottom of the slope, Kim had almost reached her, and the three undead had become thirty. Kim threw another bag to her, then, dragging the bike in one hand and Annette with the other, ran up the slope, Sholto just a few steps behind.

"My fault. My fault," Sholto said, as we finished tying on the last bike. "Should have realised. A place like that, food, water, gas in the tank. There had to be a reason it wasn't looted. I thought I was opening a door to an office. Turned out to be the assembly hall. It was packed with the undead."

"Kids?" I asked as we got in. The nearest zombie had just passed the first set of rugby posts so was still a few hundred yards and a steep slope away from us.

"Can't be certain, but I doubt it," he said. "The name on that minibus wasn't the schools. Some people came to loot the place and got infected. Or maybe they were the ones who brought the infection here. Can't say how many and can't say where from. I guess it doesn't really matter."

"No," I said, starting the engine. "I guess not."

The trip was far from a failure. We've four bikes, three kilos of canned meatballs, two of peaches, twenty tea bags, a saucepan, the towels and a dozen assorted bottles from a vending machine. I've had far worse days than that.

We kept driving until four p.m.

"This is it. All change," I said, as I brought the car to a final stop.

"We're out of petrol?" Kim asked.

"We've about five miles left. But the tracks are heading off in the wrong direction. We might as well stop here. That field looks clear, we'll head off that way and find ourselves a likely looking farm."

Eyes open for the undead, we crossed the fields until we came to a house, but it was too close to the car. Zombies were shambling along the road outside it, heading towards the train line. We cycled along paths and trekked across fields until we, literally, stumbled over our first motionless zombie, squatting unheeding in the middle of a bridle path. Brambles snaked across the ground, catching and snaring the creature.

"That farm over there looks all right," Sholto said as he cleaned his machete.

It did, until we got closer. There were at least ten undead and two bodies in the farmyard. We pushed on. It was a similar scene at a small hamlet half an hour later. We came around a corner to find eight creatures squatting by a war memorial in the middle of a small roundabout. We turned around, cut across a field, and two long, slow, miles later, found ourselves here at this golf club. Or what would have been a golf club if it'd been finished. We'd seen the chimney stacks from the edge of a copse of trees half a mile to the south. They'd ripped out the interior, and the side and rear walls. The building is nothing more than its facade and the front half of the roof, held up with scaffolding covered in plastic sheeting. Most of that sheeting had been ripped and torn over the last few months. By the time we got here we were too tired to look for anywhere else, and then the storm began.

We have plenty to burn. We have something to eat. It's so drenched in sugar that Daisy is having violent mood swings. She goes from vigorous jumping and bouncing to morose crying, but the storm is loud enough to cover that. We're all still alive, we're all together, and we are, finally, out of London.

15:00, 21st July

"You don't have to talk about what happened if you don't want to," Kim said.

"And I don't," Annette replied. "But that doesn't mean I won't. Bill needs to know, so he can write it down. That's important. Not for me. Not for you either, but for Daisy. She needs to understand, when she's older, why the world is the way it is. So I'll tell you, I just wanted you to know that I didn't want to."

"I don't think I really started distrusting them until we got to the boat," she said. "I mean, I knew they weren't nice people, but you'd let them take us in the truck, right? So you had to trust them a bit."

"Sorry," I muttered. She ignored me.

"I was so worried about Daisy, and what we'd do if we crashed and I had to grab her and run or something, that I didn't notice how weird they were being. All three of them, they were quiet. Almost… calm, yeah, that's it. I didn't really notice it until after we'd left the Abbey. It was the speed, you see. We were going so fast, and I knew that wasn't part of the plan. I looked behind but I couldn't see your car. I was going to say something and that's when I realised that none of them had said a word since they'd started the engine. That was scary. These three people, not saying a word as the truck hurtled down the road. It wasn't normal. So I didn't say anything." She picked up a branch and prodded the fire.

"It didn't take long to get to the river," she went on. "There was this one zombie by the boathouse. Stewart jumped out of the truck and fired his shotgun. That was stupid. It was louder than the engine had been. Barrett grabbed the gun and told him to go and check the boat. She told Daphne to start carrying the food and petrol in, and then she told me to help. I had Daisy in one arm, and I was trying to drag this petrol can along the ground, and I was stupidly doing what she said. I should have run, but I thought we were still waiting for you guys. Stewart got the boat in the water, and me and Daphne had made maybe five trips each." She thought for a moment. "Maybe it wasn't as many as that. I'm not sure. I wasn't really counting. I kept on looking down the road, expecting to see you any minute. I was sure you'd come." She threw the branch onto the fire.

"I'd sort of half thrown this box to Stewart, and was hurrying back towards the door when Barrett came running in. She slammed the door closed and threw boxes and crates down in front of it. She said there were too many outside and we needed to go. That's when I first got it. I was standing there, looking at all this food and I knew there was meant to be half in your car and half in the truck, but this was most of it. I mean, all the food from the Abbey was there. They couldn't have left you with any."

"We never really checked," Kim said, "but I think they loaded the car down with junk. They didn't want us to catch up."

"That's what I heard them saying, later. That Liz was meant to make sure you two didn't get to the river. They'd told her that they'd pick her up a few miles downstream. They'd drawn lots, and Liz had drawn the short straw, except I think Barrett had arranged that. Anyway, I was staring at the food trying to work out what it meant. Not that it mattered, because Daisy was on the boat and I couldn't leave her. So when Barrett sort of pulled me on board, I had to go with it. Then I got pushed down into a cabin, me and Daisy, and after that I couldn't see what happened. But I could hear them, even over the sound of the engine. I don't think they knew how loud they were being. They certainly didn't mean for me to hear them fighting over who would shoot Liz."

"Over whether they should or not?" I asked.

"No, it wasn't like that. They were arguing over which one of them was the better shot. They wanted her dead, you see. She wasn't really one of them, that was what Barrett said. But Liz 'knew', and that's why she had to die. They weren't really going to pick her up downstream. She was meant to die out there with you. Instead there she was, swimming out to the boat. They could see she'd been bitten. That's what Stewart said, she'd been bitten and was going to die, so why waste the ammo? But Barrett said she might be immune and they couldn't risk it. They had to make sure she was dead, otherwise she might tell someone. I don't know which one did shoot her in the end. But they did."

"It was Stewart," Kim said.

"Oh. Right. I think he was the better shot. He certainly thought so. He and Barrett argued about that. They argued about everything. It was weird. Like, we were on this river a few feet from the shore and at any time either one of them could have just got out and left. From the way they were yelling at each other I thought one of them would. Or that whoever had the gun would just shoot the other. But they didn't do that, either. It was almost as if they couldn't."

"And Daphne?" I asked. "Did she argue and fight too?"

"No. She didn't say anything. Nothing at all. It was like, as bad as Barrett and Stewart were, they were trying to act human. Daphne, she didn't even try to be normal."

"I remember when Chris was bitten," I said. "She wanted to just leave him there, she didn't even want to wait to see if he'd turn."

"No, it wasn't like that," Annette said, clearly annoyed at the interruption. "Whenever she'd look at me or Daisy, it was with this dead expression, like she hated everything about us, but somehow… It's hard to explain, but somehow me and Daisy were important. Not us in particular, but the idea of us. Does that make sense?"

"Yeah, I think so," Sholto said. "They were protecting children in general, not you and Daisy personally."

"Hmmm, no, I'm not sure that was it," she said doubtfully. "Anyway, Barrett came down to the cabin and said you were dead. I'd have known she was lying even if she'd tried to sound sincere, but she didn't. She said it was going to be okay and that she'd look after us and I didn't believe that either. I cried a bit, just for show. Well, mostly for show. I could hear them talking. Making plans. They were convinced everything would be all right if they could just get to Scotland. I don't know why. I think they'd just convinced themselves. I knew they'd never get there. You'd said they wouldn't." She paused, looking at me.

"They wouldn't," I said. "With all the petrol we'd had, they probably wouldn't have made it out to sea."

"They thought they could make it, but I knew the only way you'd find us was if we stayed on the river. So if they were going to try to get out to sea then Daisy and I needed to escape. I was ready to do it, too, but every time we stopped at one of the locks, they made me leave Daisy in the cabin and go and help. That's when I came up with my plan. They were stupid, you see. Not stupid about zombies, but stupid about surviving. Like, they wouldn't use the engine much because of the noise, but they had no problem using the shotgun to blow the zombie's heads off when we drifted close to the banks. That was like a game to them. It was sick. Or like at night, they'd not leave anyone on watch. That's how I did it. I just waited until they were all asleep."

"Did what?" Sholto asked.

"I threw most of the petrol and food over the side. I kept enough for Daisy, and left them a bit for the next day. Then I threw some wrappers around near where Daphne was sleeping."

"And she got blamed?" I asked.

"That's the thing. They didn't even notice. I hadn't realised, how could I? I spent most of my time down in the cabin. They weren't rationing the food. They had no idea how much they'd brought with them. Not until about lunchtime on the second day. Then they were like 'oh, I thought we had more food than that'. That's what I mean about them being stupid. I put on my best scared-little-girl act, and I told them about Kew and how it had all this fruit and stuff growing in the greenhouses, and how some of the plants had been there for hundreds of years, so they'd obviously be there still. And then I talked about the tractors and how they'd have fuel we could use."

"You'd been there before?" Sholto asked.

"Oh no, places like that were too expensive. I told them I'd been there on a school trip, but that was a lie. I got it all from the pamphlet. It had a map of the place and some pictures, and I just made up the rest."

"This one?" Kim took the brochure out of her pocket.

"That's it, with the finger paint. I knew you'd find it! It took ages to get the ink off Daisy's fingers, but at least that gave me something to do…" She trailed off again. "I thought that I'd find some way of escaping, you see. You'd find the pamphlet and you'd go up to Kew, and me and Daisy could find some house to hide in and we'd just wait for you. But it didn't work out like that. The river was blocked. Well, you must have seen that, right? And did you see the towels I hung over the side of the boat? So we had to go ashore, I thought that was our chance, except they decided they'd drive. It was the zombies. They were all gathered on the bank a bit further downstream, near where those boats had been wrecked. I said we should just run, you know. We'd have easily outpaced the undead, but the others, they didn't want to because they were afraid of being caught. And that was stupid too.

"I think it was Barrett's idea to empty the last of the petrol out of the boat and drive up to Kew. Then Stewart would find the food, and Daphne would find the petrol, and they'd just keep on driving along the river until they were through London and out the other side. Stupid, right?"

Kim and I exchanged a look.

"I mean," Annette went on, "okay, so it might have worked if they'd gone straight to Kew. But they saw this little shop on the way. The windows weren't broken and Daphne saw something on the shelves that she wanted. I don't know what, but she made them stop. They knew the zombies would have heard the car's engine, but they actually stopped. I was ready to run, but Barrett said I should go and help carry. That meant

Daisy was stuck in the car while I was outside. Stewart went inside. He wasn't gone for long. There was a shot and he started shouting 'run, run', which was a totally pointless thing to say. I barely had time to put Daisy's hat on that bin, you know, another clue. Then we were off again."

As if on cue Daisy pulled the hat off, threw it to the ground and then picked it up again.

"Did you find her ribbon?" Annette asked

"Her ribbon?" Kim asked. "No."

"I dropped that out of the car window about a mile further on."

"Sorry, we didn't see it," Kim said.

"Oh. Well, never mind." She sounded disappointed.

"They must have been furious when you got to Kew and found no food there," Sholto said.

"Oh no. There was food. Lots of it. That was the problem. I was expecting we'd have to split up and go and look for supplies. That was going to be my chance you see, because I don't think they were expecting me to try to run. But the storeroom behind the cafe was full of juice and crisps and biscuits and stuff. Wine and beer, too. Crates and crates of it. That cheered them up. But they didn't just grab what they could carry. They wanted to take it all. Then they realised that they weren't going to be able to do that, so they actually started going through it. They were sorting it, throwing aside the stuff they didn't like. That's when I grabbed Daisy. I ran to the door, but it was too late. The zombies had arrived. They'd followed the sound of the engine, of course. And then, They started beating at the door and Daisy started crying and…" She swallowed. "We were trapped. After that, something changed. It was like I was seeing the others properly for the first time, and I didn't like the way they were looking at Daisy and me. We barricaded the doors, and all right, they did an okay job at that. But once that was done, once they thought they were safe, they went back to dividing up all that food. I started looking for another way out. I didn't find one, but the storeroom had a proper reinforced door, with another door at the back that led to the tower. There was a small safe in the storeroom. I think that's why the door was reinforced. I got Daisy and locked us in there."

She smiled, but the odd shadows from the firelight turned it into a feral grin.

"It took them a while to notice," she said. "They tried to break the door down, but they couldn't. They tried shooting it with the gun, but the pellets bounced off the steel. They shouted at us for a bit after that, then they just left us alone. For days. I'm not sure how many. I think they must have been waiting to see if the zombies did just go away. But they didn't. When I climbed the tower to hang out the towels I saw the zombies. Hundreds and hundreds of Them. And there was no sign of you."

"Sorry," I murmured again. "My fault. I was sick."

"Well, I didn't know that, did I?" she snapped. "I started to think you weren't coming. Oh, it doesn't matter. Not now. They ate all their food. I think that must have been all they were doing, eating. Then they started trying to smash through the wall. They weren't very good at it, but they'd have managed it in the end. I heard them talking, just outside the door. I don't know if they knew I was listening. I don't think they cared. It was Daphne who said it, 'It doesn't matter how much she eats. There's still going to be food in there. Fresh food.' Stewart said, 'No, we agreed. After that girl, we weren't going to do it again.' Barrett said, 'It's simple mathematics. We're going to be here for weeks. We won't all survive. Those girls are already dead. It's just a question of whether we're dead too'." Annette sniffed.

"That's when I stopped listening. I'm not stupid," she said. "I know what they were talking about. I climbed up the tower again. I was going to climb down the outside, I'd carry Daisy and we'd run past the zombies. Or we'd try." She sniffed again. "I don't know if we'd have made it because when I got to the top of the tower, I saw the sheet hanging from that building. I hung up another towel and, well, then you came. Thank you for that."

"I'm so sorry—" I began.

"Never mind that." She gave a brittle smile. "We're all here together, and that's what's important."

"Cannibalism? I don't believe it," Kim said. We'd walked along to the far end of the scaffolding, which was as much privacy as we could find. "I mean, they were just winding her up weren't they? Just trying to frighten her?"

"Why would they lie? It explains why they stuck together at least, why they wanted to make sure Liz was dead."

"But, really?" she asked. "After only a few months?"

"It wasn't a few months. The first time, it was just a few weeks."

"You're saying that they actually wanted the girls with them as some kind of, what? A walking larder?"

"No. No, I think that they saw saving the girls as a way of redeeming themselves. Getting them to safety would rebalance the scales, but then hunger and time and all the rest kicked in. It wouldn't have been such a taboo, not the second time around. Besides, they each would have known that refusing would be as good as volunteering for the pot themselves."

"Oh, don't say it like that," she said, grimacing. "Annette and Daisy, they're just children, surely they wouldn't. No one would. I mean, you've been hungry, so have I, and we've never thought like that. Or at least I haven't."

"No, neither have I, but we were on our own. We didn't have the opportunity. Besides," I added hurriedly, "survival wasn't our biggest priority. For you it was getting out of your cell and getting revenge on your captors. For me it was finding out why my evacuation plan failed. Revenge and guilt, that was what drove us. All they cared about was going to sleep and waking up the next day. Everything was focused on that. For the rest, they were just acting the way they thought they should."

"I still don't buy it. Not here. Not in Britain."

We sat in silence for a time, each lost in unpleasant thoughts.

"What about Sholto," she finally asked. "What's his motivation?"

I thought for a moment.

"I don't know," I said. "At first I thought it was what he said, that he was actually glad for the end of the world. That it meant he'd escaped capture and trial, and never had to face up to the fact that he'd had years to get his revenge on Quigley, but hadn't. Now, I'm not so sure."

"Didn't you ever suspect that he was your brother?"

"Of course not. Who would?"

"But you never dug into your past, never once looked up who your parents were?"

"I was at boarding school when I wasn't up at Caulfield Hall. That's the Masterton estate up in Northumberland. A massive, rambling place. They've had the land for centuries. Anyway, the other kids would get letters from home, and sometimes, yes, I'd wonder, but I never asked. Lord Masterton wasn't a bad guy. He'd sometimes mention things, like how much I looked like my father or, if I did well at something, how proud my parents would be, that sort of stuff. Looking back on it, it was just enough to make me feel that I could ask if I wanted, but not enough to make me curious. As I got older, I thought it was something I'd look into at some point, but life got too busy. Whenever I did think about it, it was as something that could be dealt with in the distant future."

"You didn't wonder if you had siblings?"

"I assumed, or was lead to assume, I didn't. There was family, uncles, I was told, but I was also told I wouldn't want to have anything to do with them. That they'd cut off my parents when they got married. I suppose I didn't want to think about it. The Mastertons were my family. Jen was my sister."

"Was she?" Kim asked. "Was that all she was?"

"Of course."

"Oh."

"And as for Sholto," I said moving the conversation off treacherous ground, "I should have guessed something. I think it just shows how naive I was. Here was this man feeding me information on which MPs had taken what bribes when they'd been on some overseas jaunt. I'd feed it to one of our tame journalists, and we'd get a resignation and a by-election, and Jen and I would be there ready with a pre-planned comment to get us on every news show that mattered."

"And you never thought there was anything more to your relationship?"

I decided to assume her question referred to my brother. "I worked twenty hour days, sometimes more. I enjoyed it. I guess I didn't want to think about that either."

"Oh."

She was about to ask something more, but Daisy took that moment to wail. Kim hurried back to the fire. A moment later, I followed.

21:00, 21ˢᵗ July

"What *did* go wrong back at Kew?" I asked

"Your plan didn't work." Kim sighed. "Look, Bill, you knew it wouldn't."

"They wouldn't just let the girls go?" I asked.

"No," she said. "I mean that's not the part that didn't work. Do we have to talk about this now?"

"I don't know? Do we?"

"Oh don't start being passive aggressive. It doesn't suit you. You want to know? None of the plan really worked. Of course it didn't, I mean how are any of us meant to come up with plans to deal with any of this? It's all so far beyond anything we can truly understand that, at best, we're just stumbling in the dark hoping someone else might strike a light. You want the minutiae? Not all the undead followed the car. That was the first problem. Half of Them couldn't. Maybe it was more than half, maybe it was less, but all the ones on the other side of the ticket barrier, They were pushing and shoving and making more noise than ever before. So Barrett wouldn't have been able to hear your brother shout, anyway."

"But did you try?"

"What does that matter? You heard what Annette said, are you honestly saying the world isn't a better place now? No. No, we didn't try. If it's important to you, we didn't get a chance. It took nearly an hour before the road was clear enough we could get out into the street. When we did, I saw that ticket barrier shaking. I thought it was going to break and then there'd be zombies all around the building again. The barrier didn't break, I was wrong about that, but I was right about Barrett. You have to agree with that."

114

"I do. I just don't like that we live in a world where violence has become the first resort."

"You shot Stewart," she said. "You killed Sanders. Or tried to."

"That's different. Stewart would have shot us. At the very least he'd have wrecked the car. That was in the heat of the moment. It was the same with Sanders. It wasn't planned out in advance."

"You're talking about murder, Bill, when this is war."

"That's what I'm worried about. It shouldn't be, you see." I threw up my hands "Alright, fine. The world is the way it is, and there's no point wishing it was different. So what did happen, back at Kew?"

"Well, we went up to the main gates. You know, it wouldn't have mattered if we'd tried to shout. Or knock, even. They fired at us first."

"With both barrels," Sholto said. "Right through the barrier they'd built themselves. I gave Kim the M16 since it wasn't going to be much use to me, climbed up and ran along the roof, looking for a window I could force."

"So that's what you were doing," Kim said. "You could have told me."

"I thought it was obvious," he said. "There was a skylight. That's how I got in."

"I guessed that bit, because they started shooting at something inside," she said.

"Right. At me," he said. "And I didn't fire back, so they thought I was unarmed. Probably thought I was you, little brother. What was her name, Daphne? She came running out of the gloom with a carving knife in her hand. I barely managed to swat it out of the way, but she leapt at me, knocked me to the ground. She got a hand around my throat, the knife in the other and I was trying to hold her back. She wasn't a big woman, nothing but skin and bones, but she was driven. I've seen that before, people who've gone through madness and come out the other side. Maybe I'm just getting soft. After all these undead, maybe I've just forgotten what fighting people is like. I didn't forget for long. I remembered that people can feel. They can hurt. I squeezed her wrist until the bones broke. She dropped the knife, screaming. Not with pain but with frustrated anger. I didn't let her scream long. I grabbed the knife and…" He finally noticed my expression. "She died," he finished. "I started shouting for Annette. She came out of the storeroom at about the same time as they started shooting again. I took the baby, told the girl that Kim was outside, and dragged her over to the skylight."

"I fired a few shots," Kim said. "I couldn't see anything, but I wanted to distract them. I saw Sholto throw Annette up through the skylight. I mean, literally throw. It was…"

"Impressive?" he asked.

"Reckless," she said. "Then there was a scuffle. Barrett and Stewart. I guess they were fighting over the gun. All I saw were shelves falling, and then Barrett stood up, pointing the gun straight at Sholto and Daisy. That was all I needed. One clear shot. I fired. She died."

"You're sure?"

"Certain. It was a head shot. I've become good at those."

"We ran over the roof," Sholto said. "Came down the other side, and that was about when you turned up."

"I know you don't like it, Bill," Kim said, "but they had to die. In the old world there were prisons and police, but out here there's no one." She turned and stared out into the darkness. "They brought me up, sometimes. From my cell, I mean. That's what you called it, wasn't it, in your journal. My cell. I didn't give it a name. You know why?"

"Giving it a name gives it power?"

"Right. And you know that, and yet in your journal you keep calling the undead Them, with that capital T."

I shrugged, not wanting to derail her train of thought.

"They kept making up stories," she said. "About the ones they shot, I mean. That was when…. If…. If we'd not met Cannock. If it had been just me and Sanders, we'd have got together because in this sad little world of ours you'll take any kind of comfort you can find. If we'd just gone another way, headed north instead of south, we'd not have met Cannock and it would all have been different. But we did meet him. And… I don't know if they were trying to intimidate or impress me, but they brought me out of the cell and made me watch as they told stories about the zombies they were about to shoot. Except to Cannock, They weren't zombies. They were still people. He gave Them names, and Sanders soon followed. It wasn't that he changed. It was more that he gave in to something that had always been lurking deep inside. That was why I had to kill him. I couldn't let him live, you see. It wasn't what he did to me. That I can live with. It was the children. The zombie children, giving Them names and making up these stories about who they'd been before killing Them. That's why he had to die. There wasn't going to be anyone, any court or judge or anything, ever again. I was the one who had to decide, I was the one with the right, and having made that decision I had to act. It was the same with Barrett. Right then there was just me, my responsibility and now there's just us."

"Justice," I muttered. "That old expression, you know, 'there's no justice, there's just us', I always hated it. It's one of those trite self-serving aphorisms used by people too hide-bound to know that they're in the wrong."

"We did it Bill," Kim said, standing up. "Just us, alone."

Day 132, Penlingham Spa & Golf Club, Milton Keynes

04:00, 22nd July

The rain has stopped. Everything's quiet. It's time to leave.

Day 132, Laketon Heath Reservoir, Warwickshire

14:00, 22nd July

We took a detour this morning into a village, though village is a bit of an overstatement. One pub, one shop, one post-box. Even the church had a for sale sign out front.

The shop had been thoroughly looted of everything that most people could want. Fortunately for us, most people didn't want baby wipes or nappies. We loaded up on those, and were about to cross the road to check the pub when Daisy began to cry. I'm not sure what caused her to yell out. I'm certainly not ascribing some kind of sixth sense to the child, but a moment later there was a tinkling of glass as undead arms smashed through the pub window. We got back on the bikes and cycled away. There are plenty of other places to loot and plenty of undead we can't avoid killing.

We said we'd take it in turns, one of us out front, one of us carrying Daisy, one at the rear with Annette. Somehow, so far today, Kim's always in the lead and Sholto's at the rear, and I'm left carrying the baby. I'd come up with some deep meaning for that if Daisy hadn't spent the entire morning alternating between crying and grabbing at everything within reach. Just keeping the bike going in a straight line has taken all my concentration.

I don't mind. All in all it's probably easier than keeping Annette amused, something that my brother has no difficulty in doing. They've spent most of this morning hatching a plan to expropriate the Orient Express. Annette saw it a few times at Victoria station, and has grand ideas about running steam trains from the coast to the big cities to bring back supplies.

Looking after Daisy is certainly better than being out in the lead. Every few miles Kim will spot some movement up ahead, put on a burst of speed, then dismount, unsling her axe, dispatch the creature and be back on her bike and a dozen yards ahead before I can catch up. Every few miles she'll sprint ahead, then sprint back reporting that there are too many of the undead. Then we'll take to the fields and the farm tracks until we find another stretch of apparently clear road.

The ground's too wet to travel quickly off-road, but even so we've covered nearly forty miles so far today. We're about ten miles southwest of Stratford upon Avon, and forty miles due south of the outskirts of Birmingham. If we can manage the same again this afternoon, and the same again tomorrow, that'll get us deep into Wales. We could even reach Llanncanno the day after that.

That was why I thought we should take a short break at the reservoir. We could see for miles in either direction and there was nothing in sight. We had at least an hour before any undead appeared. I thought we deserved a wash and a swim. We'd just begun arguing over whether, if Birmingham had been bombed, the water would be safe, when Kim spotted the tent. It was zipped closed and something was moving inside of it. It was a shame. Otherwise, it's a nice spot too. The open water, the trees ringed with flowers.

Time to move on.

Day 132
40 miles south of Birmingham

20:00, 22nd July

We're in a house. It's just an ordinary house, there's not much more to say about it. I think we made another five miles westward this afternoon.

Half a mile after the reservoir, we came across an A-road that had been reinforced for the evacuation. We then spent the rest of the afternoon heading south and, when the road curved, southeast, before we found a spot where we could cross. The fencing was broken at least once every quarter mile. The problem was finding a spot where the fence was broken on both sides, without more than a couple of the undead on the road in between. Still, forty-five miles, that's not bad for a day's effort.

Day 133
40 miles east of Welsh border

20:30, 23rd July

Not such good progress today. Fifteen miles, maybe twenty. The day started well. We found the train line and followed it to the edge of Worcester. We'd hoped to find enough supplies in that small cathedral city to last us the next week. From a vantage point on the outskirts, it was hard to make out many details, but there was one street we couldn't miss. It was swarming with the undead. That's what it looked like, a swarm of a hundred or more zombies, moving up and down the road, going from house to house, back and forth. Whether the whole of Worcester was like that, or whether it was just that small corner, whether there were people down there and why the undead were doing that, we didn't stay to find out. Daisy started crying and we had to leave. We spent three hours backtracking through the fields to find a way around the city, and most of the afternoon getting a few miles away from it.

We found this farmhouse just before it started getting dark. There wasn't much food here, though. Someone had already stripped it of nearly everything of use. We did find a few dozen tomatoes growing around the back of a summerhouse and a couple of olive trees by the front door. The tomatoes were green and the olives were so small and tough they must be a purely ornamental variety, but food is food.

I feel bad that we couldn't stop to help whoever was down in Worcester. I think we all do, but Daisy and Annette have to come first. We have to get them somewhere safe. If there is such a place.

Day 134, Ludhill Tunnel
10 miles east of Welsh border

It was around noon that we first heard it.

"Thunder?" Kim asked.

"Must be," I answered automatically. Thunder meant rain. If it was another storm then we needed to find shelter, but the sky was clear.

"We should look for somewhere to stop," Kim said, though there was a trace of doubt in her voice.

"Can you hear it?" Annette asked, as she, with Sholto just behind, came to a stop next to Kim and I. "It sounds like the wind is ripping up the trees. Sholto's been telling me all about tornado alley, haven't you?" She turned, and Sholto smiled and nodded, but the moment she looked away, a puzzled look returned to his face. "Sounds terrifying. Come on," she added with a grin, "no point stopping here."

She was right. We headed on. The sound must have been there for some time. I'd just been so focused on Daisy I hadn't noticed it. Nor had I noticed that we'd not seen any zombies for a while, either. I knew that meant something, but I couldn't focus on what. Daisy was alternating between crying and wailing, and it was all I could do to keep hold of her and keep the bike heading in a straight line.

Kim reached the top of the hill first. I couldn't see her expression, but her shoulders slumped.

"What is it?" I called out as I neared the top. She turned to look at me. I've seen her scared. I've seen her angry. I've seen her triumphant. I've even seen her happy a few times. I'd never seen that expression of horrified disbelief before. She didn't answer me. She didn't need to. I reached the top of the hill and saw it for myself.

At first I thought it was just a massive cloud of dust, a freak weather phenomenon caused by the nuclear bombs. It stretched for miles, the dust seeming to carry right to the horizon. Then I looked down at the edge nearest us, barely five miles away down in the valley. That's when I saw the dot-like figures moving back and forth at the ragged edges of a horde millions upon millions of zombies strong.

"That's it. That's everyone," she whispered. "That's the undead of England."

It explained why we'd seen so few today. It explained, in part, why the only times I've really seen more than a few thousand in one place had been at the barricades in London or on the M4. It explained it all. They were all here, turning grass and fields, trees and stone, houses and cars and all the rest into dust and mud.

"What…" Annette began when she and Sholto reached the top of the hill. She didn't finish the question.

"Five million? Ten? Twenty?" Kim muttered.

"It's… impossible." Sholto's voice was hoarse, without a trace of his usual careless cheerfulness.

"Where are they going? Are they coming this way?" Annette asked, then the edge of desperation turned to panic as she croaked, "Can they see us?"

"No. We're too far away." I hoped. "We should go."

"Where?" Kim asked. "There's no escaping that. Where on this whole wretched little island can we go to get away from that?"

"Well, for starters, we can go back down the hill."

We'd no idea how many there were. We'd no idea what direction they were going, except that the land around us looked untouched. We went back down the hill and headed west, because that's the direction the first track we came to led.

"Farms are out," Sholto said. "Houses too, They'd just knock them down."

We were cycling nearly abreast, pedalling hard though none of us knew where we were going.

"Is it getting louder?" Annette asked.

"I don't think so," I said.

"That's good, right?"

"Not really," I said. "I don't think it's getting any quieter, either. That means we're heading in roughly the same direction."

"Do we go back, then?" Kim asked, frustration in her eyes.

"Let's stop a moment." I brought the bike to a halt and took out the map.

"We shouldn't stop," Annette said. "We should hurry before They catch us."

"We're hours ahead of it." I tried to keep my voice calm.

"So we can outpace Them?" she asked.

"We're managing about six miles an hour, which is double what They are. Probably more," I said.

"So there's no problem," Annette said, sighing with relief. "We just cycle south for a day, then west tomorrow and find a way around Them."

"Wouldn't work. We need to sleep. They don't."

"I got caught up by one of these down near Lenham," Sholto said. "It wasn't as big as this, though. You saw what it did to the land around there. I hid in a church. Say what you like about England, but you're not short on churches."

"That won't do," I said, peering at the map.

"No, I mean I was in the crypt," he said. "Some of the church was knocked down, sure, and I ended up drinking the water from the font, but I survived there, underground."

"No. It's Daisy. She'll cry. No matter what we do. And while They may not hear when They're passing overhead, once it's down to just a few hundred or a few thousand stragglers, They will."

"Then we go back south," Kim said.

"Perhaps if we only sleep for a few hours we might out distance Them," I said, "but then what? We'll still need to find food, and still have to look after a baby crying all the time in a land full of the undead."

"A tower block, then?" Kim suggested.

"That means a city," I said, tracing a line along the map. "During one night in London, thousands went by. Perhaps more. The next day there were dozens left, all still heading off in the same direction. It took days before They'd dispersed. We'd need a tower block right in the middle of a city and we'd need food for weeks, and even then…" I found it.

"So where then?" Annette cried plaintively.

"Here. The train line. You see it. The grey line." I pointed to the map. "There's an old branch line about here."

"Where?" Kim asked.

"Between here and here." I pointed. "It's not marked because that branch was closed years ago. But it leads to a tunnel, here. That was closed as well, but they were going to open it up again. They'd sent engineers in to assess it. That's where we go. Then we'll wait until the horde has passed over us, then we wait some more, and then we keep going. We're going to get to Wales and to that beach, and I'm going to get you onto that boat."

"That's thirty miles away," Kim said.

"Then we should get moving," I said.

It took an hour to find the train line and it was a terrifying hour. We came across a large pack of the undead. They were strung out in ones and twos, a hundred yards apart and on the road we needed to travel along. The thundering roar of the horde that was acting like a siren to this smaller pack drowned out any noise we made. They didn't notice us until we'd cycled past. Then They snarled and dived and sometimes just fell forwards in their eagerness to get at this fresh prey that had so wittingly appeared in their midst. Then, we reached the old train tracks, and as they curved away from the road, we escaped the pack and were alone once more.

The tunnel was exactly where it should have been. The entrance was sealed with sheet metal bolted to the brickwork. In the middle stood a small door, held closed with bolts and three padlocks. We used the powder from two of the remaining cartridges to blow the locks. I don't think I ever really knew what pitch black really meant until I stared into that dark tunnel.

"It's empty?" Kim half said, half asked.

"Wait. Listen," I said. We all did.

"I can't hear anything," Annette said after a tense thirty seconds.

"No," I said, "and the sound of that gunpowder going off would have drawn Them here if there were any inside."

"Still, I, I don't know," Kim said. "We could get back to London or
—"

"It's too late. Look," I pointed at the grey cloud on the horizon. "The horde is getting closer. It's this or nothing."

"He's right, come on," Sholto said, stepping inside. "Pass me the bikes."

I waited until he and Annette were inside, and then handed Daisy to Kim.

"Here, take her for a moment." Then I emptied my bag onto the ground. "And take that stuff inside. Grab some wood from out here to burn. I'll be back in an hour."

I ignored the questions and shouts of protest, grabbed a bike, and cycled back the way we'd come.

It wasn't anger, frustration, irritation, insanity, or anything else, not this time. It was just mathematics.

I don't know if I'd been thinking clearly when I remembered the tunnel, but I had been since we'd set out for it. It was instinct that said turning back just wasn't going to work. Nearly cycling straight into that horde was as good a sign as any other that our luck had run out. Another week or more roaming the countryside would only end with us trapped, dead, or worse. That's why I was sure the tunnel was the right place to be. If we could survive just a few days, we'd be able to continue on to Wales in the knowledge that all the undead were behind us.

Reading it back, it does seem like I might be hoping for too much. But as we were cycling along the railway track, I didn't have time to think about what would happen when we left the tunnel. I was fixated on the number of days we'd have to spend there. We'd enough food for three adults one, child, and one baby for four days, assuming none of the adults ate much.

I'd tried to work out how big the horde was, but there were just too many variables. All I had to go on was gut instinct based on what I've experienced so far and that said we needed enough food for a week. At least. Wherever that horde has been, nothing will grow. There will be nothing left intact to loot. There will be nothing but a dusty barren desert.

I can't do much about that, but enough food for the five of us for four days is a different way of saying enough food for four people for five, and five days is nearly six, and six days is nearly a week and that might be nearly long enough. We needed more food or fewer mouths.

That's why I cycled away, simple mathematics. I had to look for more food and not return if I didn't find it. Don't get me wrong. I planned to get back to that tunnel. I'd spotted the farm on our way here. The sight of those trees laden with fruit had been what had started me calculating.

The farm turned out not to be a farm, but a small family home built on the edge of farmland. A huge fence separated it from the fields, belonging, I assumed to the much grander, much older building on the crest of the hill half a mile away. I took that in and discounted it as unimportant compared to the rising dust cloud approaching from the east.

I jumped off the bike and dragged back the iron-gate covering the drive. Inside, on a lawn dotted with a rotting trampoline and a rusting swing set, were three apple and two wizened pear trees. Perfect. I shook one and started gathering the fallen fruit. The bag was filled in a matter of seconds. It wasn't a large bag. I needed another. There was only one place I'd find one. Inside.

I looked up at the sky. I couldn't be certain, but the dust cloud seemed nearer. There was no time for stealth. There was no time for thought. I crossed the lawn, reached the back door and threw it open. The door led into a utility room crammed with tumble driers and washing machines and a long oak table. On the other side of it was a zombie.

Its mouth was already snapping at me as it tried to walk through the wooden table. I'd left the pike back at the tunnel, but it wouldn't have been much use in a room with such a low ceiling. I pulled out the hatchet with my right hand, while my left went to the edge of the table. I slammed it back a few inches. That was enough to push the creature off balance just long enough for me to edge round the table, bring the axe up, and then bring it down.

There was a noise behind me. Another creature stumbled through the doorway, its hands flailing in front of it. The blade came up and down on the creature's temple, splitting its head in two. The second zombie died.

I took a breath, then kicked at the body, moving it away from the doorway so I could get past. But it was a family house, and a family is made up of more than just adults. There were two children. A boy and a girl and neither could have been much younger than Annette. Back in London, when I'd found a house like that, I'd turned and ran. But now I understand. They had been children. They weren't any more.

It wasn't killing, that's what I'm telling myself. I know that it is the truth, I just find it hard to accept.

There were two other bodies in the house. A young child and an old woman. They were properly dead. The child had been laid out in a cot, perhaps dead of some natural cause. The old woman was locked in an upstairs room. After I broke down the door, and saw her body on the bed, unmoving, I didn't investigate any further. There wasn't time.

I found an old sports bag at the bottom of a wardrobe and threw in some of the clothes hanging above it. I went back down to the kitchen and filled the rest of the bag with every packet and half-filled jar there was left. There weren't many. I opened the drawers until I found some green plastic bin bags. I opened one and threw in matches, toilet paper, tea-towels and anything else I saw and thought might help us through the next week. Dragging the bags behind me I went outside, pulling a couple of jackets off a hook as I went.

I filled one bin-bag with apples, then started tearing at the vegetable patch. I vaguely registered that it had been tended recently, that it can't have been long since the people inside… I pushed that thought away as I thrust fistfuls of leaves, greens, roots, and soil into the bag. I didn't even notice what I was putting in. I only paused when I noticed the ground was shaking. I looked up. The dust cloud was closer. Much closer. I grabbed another handful of leaves and pulled up the world's smallest carrots.

"What the hell, Bill?"

Startled, I dropped the bag. It was Sholto.

"You followed me," I said.

"Of course I followed you," he said. "I came here, to England, didn't I?"

"We need food and clothes and everything else to survive the next week, you see," I said. It came out more manically than I intended.

"Right. Is that what's in the sacks?"

"Apples. Mostly apples. And whatever else I could find. Carrots, see?"

"How are you going to carry it?" he asked.

"What?"

"You've got five sacks full."

I hadn't thought about that.

"Here." He started picking up fruit. "Let's finish filling this bag, and then we'll go, okay?"

There was kind desperation in his voice. He must have thought I'd lost it. If anything I was finally thinking sanely, though I guess that's what an insane man would say.

When we got back to the tunnel Kim was standing grim faced outside it, the M16 held menacingly in her hands. She didn't even wait for me to get off the bike before she slapped me. I deserved it. Then she turned and walked inside.

She and Annette had gathered wood for a fire. By its light, after we'd secured the entrance, we took a look at my haul.

"Lots to eat," Kim said, carefully. After a moment she added, "Food. Shelter. Fire."

She was making a point. I couldn't work out what. Annette did.

"There's no water. Nothing to drink," she said.

"Here, food and water all in one biodegradable package," I said, handing her an apple. I felt lightheaded. I gingerly put my arm out, searching for the ground as I sat down. "It's dark in here. Didn't one of those bikes have a light on it?"

"I thought we'd save that till later," Kim said.

"Right. Sure." It was odd, sitting around a fire inside a tunnel. I closed my eyes, and rested my head on the cold, damp ground. "The problem wasn't food. It never was. It was always water. But water needs to be carried, doesn't it? Carried and boiled. But apples, they're eighty five percent water, aren't they? Or is that people? It's one or the other."

128

I don't know if I said anything else. I fell asleep.

But not for long. I was woken when a lump of something hard fell from the roof, onto my leg. The tunnel was shaking. The undead were close. I heard sounds, too, an irregular banging, not far away.

"You all right?" Sholto asked.

"Sure. Just tired."

"They're outside," Kim said, gesturing back up the tunnel. "At the door. After you passed out we went out for more firewood."

"You brought back dog biscuits," Annette said, holding up a packet.

"I did? I just grabbed anything that looked like food."

"I mean, dog biscuits?" she repeated, in a tone that mixed disgust with disappointment that I'd not found anything more enticing.

"They're not made of dog. Are there enough?" I asked.

"For you? Plenty, because I'm not eating any of them."

"I meant food. Do we have enough?"

"For over a week," Kim said.

I hope that's enough.

Day 135, Ludhill Tunnel
10 miles east of Welsh border

01:00, 25th July

The incessant banging at the door stopped an hour ago. It has been replaced by an intermittent slamming thump as one after another, scores at a time, the living dead walk, or are pushed, into the doors. Each echoing, metallic reverberation signals the horde's slow progress up and around the embankment and over the hill above us.

The doors are holding. There is nothing else to say, and nothing else to do.

04:00, 25ᵗʰ July

Sleep is impossible. Bang, thump, a ringing of metal, a cracking of stone, the breaking of bone, it's the worst kind of symphony and the tunnel acts as an echo chamber.

07:00, 25ᵗʰ July

I think I heard a tree fall.

08:15, 25ᵗʰ July

Yes. Falling trees. Those must be the ones running alongside the embankment being knocked over.

15:00, 25ᵗʰ July

"What if those trees are blocking the entrance?" Kim asked.

It was a good point. In the dim firelight, I could just make out Sholto shrug.

"Doesn't matter," he said.

"How do you work that out?" she asked.

"This is a tunnel, not a cave," he said.

It took a moment for the meaning to sink in. We all turned to stare down into the darkness behind us. Suddenly it seemed ominously forbidding.

"How long is it?" Kim asked.

"Five hundred metres. I think," I said.

"We should check the other end," Kim said.

"Yes," I agreed. None of us moved.

"If there was something down there, we'd hear it coming," Annette said. "I mean, wouldn't we?"

"Probably," Kim said.

"And it would see the light from the fire?" Annette asked.

"Probably," Sholto said.

"And they would have stuck those metal sheets over the other end, so nothing could get in?"

"Probably," I said. What I was thinking, but wasn't going to say, was that if the builders hadn't, if the other end of the tunnel was open to the outside and it was just luck that had kept the undead wandering up the tunnel, then there was absolutely nothing we could do about it.

"There's no point hiding from the monsters in the dark," Sholto said decisively as he stood up.

"Wait," I said. "I'll go."

"Yeah, sure."

"No, I'm serious. If I'm bitten then it's not the end of the world. If you are…"

He hesitated for a moment. "We'll both go," he said.

"I can manage on my own," I said.

"Then I tell you what," he said. "I'll let you go first."

The torchlight barely reached twenty feet ahead. It did little more than add a silver silhouette to the potholes that riddled the tunnel floor, but it was infinitely better than stumbling in the dark.

The rails had long since been removed, leaving nothing but the occasional rotten wooden sleeper. After I stepped on one that crumbled into a bloom of dust, I kept to the sounder footing of the rubble at the side of the tracks.

Step by step, inch by cautious inch, I moved slowly down the tunnel. I tried to listen, but I could hear nothing over the continuous drum roll of the undead. I told myself the sound was coming from outside but it was impossible to believe with the floor shaking, and a shower of dust and dirt raining down from above. At any minute I expected to see hundreds of ghoulish mouths snapping up and down at the edge of the light. And I knew, if I did, that would be the last thing I'd ever see. It was the worst kind of torture.

Then I came to a door built into the side of the tunnel. It's of the same construction as the door at the tunnel entrance, made of sheet metal held in place with padlocks and bolts.

"What is it?" Sholto muttered.

"A door."

"I can see that."

"I don't remember there being a door here," I said.

"You've been down here before?" he asked.

"No. I meant I didn't remember seeing any doors on the plans. Except they weren't really plans. They were going to re-open this tunnel. Part of an express route. Commuters, you know? There was a big press event, champagne and canapés and all that. There was a model and there were maps, and that's why I knew where the tunnel was. That and it cuts through two marginal constituencies. But the model didn't have a door halfway along."

"Right. Is it sealed?"

I didn't want to check. It's stupid I know, a Heisenbergian fear. As long as I didn't check, the door might be closed and so I wouldn't have to do anything about it. But if it wasn't… I hesitated too long. Sholto pushed past and tugged at the padlocks. The door shook with an echoing gong.

"It's secure. Let's keep going," he said. We did. After twenty yards we passed another door. Exactly twenty yards after that was a third. Then there was nothing but darkness that lasted an eternity, but was over twenty minutes later when the light became suddenly truncated. We'd reached the other end of the tunnel.

"We're here." I breathed out. And I relaxed a bit more as I played the light up and down the edge of the metal, checking that it was truly sealed.

"Turn the light off," Sholto suggested. "See if the daylight makes it through."

I did. It didn't.

"Well," he said with a deep sigh, "that's all right then."

I laid my hand out against the metal. It was vibrating slightly and felt warm to the touch. The freight train rumbling of the horde was louder here. I thought I could make out the crack and snap of bones over the ceaseless tramping of feet. I didn't care. The tunnel was sealed. We were safe.

Then I really understood what I'd seen. I turned the torch back on, and slowly, methodically, played it up and down the tunnel entrance. There were three large sections of metal, two across the bottom, one at the top, each welded to the other. I ran the light along each seam, letting it fall on every inch.

"What is it?" Sholto asked.

"What do you see? Or, to put it another way, what don't you see?" I asked.

It took him a moment to realise. "There's no door."

"There's no door?" Kim asked, when we'd returned.

"So we're trapped?" Annette asked.

"Not necessarily," I said. "Let's start with the good news. The tunnel is sealed, so we're safe for now."

"But if the door is blocked by trees or something, then we are trapped," Annette said.

"I don't know," I said, tired once again. "I really don't. My knowledge of this place is from a couple of hours spent standing in an overheated room with a few maps and an engineer's model of what the valley would look like if they re-opened the bridge."

"You know more than we do," Kim said, almost accusingly. "You picked this place."

"Okay. The tunnel is halfway up one side of a shallow valley. At the bottom of the valley runs a river. It would have been simpler to build the train along the bottom of the valley, but the land on the other side was owned by some Victorian Earl. He'd made his fortune when some bubble burst. Or he'd created the bubble, or… it doesn't matter. The point is that he didn't want steam trains spoiling his view so they dug out this tunnel, stuck in the tracks, and then covered it over again. That was pretty common back then. Fast-forward a hundred years and it gets closed down, because who needs trains in the age of the automobile? A few decades after that, and a few boundary changes and the tunnel runs through two marginal constituencies. Re-opening it, and creating a fast train link, would revitalise the area and secure two seats for whichever government can claim the credit."

"How does that help us?" Kim asked.

"No idea," I said stretching out and closing my eyes, "but now you know as much as I do. So let me know if you can come up with anything."

19:00, 25ᵗʰ July

No one has.

Day 136, Ludhill Tunnel
10 miles east of Welsh border

05:00, 26ᵗʰ July

For breakfast we are serving Orange Apple Surprise. To make this you'll need about five apples, two carrots, and a cucumber. First, peel the apples. Now, eat the peel. Next, put the apples into a saucepan. Don't worry about maggots and caterpillars. Those are just protein.

Add a splash of fruit juice from the tin of peaches, but only a splash, because any more would be a waste. Place the apples in the saucepan and put to one side. Remember to put the lid on, because falling grit doesn't add to the flavour. Now peel the carrots. Eat the peel, soil and all, because there's no water to spare for washing. Cut the carrots up into the smallest pieces possible with the fruit knife, the one blade that hasn't been used to kill the undead. Place the carrots into the saucepan. Remember the lid.

Chop up the cucumber. Don't worry about the size of the chunks. During cooking it will boil down to nothing but water and skin, and that skin is going to be about the closest thing this dish will have to texture. Add herbs and spices. Seriously, add lots, because that's the only way you'll cover up the flavour of dirt and dust that covers everything.

Place the saucepan on the fire and cook. But don't leave it. This is the difficult part. You don't want the steam to escape, so hold down the lid during cooking. To reduce burns, or to make sure that everyone gets an equal share of them, take it in turns.

After about twenty minutes, or when you smell burning, whichever comes first, take the pan off the fire. Now wait.

And keep waiting.

Wait until it has cooled down to tunnel temperature. Remember, we don't want to waste that precious steam! If you've done it properly the dish should now resemble a green-flecked orangey mush. Now close your eyes and eat it as quickly as you can, preferably without letting any of it touch a taste bud. Try to digest.

Best served with one dog biscuit per person.

12:00, 26th July

Nicole Upton, Minister for Trade and Development. That's who that woman was, the one I thought I recognised down by the boat. The zombie I killed. She was in the eight member emergency cabinet with Jen, though I don't recall what her role had been. I'm not sure I even knew.

Perhaps it wasn't her. I mean, the face was dried out, stretched and scarred. Perhaps it was just someone who, in death, looked like her. That doesn't say much for what she looked like in life of course. Ah well, whether it was her or not, it doesn't matter.

17:00, 26th July

They're still overhead. I keep thinking They should have passed by now. That's the difficulty, I keep thinking of the zombies as marching in a column. It's not like that. The horde has no order. It is not going to or coming from anywhere. It's a great roiling storm, moving inch by inch over the countryside. It could be gone in hours. It could then return or even just disperse. Or it could stop, right above us, waiting for some distant movement to reanimate first one, then all. Or stop until it hears some distant sound or, worse, the nearby sound of a baby crying.

That's my real fear now, that I've trapped us all down here. And it's no comfort that there was nowhere else to go, and had we stumbled about out in the wasteland our best hope would have been to become trapped somewhere else. The reality, I'm sure of it, is that we would have died.

I tell myself it would have been little comfort had we died being able to see the sky. Something deeply primitive inside of me tells me that's not so.

Day 137, Ludhill Tunnel
10 miles east of Welsh border

03:00, 27th July

It goes on. I can't sleep. We're trying to maintain a normal routine, but there's nothing to do but sleep and talk. Daisy whimpers a lot, but she's not crying anymore. Out loud I say that she must find this constant vibration soothing. I don't believe it, nor does anyone else, but words are the only reassurance we can give one another.

"What was New York like?" Annette asked my brother.

Sholto sighed. "It was like… it was unlike anything I'd ever seen. Anywhere. You can talk about chaos and the breakdown of law and order. You can call to mind images of people running from bombed out buildings, you can picture war zones and killing fields and all the worst atrocities in history and you won't even come close. Then, even then, even in those worst times, people knew that if they ran, sooner or later they would come to safety. They knew that out there, somewhere in the wider world there was some spark of kindness, even if it was nearly impossible to believe it among the bleak inhumanity surrounding them. It may have been small, but even then, there was a small spark of hope. Not so with the outbreak. There was this one moment, you saw it all the time, when people first saw a human turned into an inhuman killing monstrosity. Something that couldn't be reasoned or bargained with, something that couldn't possibly exist yet was standing there in front of them. That was their Rubicon, the moment they crossed the line between society and self. The moment when all that was left was to run, not to anywhere because nowhere could really ever be safe, but just to run because all they could do, their only hope, was that they could run faster than the person next to them."

"That's what it was like for me," Kim said. "When I got out of that motorway, there were people around me, all the same, all just wanting to get away. I didn't recognise it at the time, but that's what it was. Calculated suspicion. It was masked by fear, but it was there. No one offered to help, no one tried to organise anyone else or work together. Even the people travelling with their friends or their families, they weren't truly *with* these other people. They were all alone, just sometimes going in the same direction."

"I was lucky," I said. "I missed all that. I had the hope of rescue to keep me going until I became so caught up in my own personal survival that other people only existed in some mythical enclave. In those videos you sent me, the people who fought back were the ones who died. Sooner or later, and usually sooner, they got swamped because when they stepped up, they stood alone."

"And most of the rest died anyway," Kim said. "So it didn't matter, did it? Stand or run, It was all the same in the end."

"Yeah," Annette said, in that exasperated tone she'd copied from Kim, "but what I meant, what I was actually asking, was what New York was like before. You know, the theatres and the restaurants, and Central Park and everything."

"Oh." Sholto sounded chagrined. "Well, it was like no other place on Earth…"

He spun story after story until she fell asleep. If you were to believe him, the streets were paved with fame, the hot-dogs were one hundred and ten percent beef, and the snow was always white, right up until it melted on the first day of spring. And throughout all of the stories, the noise from the undead continued above us.

15:00, 27th July

Daisy is worrying me. She's quiet. Too quiet. There's nothing we can do. I hate that.

17:00, 27th July

I'm not sure. It might just be wishful thinking, but perhaps the noises from outside are lessening.

22:00, 27ᵗʰ July

I'm certain. It's another one of those good news, bad news situations. I went to listen by the front door and now I can make out the sound of individual zombies. That, surprisingly, isn't the bad news. Daisy is worryingly quiet, but we've moved down the tunnel anyway, just in case she cries out. I'm hoping it's the darkness. I'm hoping that's all that is. I can't do anything about it, and that's what I repeat to myself. But that's not the bad news either.

I went to listen by the tunnel entrance, and while I could hear the undead, They were not close. Rubble, dirt, trees, the bodies of trampled undead, whatever is blocking the door must be heavy.

Day 138, Ludhill Tunnel
10 miles east of Welsh border

03:00, 28ᵗʰ July

"It's obvious what's behind the door, right?" Sholto asked, rhetorically.

Now that the noise from outside has died down we've all become aware of this irregular thumping noise far closer. It's coming from behind the three closed doors in the middle of the tunnel.

"They must be ventilation shafts," I said.

"I say we leave the doors closed," Kim said.

"I agree," Annette added.

There was another thump. Then another that sounded more like the cracking of bone.

"Agreed," I said.

07:00, 28ᵗʰ July

We've done a stock take. We can stay here for another three days. No, that's not what I mean. In three days we run out of food. Frankly, I don't think we can wait that long. At the very least we need to find a book on paediatric medicine. If I'm honest, I doubt we'll find anything more useful than that. We'll be lucky to find any medicine anywhere, certainly none we'd know how to use. No, we need to get Daisy out into the fresh air, find her some fresh food and fresh water, and hope she livens up.

That being said, while the undead are still going past we can't. If we could see outside, if we had a clear road, we could try cycling past, but we can't see outside, and whatever it's like out there, I doubt the road is clear.

11:00, 28th July

"We could try climbing up the ventilation shaft," Sholto suggested. I stared at him. I don't think he could see me and he certainly couldn't see my expression.

"There are zombies in there," I finally said.

"We'd have to kill Them first," he said.

"Have you considered just how many there might be?" I asked. "Just think about how long we've been down here, how many there must have been in that horde. One million or ten, it doesn't matter because that ventilation shaft must be full of Them by now."

"It's not," he said, and I swear he sounded smug.

"How do you know?" Kim asked.

"You can here bones cracking," he said. "That means it's a long fall onto a hard surface, not a short one onto a pile of bodies."

There was something in that, but I thought he was missing the wider point.

"So even if there's just a few dozen or a few hundred, then what?" I asked. "One of us just goes in there and tries to take Them all on?"

"You're forgetting these," he said fishing out one of the incendiary canisters he'd brought from Lenham Hill.

"Those. Right." I had forgotten. "So, what? We throw one in, hope it works, and then hope it burns out every last one of the undead? What if it burns down the door?"

"It probably won't," he said breezily. "This stuff is designed to burn hot and quick."

"So it isn't going to turn everything to ash? In which case how do we know it will actually kill one of the undead? So what if their skin burns? So what if their lungs are singed, their eyeballs—"

"Bill!" Kim snapped, glancing towards Annette.

"Sorry," I said. "I mean it could burn the zombies, but They could still be a threat."

"Probably not much of one," Sholto replied.

"Fine. Fine. Let's say it works. What then? How do we climb out?"

"Have you a better idea?" he asked.

"Well, as a matter of fact, yes. I was just going to wait until it was a bit quieter and try the front door."

19:00, 28th July

I spent all afternoon sitting by the tunnel entrance, listening. Sholto did the same at the other end of the tunnel, Kim and Annette at the doors to the ventilation chambers until the bike-light finally died. That was at about five this afternoon. We'd let Annette use it, while we'd done our best with branches lit from the fire. They offered little light but some comfort in this dark and suddenly near-silent world. But the fire had gone out when Kim and Annette went back to it and we've no more matches. We could try to get a spark from the flint in one of the disposable lighters littering the bottom of my pack but that would only delay the inevitable for a few short hours. It is time to leave.

We reconvened and decided to try the door. It opened, but only a few inches, letting a drift of soil and leaves fall down onto the tunnel floor. And we *could* see them. There is sunlight out there, enough to write by.

We pushed and barged and charged at the door until our shoulders were bruised, but that only moved it another six inches. A tree, or perhaps two, have fallen right in front of the entrance. Will the incendiary burn through it, or, in the open air, burn too quick to incinerate the still green wood, or will it find enough fuel to create an inferno and suffocate us all? Tomorrow morning, just as soon as we see the sun's first light, we will find out.

Day 139
Somewhere near the Welsh border

07:00, 29th July

We got out. Now we need to get away.

13:00, 29th July

There was a church here a few weeks ago. Now there's just a half ruined tower and a single, well polished marble step. I think, perhaps, it led up to the altar. Everything else has gone. Prayer books and organ, gold and brass, glass and stone and wooden pew, it's all gone. Knocked down, then trampled into dust. All except the tower and this one step.

I can't tell you the church's name. I can't tell you the denomination. I can't even tell you where we are. We've been walking for six hours. The ground is just too uneven to cycle. Six hours. We've covered fifteen miles. Perhaps less. Perhaps twelve. It's impossible to tell. There are no landmarks anymore. No signposts, no hedgerows, no trees.

It was as if a flood has passed this way, leaving a thick layer of dirt and cloying dust covering everything, creating irregular barrows over the rubble of civilisation. Sticking out of those are jagged shards of metal, too twisted to tell if they came from cars or buildings. When the sunlight catches an untarnished edge, they glitter and gleam, a mocking reminder of the streetlights that must once have stood here. Wherever here is.

Six hours, fifteen miles, and no sign of life. Nothing but the ever-present undead.

Every few yards, out of the ground or the side of one of those hillocks, a hand will twitch or a mouth will snap.

At first, we tried to kill the undead for no other reason than that is what we do. We stopped when Annette joined in. No, that's not the right phrase, it suggests she was doing it for fun. Where Kim, Sholto, and I were acting more out of reflexive habit, lifting a blade up and then letting gravity bring it down, putting no more effort into it than a slight twist to the shoulders so the edge fell true, Annette acted out of a far more primal rage.

There was a wall that was still standing. We were using it as a marker. In this monotonous hellscape, it was the only landmark for miles in any direction. When we got closer we saw it was just a side wall from some building, though whether it was an office or farm or town house, none of us could guess. There was nothing special about it, not to me, and no reason to stop there. As we went past, Annette grabbed the hatchet from my belt, and ran ten yards to a zombie ineffectually trying to claw its way out of the dirt burying it up to its chest. Before any of us could react, she was swinging the hatchet up and down, over and over again, screaming with each blow, "It's all wrong!"

She's been quiet since then. That's not usual. But she's only thirteen. We're a lot older and we all have our moments.

This morning, we took cover halfway down the tunnel, while Sholto threw the incendiary out through the door. I was expecting an explosion like in the movies. A bang, a crash, and then it would be over. It wasn't like that. There was a 'whoosh', then a sudden rush of wind as the air was sucked from the tunnel, then a roar as the fire took and expanded. The wind grew stronger, forcing us all down to our knees. It was next to impossible to breathe.

Then, up ahead, we saw a glow. Faint at first, but getting brighter by the second, the metal sheets covering the tunnel entrance began to glow around the welds that joined them together. Red, then orange, then white. Then it seemed to spread, taking in the outline of the door. The metal buckled and cracked with a sound louder than the undead had been these last few days. Blue flames licked upwards around the tunnel roof, and then, all at once and with no warning, the metal buckled and cracked and collapsed.

The wind suddenly stopped. The flames outside grew brighter, turning white again, but this time just for a fraction of a second. Then the white light at the end of the tunnel dimmed to yellow and orange, and I could make out the burning skeletons of the trees outside. I didn't dwell on the symbolism too long, because I found I could breathe again, but that first lungful was mostly smoke. Annette was coughing. Daisy was wide-eyed and pale. We had to get out of there.

The metal sheeting once covering the tunnel mouth had collapsed onto the charred remains of fallen trees. It formed a rough ramp up the side of the embankment. It was still glowing in places, but we had no choice. We threw ourselves out of there as fast as we could. We all got burned. All of us. The soles of our shoes are melted. But we got out, and we got away. We only lost two of the tyres. That's not bad going. But we can't cycle, not even on the wheel rims. And we can't stop. Not yet. Not here.

20:00, 29th July

A tree. We saw it from half an hour away and we came here because it was the first living thing we'd seen all day. All the lower branches have been broken off, and it's been pushed to a forty-five degree angle, but it is still alive.

Another ten minutes and we'll have to go on.

Day 140, Wales

03:00, 30th July

We're on the roof of a grain silo. There's no grain, naturally. But it was still standing and we needed to stop. It's hard to see in the dark, but we did see odd patches of grass thrusting up above the dirt. We've seen more trees and more broken walls. We're reaching the edge of the ground the horde travelled along.

12:00, 30th July

When the sun came up, we saw that only a few hundred yards from the silo everything looked normal. There is a physical line gouged into the earth, through the middle of an abandoned field. One side is carpeted with a vivid red and blue display of cornflowers and poppies, on the other is bare, uneven earth.

143

We searched the farms until we found a couple of spare tyres to replace the ones burned when we left the tunnel, and then we were back to cycling almost as if everything was normal. And what does it say that life ten days ago counts as normal?

We continued on until we came to this village. The two pubs on the village green had both been looted, but no one had thought to check the garden centre on the outskirts. The vending machine was half full. Flavoured, sparkling, sugar water has never tasted so good.

"I'm worried about Daisy," Kim said. "I was thinking we could find a hospital and…" She trailed off. "It's not going to work, is it?"

"This village in Ireland, that's where we've got to get to," I said. "The submarine would have had a doctor, and I'll grant you that they probably don't have to deal with many infants in the Royal Navy, but that's our only chance."

"Will we make it? In time, I mean," she asked.

"It doesn't matter. If they're not there then they'll have left directions or a radio or something."

"But what if they haven't?" she asked. "What if no one comes? What if they're already dead?"

"We'll find a GP's somewhere. Find a book on paediatric medicine, work out what's wrong and find out what she needs. It'll be okay."

I hope.

Time to move on.

Part 2:
Rendezvous, Rescue
& A Request

Wales

2nd August

Day 143, Llanncanno Safe House

03:00

For once my plan worked. We reached the rendezvous about eighteen hours ago, a day ahead of schedule.

"There it is," I said. "The beach."

"Well, what do we do?" Kim asked.

"We have to help. Don't you get it? It's a flag house, we have to!" Annette said.

We'd barely stopped since we left the tunnel. Daisy was coughing when she wasn't completely silent. We cycled and tramped across fields and tracks. We threw away nearly everything we'd been carrying. We kept going, stopping to sleep only when it was too dark to see. When Annette was too tired to carry on, we got rid of her bike and she rode, uncomfortably, on Sholto's cross-frame. I don't think any of us noticed how lush the land was around here, not until we caught that first scent of saltwater. That gave us the strength to continue, travelling on by starlight. We saw the sea and followed the coast road until we reached a copse of trees about a mile from the beach. We stopped, near collapse, and I'll admit we all dozed as we waited for dawn to bring enough light to confirm we were in the right place.

In front of the trees lay a handful of fields broken only by the occasional stone wall. Beyond that lay a short farm track, running east to west, that ran from the coast road by the beach up into the hills. On the corner where the track met the coast road, its rear windows overlooking the sea, were three buildings. An old cottage, with a new extension, was bracketed on either side by two whitewashed barns that formed a rough 'U' around a paved area complete with a picnic table. At the edge of the property, in clear view of the main road, was a large sign. It read, 'Llanncanno Outdoor Pursuit, B&B and', the rest of the words were illegible, as they've been painted over with 'Safe House. Survivors Welcome.'

Flying from a telegraph pole a dozen yards from the driveway was what might be called a flag but what, six months ago, was certainly called a bed-sheet. For good measure the words 'Safe' and 'Hose', had been daubed onto the barn walls. In case the misspelling was enough to put someone off, the windbreakers down on the beach had been covered in more bunting than I've seen since the royal wedding.

Next to the sign was a driveway leading to a slope and a small car park. Beyond that lay another slope and the three buildings. Around those stood the undead.

"I can count twenty, so I'd guess there's thirty," I said. "Perhaps thirty-five. Depends how many are on the far side."

Most of the undead were gathered around the cottage. Bloody-brown smears marked where the undead had beaten their fists against the whitewashed walls in an attempt to get at whoever was inside.

"Another safe house," Kim murmured. "Are you sure it's the right beach."

"The sign says so, doesn't it?" Annette snapped. "Llanncanno. This has to be the place."

"We're in the right place," I confirmed. "Just a day early. Do you think those are the people we're meant to catch a lift from?"

"Either that or they're more people waiting for a ride," Sholto replied.

"We could wait for the boat," I suggested, "and hope they've some way of getting rid of the zombies."

"Like what?" Kim asked. "Isn't it meant to be a fishing trawler? Or are you hoping that this community is going to spare a nuclear submarine to use as a taxi service?"

"What if the boat comes, and it sees the house and it can't do anything and so it goes away?" Annette asked, anxiety in her voice.

"They wouldn't do that," I said.

"You don't know that. You can't. You don't know what they're like. Neither," she said, forestalling a comment from my brother, "do you."

"There's a more likely scenario," Kim said. "That boat will be noisy. It'll come close to shore, those zombies will hear, and They'll flock down to the beach. Do you see the fence ringing the property? It's about three feet high and built to keep out sheep. I think thirty zombies would knock it down quickly enough. Then it would be a race between the zombies and the people in that house. The people would get down to the beach first, right? It's only a few hundred yards. Then the boat will leave, but what about us? It's a mile, right? We'll be halfway there, the boat will have gone and we'll have all those undead right in front of us."

"You see?" Annette said. "We have to help them."

Sholto took the scope and began to methodically scan everything in sight. "There are no other zombies around here. None that I can see. Or Hear. So where did they come from? I mean, this is the middle of nowhere, right?"

"Time," I said. "One follows another and another follows that one. Sooner or later—"

"No," he interrupted. "Statistically speaking, I can't see how you'd get thirty surrounding a house if there weren't a few dozen or so coming up from the beach or these fields."

"That's got to be time, too. Let me see." I took the scope. "Those must be all the undead within earshot."

"So they're not flag people?" Annette asked. "They're just like us, and they went there because the sign said it was safe?"

"Perhaps."

"They could be just like Barrett," Kim said.

"Or just like us," Annette said. "You can't know."

"We could try to communicate with them," I suggested half-heartedly. Other than the stone walls and the foot high grass there wasn't any cover between our copse of trees and the house. There was a good chance they'd not see us signal unless we got close enough that the zombies would see us too. And that was assuming that my brother remembered enough Morse code to send a coherent message, and that someone inside the house also knew the code.

"And what message could we possibly send?" Sholto asked, as if reading my thoughts. "Would we ask them if they wanted help?"

"We can't wait here," Kim said. "We're almost out of food."

Water had been surprisingly easy to find, at least while we were travelling through the Brecon Beacons, but filling a stomach with water can only fool it for so long. The last stash of food we'd found at a hiking supplies store had been just enough for Daisy, with nearly enough for Annette, and no more than a mouthful for Sholto, Kim and I.

"We could cycle down to Cardigan, that's about fifteen miles from here. Or Fishguard, that's about thirty," I suggested, but without enthusiasm. The villages and houses close to the coast that we'd looked in had been looted with more efficiency than those we'd seen inland.

"And then what?" Annette asked. "What if we don't make it back in time? What if we do and the boat comes and they kill all the zombies? Do we just go down to the beach and ask for a lift. Because they may not be like Barrett. They may not be like those men in the house where you met Bill," she added to Kim. "But isn't that what they'll think we're like if we just stay up here and watch? You see, we're not just asking for a lift, we're asking to join them. We want to go and live with them in their village, right? Well why should they let us? Why should *their* doctor help Daisy if we don't go and help *them*?"

"She's right. We've retreated until we've got the sea at our backs," I said. Annette opened her mouth. "Or at our side. It's a figure of speech," I added. "It means there's nowhere left to go."

"Then we're going to help?" Annette asked, brightening up. "So what's the plan?"

"Not we. Sholto and I will go. You're going to stay here with Daisy. You too, Kim."

"Oh no," Kim said, "If anyone is staying, then it should be you. I'm far better in a stand up fight."

"Exactly. Someone has to look after Daisy and Annette if this goes wrong. Someone who can run a mile down to the beach while carrying a baby. That's not me."

"I don't like it," Kim said. I just shrugged.

"What is the plan, then?" Sholto asked.

"No plan," I said, standing up. "There's no time. We'll just go down there, and hope the people inside come out and help."

I felt strangely calm walking across the fields towards the house. I was freed from responsibility, from planning, even from thinking. All I had to do was act. All the complexities of survival had come down to a simple matter of life and death, and one that didn't involve Kim and the girls. She'd keep them safe, and if I died, I would have done so trying to help others. And if that doesn't count towards redemption, then what does?

"There's a wall, just in front of the road," Sholto said. "I say we go down to the road, lure the zombies away from the house, then fall back behind the wall. They shouldn't be able to clamber over. If we take our time, be careful, be cautious, we'll be all right."

"Sure. Sounds good." I almost didn't care. Almost. What Annette had said came back to me. I'd dismissed it, initially, as words masking her anxiety for Daisy's health and our own desperate situation. It wasn't though. She genuinely meant it. She wanted to help, and would probably have tried to help them even if she'd been on her own. Helping others is what she does. That's why she saved Daisy. It's why she was certain we'd come and rescue her. She's a remarkable girl.

"They'll see us soon," Sholto said. We were in the last field. There were just a few hundred yards between us and the last stone wall, then just another fifty yards of road, driveway, and car park between the wall and the undead.

"We've a bit further to go yet," I replied.

"You got a battle cry?" Sholto asked.

"No. Sometimes I apologise. I picked that up from Kim. Is there a family motto or something?"

"Not really." He thought for a moment. "You could try 'Qui Fraudem, Adipiscitur'."

"Meaning?" I asked.

"He who cheats, wins."

I nodded. I might even have smiled. I thought, then, of all the questions I could have asked him about our family history, but then I realised there was only one question that really mattered.

"Did you really come over here because of me?" I asked. "I mean, how much of it was about revenge or finding Quigley or that scientist?"

"I'm here with you now aren't I?"

That was good enough for me. We reached the stone wall.

"I've forty-three rounds left," he said, unslinging his M16.

"That might do it." I'd left the pistol and its last few rounds with Kim. We climbed over the wall.

"I'll take the left then, you the right?" he asked.

"Sounds good."

He looked at me, I at him. He nodded, I nodded back. He headed off to the left, I to the right.

I kept my eyes fixed on the small patch of clear ground I was intending to make my stand. As it grew nearer, the idiocy of what we were about to do began to sink in. An all or nothing frontal assault to save a child, it was absurdly romantic in the most old-fashioned sense of the word.

We reached the road at about the same time, and without the undead noticing us. We were about a hundred yards apart, each about the same distance from the drive leading to the car park. Waiting for the zombies to realise we were there, I started to feel foolish. I wondered whether I'd have to start shouting, just to get the attention of the undead. I looked over at my brother, intending to signal my intention, when he solved the problem by firing.

It was a single shot and it took a zombie in the back of the neck. The creature stumbled and half spun forwards, falling into two creatures in front. Sholto fired again, the bullet struck just above the creature's ear. Even from close to seventy yards away I saw the spray of gore arcing up over the pack, as the back of its head exploded.

Before its body had fallen to the ground, They began to turn around. Not all together, but one by one, in quick succession. And just as quickly, They began to lurch towards us.

I checked that the hatchet was loose in my belt, then lowered the blade of the pike so it was level with the ground. I'd try to hook the creatures, knock Them over, then stab Them through the skull. That had worked before, and if it didn't work now, I'd retreat until I could climb back over the stone wall. I played out that scenario, over and over, as the zombies got closer and closer. The pike grew heavy. I'd forgotten how slowly They moved. They had to cross the car park, and then reach the driveway. The fencing would funnel Them out onto the road, but then I'd still have to wait for Them to cross the fifty yards or so of road.

There were three out front, five behind, then two, then the rest. Would They split up, half heading towards me, the rest towards my brother? I'd no idea. He fired. Another creature went down. He fired again and hit a shoulder. And again, and this time I couldn't see any effect. I realised that there was no reason for the undead to come towards me. Sholto was the one with the gun. He was the one making the noise. I started limping towards the driveway.

Sholto fired. It was a good shot. It was a great shot. The bullet smashed through a zombie's open mouth and blew the back of its head apart, sending its lank pigtails, still attached to skin and bone, flying off in opposite directions. For some reason one of the zombies was faster than the others. It staggered forward, a dozen paces ahead of the pack. I took another step, checked the position of the other undead. They were a dozen paces behind. There was a shot. I didn't look to see if it was a hit. I took a breath and readied the pike.

The zombie was twenty feet away. It had been scalped. That's the only way of describing it. Hair and skin had been cut off, revealing white bone like a macabre parody of a tonsure. Someone must have tried to kill it. They'd missed and, probably, they'd died. A few errant strands of hair remained, twitching back and forth each time the creature's shoulders flexed and its hands grasped out at the gap between us.

There was a shot.

I checked my grip, reminded myself that I had two fingers missing. The zombie had reached the edge of the slope leading down the road. I took another pace, swung the pike and looped the head under the zombie's ankle. I pulled. It fell. I skipped forward, plunging the spear at its skull. The creature rolled. The point jarred against concrete.

There was another shot.

I didn't look to see, I was too busy regaining my balance. I pulled the point back and was about to try again, but it was too late. The creature was halfway to its feet, and two more zombies were now at the top of the slope. Gravity helped Them on their way, as They half fell down the incline, knocking the creature that had fallen back down to the ground.

I skipped back a pace, and another. I looked at the pack. There were eight or nine all close together, all close to me. I didn't waste time counting properly. Behind Them came the rest, and it suddenly looked like a lot more than thirty zombies. There was another shot.

Focus, I told myself. I stepped back another step, and glanced at Sholto. So far, all the zombies heading down the drive were coming towards me. That was good, I told myself. I could lead Them away and my brother could thin Them out. There was another shot. I risked a glance over my shoulder. The stone wall stood twenty yards away. I could make it. It was going to be okay. I repeated the words over and over, in the hope that would make them true. My earlier stoicism was gone. I really, *really* didn't want to die.

Another shot. Climbing the wall was going to be the tricky part. Then three shots in quick succession. I glanced over at my brother. I could no longer see him. The undead were in the way, but there didn't seem to be so many, not right in front of me. There were seven. Or was it six? There was another shot then three, then a burst, and I cursed. Sholto should be saving his ammunition, making each shot count, not wasting them like that. But he would know that. He must be in trouble. I had to help him. I'd have to climb over the wall and run down the length of it to where he was. Another single shot and this time there were definitely only six, and how did my brother get the angle for that last shot? I didn't have time to work it out, because that creature with the scalped head, the one marginally faster than the others, was out in front again, only six paces away.

I swung the pike up, spear-point forward, and skipped half a step to change my footing. I plunged the pike forward. The point smashed up through the zombie's cheek. Its skull almost seemed to crumble as the creature collapsed, dragging the pike with it. I barely managed to keep my grip. In the half second it took to pull the weapon free, the pack had advanced, and now they were a pushing shoving scrum of arms and teeth, barely a pike's length away. I skipped backwards, and again. I was in the middle of the road. If I wanted to get to the wall I needed to get some distance from Them. There was another shot. A zombie collapsed. Another shot. There were four zombies left in front of me. Then a rapid burst, and there was only one. I stopped retreating.

I swung the pike up, scoring a line through a faded flannel shirt. The creature didn't notice. I swung again, the blade bit deep into the zombie's neck and stuck there. The zombie fell, brown pus spraying out onto the asphalt, and it took my pike with it. The shaft hit the ground as the zombie toppled forward. The wooden handle splintered and broke. I pulled out the hatchet. The nearest zombie was at the top of the drive, but moving back towards the house. I stalked towards it, but only managed three paces before it collapsed. There was a volley, then another. I looked over at Sholto, half thinking that he must have had more ammo than he'd thought, but his gun was lowered. There was a third volley and I realised the shots had come from the house, and the pack was now heading back there, towards the sound of gunfire.

Hatchet in hand, unsteady from an excess of adrenaline and a lack of sleep, I followed.

As I got closer, I made out five rifles pointed out of four windows on the upper floor of the main building. Then the volleys stopped. There was one last shot, and a zombie wearing the remains of a lurid pink tracksuit collapsed. Then all was silent except for the hammering of undead fists against wood and stone.

When I'd climbed the incline to the main gate, I realised why. What I'd taken as a dark band of paint ringing the house at about the level of the ground floor ceiling was actually the shadow from a ledge. It was about three feet in width, and judging by the window boxes, had held a profusion of trailing plants. Now, it prevented the people in the house from firing down at the undead immediately underneath them.

"There were more around the other side than we realised," Sholto said, walking up to join me. Twenty zombies lay dead in the car park and out on the road. About the same number, two or three deep, were once more gathered around the house, beating and clawing at the walls.

I could just make out faces in the window, and thought their expressions seemed expectant. It was Sholto who worked out what they were expecting. He started shouting, bellowing out the words to some old protest song. Even under the circumstances, I thought that was in bad taste. I stayed silent. He was making enough noise for the both of us.

Heads at the back of the pack slowly began to turn. By the second chorus, seven zombies were heading towards us and another dozen were faltering at the pack's edges uncertain as to whether we, or the house were the more enticing prey.

The closest of those seven was fifteen feet away when there was a ragged burst. They fell. Only one tried to get up. Its jaw had been shot away. Its head nodded back and forth as if it couldn't understand why it could no longer bite down. Sholto aimed, pulled the trigger. His rifle clicked empty. I darted forward, swinging the hatchet up and then down. The movement was enough to get another four moving away from the house. Sholto had stopped singing, and I clearly heard, coming from the house, the words, "Aim first, Donnie. Remember to aim!"

There were four shots. The zombies fell. There was a brief lull. The undead had all returned their attention to the house. My brother started singing again, but without the same vigour as before. Only three creatures moved far enough from the building to be shot.

There were about fifteen left when, at the same time as she started climbing out onto the ledge, a woman called out, "Get Closer! Keep singing. Shout!"

"Get back in Carmen," another woman, still inside, called out. "It won't take your—" The ledge cracked. It split. Amidst a shower of splinters and stone, the woman fell down into the pack of undead.

"Come on," Sholto roared, but I was already limping forward as fast as I could, as the undead crowded around the woman, and she disappeared from view.

There were a few shots from inside. Bullets skittered on concrete and smacked into the stone wall of the barn. A few undead fell, a few more spun backwards before renewing their efforts to reach the prone woman. Then there was a long drawn out burst. The woman had been lucky. She'd managed to hold onto her rifle. She emptied the magazine. Two of the creatures collapsed on top of her, and together with the remains of the ledge, that offered her some temporary protection from the clawing hands of the pack.

Sholto reached the undead, his machete cleaving up and down and left and right, at about the same time as the door to the house flew open. Three men came out. One held a sword, one a rifle, and another a short-handled spear. I didn't have time to take in any more details because I'd reached the edge of the pack. With the woman on the ground, with Sholto yelling and ululating, the creatures didn't even notice me. The hatchet came up and then down. I swung. I hacked. I pushed and kicked and punched and hewed. It was all a blur, a great mass of gore, interspersed with brief moments of clarity.

The hatchet stuck in a creature's forehead. The blow hadn't done enough to kill it, so I was warding it off with one hand, while trying to pull the axe free with the other. I'd just turned my head, and saw this second creature just inches away when, out of nowhere, the man with the spear appeared, stabbing it through the zombie's eye. I wrenched the hatchet free, and hacked at the creature until it fell. I had barely enough time to register that the man who'd come to my aid was old, not aged by recent experience, but genuinely old, before there was another zombie in front of me. My axe went up, my hand went out, and the fight went on.

And then, moments that seemed like years later, it was over. My eyes darted around, my hands moving up and down, looking for the next opponent, but They were all dead.

I glanced over at Sholto. He was doing that same jerking back and forth, scanning the ground for threats. He'd lost his machete at some point and had resorted to using the M16 as a club. The barrel was bent, the butt covered in gore. He stared at it for a moment before throwing it away in disgust. He shook his head, as if clearing it, then ran over to the side of the house and the woman who'd fallen from the ledge.

"Carmen? You all right?" the old man called out.

"Fine. Fine. Bruised my ego, that's all," the woman called from under the bodies, as Sholto started dragging Them off her.

The man with the sword was young, with a scraggly red beard that matched the colour of his sunburned scalp. Wearing a camouflage jacket and carrying a rifle slung over his back, he might have seemed intimidating if he'd not been moving erratically from body to body, the sword waving in a haphazard figure of eight, brown pus dripping from its edge, as he checked for the still-living dead. He looked like I felt, shocked and dazed.

The third man, the one who'd come out of the house with a rifle and still held it with a calm professionalism that just highlighted how the rest of us were still just experienced amateurs, took pity on him.

"You are all right, Donnie. It is over." He spoke softly, enunciating each syllable in a cultured Parisian accent. With a face that had more creases than lines, and erratic patches of grey in his hair, I'd safely guess he's on the wrong side of forty. His body on the other hand had a wiry athleticism that mine had never even approached.

"Yeah. Right. Thanks Francois," the young man, Donnie, muttered in an Irish accent with that transatlantic lilt of a Dubliner.

"Good. Now put that sword down and go and help that man with Carmen."

I watched, unmoving, seeing it all but not really taking it in.

"And how about you?" the old man asked. I'd not noticed him approach. "Are you all right?"

"I'm..." I raised a hand to wipe the sweat from my eyes but saw it was covered in blood and gore. I'd cut it somehow. I looked at the blood and saw the cautious concern in the old man's eyes. "I'm immune." I said.

"Ah," he relaxed. "Me too. And it was a shock finding out. Like being born again, 'cept into a nightmare you can't ever be sure isn't Hell. George Tull."

"Bill." I'd half extended my hand in that old familiar gesture before I remembered.

"Later," I said. "After I've had a wash."

"Well we've water enough for that. And thank you, Bill, for your help. I'm grateful."

"It doesn't look like you needed our assistance."

"Unexpected help was rare enough in the old world, out here it's about the only thing of any worth. So, thank you. Introductions then. Carmen's our wannabe acrobat, Donnie's the chap who didn't realise that even though the dead are walking, you still have to use sunscreen. Up at the window that's Marcy, our doctor. And that's Francois."

"I... We..." I didn't know what to say. This wasn't like meeting Kim, or like when we found the girls, nor even when we found Barrett and the others. This was something different. It was as if we'd walked into someone else's story. I put it down to the shock of suddenly realising I was still alive. Then something the old man had said registered.

"You have a doctor?" I asked, but he didn't get a chance to answer because there was a shout.

"Mister Tull!" It was Donnie. The old man stiffly walked over to him.

Sholto had pulled the bodies away. The woman, Carmen, was now sitting with her back against the wall, my brother's hands clutched tightly around her thigh.

"We need some bandages. Something to clean the wound," he said.

"It's nothing," Carmen said, I could hear it now, the pleading disbelief. "It's just a scratch."

"Marcy!" the old man bellowed. "Marcy! Get out here."

"I would if someone would help me," a voice called back from inside.

"Donnie, go and help her," George Tull snapped, and whatever had driven him over those hectic last few minutes seemed to drain away, making him suddenly seem little more than an old man wearing gore stained clothes.

A few moments later Donnie came back out of the house, helping a woman with a bandage around her ankle, and a large blue bag hanging over her arm.

"Right, lower me down so I can see," she said, after Donnie had helped her over the litter of bodies around the house. "Move your hands, please," she said to my brother, the tone brusque and professional. "Right, I'll have to clean and bandage it. Carmen, look at me. Carmen? Have you been bitten before?"

"What? No. I mean…"

"Has she?" Marcy turned to look at the old man.

"No idea."

"Anyone know?" she asked. Donnie shrugged, Francois just shook his head.

"Well, you haven't turned," the doctor said, turning back to Carmen. "So you're probably fine. But we're going to wait and see. That's our procedure." She glanced briefly up at Francois. The two exchanged a look that said they'd been through this before.

If I'd been looking for a sign as to whether we could trust these people, those words and that look were as close to one as I was going to get.

"I'm sorry—" I began, addressing Carmen, as the doctor began to clean and bandage the wound.

"You're standing in my light," the doctor said. I stepped sideways. I wished I could crouch down and address the injured woman at eye level, rather than towering over her like that.

"We had no choice," I went on. "We're low on food. But it's more than that. We do need help. Medical help. There's a baby, she's sick."

"There are more of you? Where?" the old man asked.

"A baby?" Carmen asked.

"What do you mean by 'sick'?" Francois asked.

"He means is it contagious," the doctor clarified.

"I've no idea. She's not got a fever, and none of the rest of us got sick if that means anything. It might be smoke inhalation, but she was like that before the fire."

"We were trapped in a tunnel," Sholto interrupted, and I was grateful he did. I knew I wasn't making much sense. "We set a fire to escape. We all got burned, though Daisy was withdrawn before then."

"Well, where is she?" the old man asked.

"Safe, about a mile away."

"Safe? They're not safe out here, not on their own. All of that shooting's going to have carried for miles."

I looked over at my brother.

"I'll go and get them," he said.

"Not unarmed you won't," the old man said. "Donnie, you give him your rifle. Francois, you go with him. Be quick now."

My brother took the rifle, hesitated a moment, checked it was loaded, then fired a shot into the body of one of the undead. He nodded thoughtfully to himself.

"Right, let's go then," he said, and hurried off towards the distant trees. The Frenchman followed.

"Not many children made it," Marcy said. "There can't be more than —"

"Twenty-three," the old man interrupted. "There are only a few hundred of us, but only twenty-three children."

"Where?"

"Ireland," the old man said before anyone else could reply. "We've secured a stretch of coastline, and a decent sized village. There's an old school there. Every day, everyone sees it, the empty classrooms, and you can't help but wonder about the future, and think on the past."

"That's all I can do," the doctor said. "We just have to wait."

"Not out here," Carmen said. "Not if there are children."

"You and me, lass," the old man said. "We'll go into the barn and wait there. Donnie, you want to give me a hand?"

Between them, they carried the woman into the barn, leaving me alone with the doctor. There was an awkward moment's silence.

"Dr Marcille Knight," she said, carefully lifting herself up.

"Bill. It's good to meet you, doctor."

"Marcy, please. Snap."

"I'm sorry?"

"The legs. How did you get yours?" she asked.

"Oh, that. Before the outbreak. I fell off a staircase. You?"

"Jumping out of a window a couple of days ago. Oh hell," she added, "We forgot Leon."

"Who?" I asked, turning to look. A man, rifle held across his body, was running down the road at a pace that would have won him gold in any marathon. He didn't stop until he reached the top of the drive. He took one long sweeping glance around, taking in me, the bodies of the undead, and then the distant figures of Sholto and Francois.

"Where are they going?" he asked, in a French accent far gruffer than Francois'. He didn't even sound out of breath.

"There are more of us. A woman and two children," I said. "They're going to collect them."

"Ah," he said nodding. "The old man?"

"With Carmen in the barn," Marcy said. "She was bitten. Donnie's helping him."

"Ah," he said, this time with a trace of sorrow.

"One of the children, it's a baby," Marcy added.

"Oh?" He seemed to think about that for a moment, then he looked around at the bodies once more. "I will go back to Gwen." The words came out slowly each enunciated with meticulous care, as if he was unsure they'd be understood, but then he turned and ran back the way he'd come without waiting to see if we had.

"He and Francois are French Special Forces," Marcy said. "Or were. I was in Mali. At a refugee camp. They dragged me onto their plane. The last one out."

"And Francois is the captain and Leon's the sergeant?"

"It's the other way around. Except Leon's a colonel. Or was, back when nationalities and ranks mattered."

"And they got you out of Mali? How did you end up here?"

"Now that is a very long story, but if you asked Leon, he'd find a way of telling it in less than ten words."

"Where's he going though?" I asked. "Who's Gwen?"

"Oh, right. Gwen and Leon were on truck duty. We drove here, it was a supply run, of sorts. Of course the undead, they follow, don't they? They always do. We lured the zombies away from the trucks, and up here. We came up that road, you see." She pointed along the coast. "The way you came. That's why Mr Tull was worried. If there were more zombies following us than we thought then that's where They'll be coming from. Anyway, the plan was that tomorrow morning we'd signal. Gwen would sound the horn until the undead start heading away from the house and then we'd shoot Them."

"So you really didn't need our help at all."

"I wouldn't go that far," she said. "There were twenty of us a week ago."

Before I could think of anything else to say, Donnie came out of the barn. He looked resigned more than upset.

"I don't get this life, this world. It doesn't make sense. None of it does. Immune or not immune…" He shook his head. "Hi. I'm Donnie."

"Bill," I said, and went through the 'can't shake hands now' business all over again. Then we talked about nothing for a while, as we waited for Kim and the girls.

"Kim, Annette, Daisy," I said, by way of introduction when they got closer, skipping over my brother as I was completely unsure how to introduce him. When they reached the house, he didn't help me out. He just stood smiling behind everyone else. But no one asked who he was. They were all far too interested in Daisy.

"We'll take her inside and I'll have a look at her," Marcy said.

"Will she be okay?" Kim asked.

"She'll be fine," Marcy said. "There's a boat coming here tomorrow morning. You're lucky you stumbled across us. That'll take us home, and we've a hospital there. She'll be fine, but I'll take a look at her now. If you want to bring her in here," she added to Kim.

"I'll come too," Annette said.

"No, dear," Marcy said, firmly but kindly, "not until after you've cleaned up. We've no spare clothes here, I'm afraid."

I looked down at myself, and then over at Kim, Sholto, and Annette. I suppose it's natural that we didn't really notice. Our clothes were singed and covered in dirt, except in the places where they're ripped or burned through, exposing the grime covered skin underneath.

"I can wash after," Annette said.

"No, I think the doctor's right," I said. "We could all do with a clean."

"There," Marcy said. "Listen to your father."

"My father?" Annette giggled, Sholto grinned, and even Kim rolled her eyes.

"We found each other on the road," I explained.

"Sorry," Marcy said. "I should have realised. It's old habits, you know? Well, come on then. There's an old shower room, you can wash in there. Back when this was a…" The doctor's voice faded as, carrying Daisy, she led Annette into the house. Kim gave me a brief look, full of meaning that I completely failed to understand. Then she shrugged and followed the doctor inside.

"We should move these away from the door," I said, gesturing at the undead.

"And I should go and check on Leon," Francoise added.

"He's already been up here," Donnie said.

"He has? Of course he has. And I bet he ran too. Of course he did. That man, he learned to run before he could walk."

Donnie and Francois exchanged a smile at that private joke.

"Which direction was that?" Sholto asked.

"Over there." I pointed.

"The east, right," Sholto nodded. "And will he keep a watch for the undead?"

"Of course!" Francois sounded affronted at the question

"And we came up from the south, that leaves the north," Sholto said. "I'll go that way, and see how many zombies heard the shooting."

"I will go with you," Francois said. "What's that expression? Two knives are better than one."

I was glad I didn't have to go and traipse around the countryside, right up until I looked down and saw the undead still littering the courtyard, and now there was only Donnie to help move the bodies.

After three quarters of an hour, I decided we'd done as good a job as we were going to, and stopped. Donnie happily concurred, fetched a couple of buckets of water and an old bar of soap for me, then he went to check on Carmen and the old man.

I was halfway through washing when Kim came outside.

"She's not sure," she said, quietly.

"About Daisy?"

"She doesn't know what's wrong. The food, the smoke, the water, it could be anything. It could be nothing. But she says they've a hospital, and power to run the equipment. She said a lot of other stuff, but I didn't really…" She took a deep breath. "They have electricity, Bill. And a school."

"Do you trust her?"

"She seems normal. Like a normal doctor doing normal things. You know, off-hand, brusquely professional, and insultingly dismissive."

"You don't like her?"

"No, I'm not talking about likes and dislikes. I'm saying she's not changed. Not like us. Not like me."

"There's something else, a 'but', isn't there?"

"She's secretive. There's something she's not saying."

"I got that impression, too. It's the old man who's in charge. And that's odd in itself."

"Old man?"

"George. And he is old, he went into the barn with Carmen, the woman who was bitten, to wait and see if she turns."

"Oh, right."

"We could still leave," I said neutrally. "If you wanted."

"No," she said after a moment. "We're all secretive, they've just met us. They don't know who we are. They seem to want to protect the girls, and that's got to be good enough."

"Good," I said, lifting the bucket and dumping its contents over my head. Now there was just the question of whether I'd be staying with them or going off to find the scientist on my own.

As for the trifling matter of who we were and whether or not these were the same people Sholto had arranged his rendezvous with, where I'd been circumspect, Annette hadn't.

"So, he's the infamous Sholto, and you're the brother he went off to find," Marcy said, almost as soon as I walked into the kitchen. "Annette told us," she added. She sounded amused.

"You've heard of my brother?" I asked.

"The man who tried to save the world? Who hasn't? At least in our little world. Give it another couple of years and he'll be a folk legend."

I couldn't tell how serious she was being.

"There's some stew. Or tea," Annette said sounding slightly apologetic, but only slightly. "I made a pot."

"How did you hear about Sholto, then?" I asked the doctor.

"From his friends. Sophia Augusto and Mister Mills."

It took me a moment to place the second name.

"Captain Mills of the Vehement?"

"Except he's decided that he's a civilian. He's still in charge of the submarine, but at the moment that means little more than deciding whether to scuttle the boat now, or wait to see if the winter storms will do the job for him."

So everything my brother had said was true. It was real.

"And you have a hospital and a school?" I asked.

"And some of the mod cons. Electricity's a bit ropey, so hot showers are limited to one per week."

"They're rationed?"

"We don't use that word. Not after… well, after all that happened. It reminds people of the other things. You know, the muster points, the evacuation and all that."

"Oh, right, yes of course." I didn't know what to say.

"And a boat will be here tomorrow?" Kim asked loudly.

"Like I said, tomorrow morning. And you guys can get a lift with us, but there is the small matter of getting through until it arrives. Someone should be on watch. Would you mind?" the doctor asked me. "You can get up to the roof from the skylight upstairs. I'll send Donnie up to join you, just as soon as he comes back from the barn."

That's the moment I'm going to remember, the image I'm going to take with me. Kim collapsed in a chair, sipping from a mug, Annette at the table, eating a fourth bowl of stew and Daisy, lying on a couch, snoring quietly.

"So if you've got this community out in Ireland, what are you doing over here?" I asked Donnie when he joined me up on the roof about twenty minutes later. "Marcy said something about a supply mission so I take it you're not just waiting for my brother."

"Ah, no. It's a bit complicated, but the old man said I should tell you. The only boat big enough for our supplies is the Santa Maria, and since Sophia insisted on coming here to meet your brother it would be more accurate to say we were catching a lift with you."

"Oh. What kind of supplies have you got?"

"Four armoured personnel carriers," he said.

"What on Earth for?"

"Ah, well, this is the complicated bit," he said. "You know the story about the nail and the king? How for want of a nail the horseshoe was lost, for want of a shoe the horse bucked, and the king fell off to be eaten by the undead? Well that's the problem we've been having. Plenty of horseshoes, horses, kings, and all the rest, but no nails. Metaphorically, I mean. We do have a few horses. Four of them, scared witless, the poor beasts. They were locked in their barn surrounded by the undead when the old man found them. You know, now I think about it, that can't have been that far from here."

I coughed.

"Right, right, the APCs. Well, we've got enough diesel to keep the Santa Maria and a few other boats going until the spring, maybe longer. Probably. We've enough to spare to keep the generator in the hospital running, and a little over so that everyone can have a few minutes under a hot shower once a week, but that's all. Everyone who arrives at our little community, whatever personal hell they've been through, knows the only guaranteed protection against the undead is having at least fifty feet of water between them and land. They don't want to get off their boats, and we've so much food to spare it's hard to persuade them that planting crops can't wait until next year."

"You've food to spare?" I asked.

"And ammunition, and enough diesel to run a fishing trawler. When the Santa Maria goes out, it comes back with its nets full. And what would

166

be the point of not sharing it? That's what Sophia says, and the mayor agrees, and if Leon doesn't, what does that matter? We are a democracy."

"So what's that got to do with the Army vehicles?"

"The mayor says it's a problem of economics. On their boats, people have food, shelter and security. What incentive can you give them to come ashore and do a hard day's toil on the land, or take the risk of helping on a supply run? Money doesn't mean anything, and everyone thinks food and shelter is all they want. So we have to pay them with something they don't have, and don't realise they want. Electricity. The mayor thinks that if they have lights and televisions and all the rest, even if it's just for a few days, they'll be willing to break their backs for more. We have the diesel, but like I said, that's allocated for the boats. Sophia won't allow it to be diverted, nor will Mister Mills, and together the two of them form quite a voting block. I think she's right. Hence this trip."

I waited for him to go on, but he seemed to have finished.

"How does coming over to England to collect four armoured vehicles help?" I asked.

"Because we need more fuel. The trouble isn't so much in finding it, but getting it out again. That means we need a way of clearing the roads, and keeping them clear so a load of tankers can get through. That's what the armoured cars are for. I'd have preferred we brought back one of the tanks, but Leon said no. Since he and Francois are the only people who know how to drive one, it's a bit of a moot point. Shame that."

"And the fuel dump, that's somewhere near here is it?"

"Ah, no. Not really. It's at Belfast International Airport."

"Belfast? You've come all the way over to Britain to find some armoured vehicles, just so you can go back to Ireland to drive them to Belfast?"

"Ah, well." He sounded puzzled. "Do you mean why don't we find some vehicles closer to the airport? We looked. We've looked everywhere." He sighed deeply. "Where we found one or two or a half dozen there's been no fuel. We didn't need to just find the armoured cars, but we also needed to find a fuel supply near them. I told you it was a horse and a nail problem."

"So you found a stash of diesel somewhere near these APCs? Well, why didn't you just bring back that diesel for people to burn on their boats? Wouldn't that have been easier than trying another trip to the airport?"

"Ah, no, I see. Sorry, I didn't quite make it clear. It's not diesel we're getting from the airport. It's aviation fuel. And we're not just talking about a few tankers. We're planning on bringing out seventy of them. One big trip, one big risk, that's the plan. There are a load of fuel tankers at the airport, and a depot half a mile down the road. That's why we needed the armoured cars."

"And boat engines can run on aviation fuel?"

"If you've got a group of engineers used to keeping the nuclear engine of a Trident submarine working, then something like that isn't a problem."

"Seventy," I murmured. "That would require nearly everyone in your little community."

"It's certainly a big undertaking."

"But you've only brought back four armoured cars."

"Well that's where this has all gone a bit wrong," he said. "There were twenty of us a few days ago. We'd planned on bringing fifteen vehicles back. Then… well, you know how it is out here."

We sat in silence for a moment. I let it last as long as I could, but macabre curiosity at this bizarre plan got the better of me.

"Fifteen APCs? How big is this trawler?"

"Oh, the Santa Maria's a big beast, but we were planning on towing the vehicles on barges."

I ran the plan over in my mind. Whichever way I looked at it, it didn't make sense. There had to be a few pieces he'd not yet told me.

"Isn't there anywhere closer to this village?" I asked.

"Village?" Again he sounded puzzled, and again only for a moment. "We've looked. We really have. We've tried airports, refineries, military bases, and depots. We've looked in Ireland, England, Wales, even the French coast. Belfast is the best option."

"Why not just look for more diesel?"

"And put it in what? The only thing we'd have to transport it in is the

Santa Maria's fuel tank. Then where would we store it? We'd end up using the trawler as a floating petrol station, which would leave no one to do the fishing or the supply runs. Believe me, we've looked at it from every angle. We even tried it, down in Cork. There was an explosion that killed twelve of us. We lost more just getting back out to sea."

"You mean to the coast?"

"Hmm?"

"Nothing. It doesn't matter." And I decided it didn't. Whatever happened, none of us would be joining them on their excursion to the airport. I decided to change tack.

"This mayor, who is she, some politician from the old days?"

"After that evacuation and Prometheus? Hardly. She's the compromise candidate. We're a nation of blocks, you see. There's Mister Mills and his sailors, Leon and his soldiers, Sophia and her refugees, then some people from Ireland, others from Britain and a lot from pretty much everywhere else. We needed some kind of government, and out of all the possible candidates, everyone objects to her less than they object to anyone else."

"Well that hasn't changed, at least." We sat in silence for a while, staring out at the fields. In the distance I thought I could make out a figure staggering down a hill. Gravity was angling it away from the house towards the north.

"Leon and Francois are soldiers. The old man, I take it he's in charge?"

"He's the power that pushes the throne," Donnie said cryptically.

"And Marcy's a doctor so I can see why she'd be here. What about Gwen?"

"She's a long haul trucker. Knows every side road, short cut, and low bridge this side of Krakow. She was near Warsaw when the world collapsed. She did a deal with the driver of a diesel tanker. She ran her rig in front, clearing the way, in exchange for enough fuel to keep the rig on the road. They made it down to the Channel Tunnel just in time to find it had been blown up, and then drove around just long enough to know they had to get off the continent. They made it down to Monte Carlo, picking up a half dozen others on the way. They stole some rich kid's yacht and drifted out to sea. Then there's Carmen, now she's…" He trailed off.

"Do you know her well?"

"What? No, not really. She turned up about three weeks ago, just before we were about to set out. She volunteered. Said she couldn't settle. It's not that uncommon. Some people, after spending a few months out in the ruins, can't accept that they've found somewhere safe and are driven by some nameless necessity into going back out. Since we were planning the trip, she said she'd come along." His voice caught on the last few words, and I was suddenly reminded just how young this man was.

"I am sorry about that," I said. "But what about you. Why are you here?"

"Me? Oh, that'd be down to my specialised knowledge."

"Really?" I was intrigued. "What kind?"

"I found the APCs, and the diesel. Well, me and Leon. I knew about Belfast, too. I used to work there, at the airport. Nothing important, I just ran a coffee and sandwich place. That's where I was, when the outbreak hit."

"Really? What was it like?"

"It was crazy," he said. "Some planes were allowed in, but not many and none were allowed out. No people were allowed in, either. I could have gone home, but what for? The airport seemed safe, and I'd more food in the shop than I did in my cupboards. So I stayed, and kept on doing almost exactly what I'd been doing before. At any minute, I was sure there was going to be an announcement that everything was going to return to normal. There wasn't. The news just kept getting worse, and each day, though I didn't notice it at first, there were fewer and fewer people at the airport. The few planes still flying were just running a shuttle service to Britain. There were plenty of aircraft parked on the tarmac, and there was plenty of fuel. I started asking around, seeing if anyone was planning on flying off somewhere. But the only people who were interested had no more idea of how to fly a plane than I did, let alone where they should fly to.

"I decided I should leave before I was kicked out. The only place I could think of that might be safer than the airport was a cabin a friend of mine had near Slievenamon, down in the Republic. It had no electricity, no phone, and no heating, but it was remote. That was important, because when those planes did come in, they were met with soldiers who'd go on board before anyone was allowed off. Increasingly often there was gunfire, and only the soldiers disembarked. I grabbed the last of the food, borrowed some fuel for my car, and headed south. I thought I'd have trouble crossing the border into the Republic, but the checkpoints were all abandoned. I got to the cabin, and I waited.

"The days all blended into one, you know? I sometimes picked up a few words on the radio, but it was never good news. I started to think that I should try to do something. It seemed wrong that I was safe while the world had fallen apart. I'd no family in Ireland, not in the Republic or up in the North, at least none that I cared about. But I did have family over in England, and this idea came over me that I was the only person in the entire world who cared what happened to them. If I didn't go and see, then who would? But how could I get there? And what would I do if I did? That thought would have driven me mad if there hadn't been a knock at the door, and it actually was a knock. It was Leon and his unit. They'd spotted the light from my fire and driven up to investigate. I'd not even thought to cover the windows."

"Marcy said that Leon was a colonel in the French Army?" I asked.

"In Africa. Special Forces supporting the peacekeepers, and that's another grim story. Their base was next to the refugee camp hospital Marcy worked in. From what they've said, it wasn't anything more than a concrete bunker that, on a good day, had four patients to a bed. A five-year old boy needed an operation, and Marcy didn't have the equipment to perform the surgery in the camp. She smuggled him into the military base to do it there, and was just sewing him back up when the outbreak hit. Orders had come through for the unit to leave everything they couldn't carry, and get on a plane back to France. Leon offered Marcy a ride. By the time they were airborne, a plane had crashed into the airbase they were meant to be landing at. By the time they reached Paris, even Charles de Gaulle was gone. They were redirected to Shannon, along with a whole load of EU military flights. Just before they landed, Leon received a message. They should wait and be ready. That was the last they heard from France.

"No more orders came through, but too many planes came in, with too many infected. They tried to quarantine the runways. It didn't work. They pulled back and tried to maintain a ring around the airport, and then they were pushed back further. With ammunition running low, when the power went out, retreat turned into a rout. They'd been in touch with other military units and knew that some people were still holding on over on the east coast. They commandeered some vehicles and headed across the country. They must have got lost, because they ended up knocking at my door."

"That was lucky."

"It was, but surviving is as much luck as anything else. Leon said he was taking his men east, towards the Irish Sea. He asked if I wanted to go with him. I had nothing to offer them, and yet he asked. I still don't know why. We reached the coast, and it seemed like everything might just work out. I'd told Leon about my family in England. About how I thought they must be dead. He said nothing is ever certain. Which, when you're talking about life, death, and the undead, could mean two very different things. But he did say he wanted to go to England, and asked if I'd like to travel with him. No," he corrected himself, "asked isn't the right word. I think he was finding a reason that would allow him to leave his men and all the refugees we'd picked up. We took a dinghy and reached Wales about the same time, we found out later, that Francois, Marcy, and the rest made contact with the Santa Maria.

"I looked for my family. They weren't there. There'd been a battle, of sorts, and there were bodies everywhere, but no sign of either of them. Then we went to Cambridge. That was where Leon wanted to go, to a house just outside the city. He didn't say who lived there, and it was clear from the street what was inside. He insisted on going in alone. A few minutes later he came out again, and he's never said who lived there. Maybe that's for the best. We've all got so many of our own horrific memories that we don't need each other's as well.

172

"After that, we drifted around for a few days. He didn't seem to want to go back to Francois, but nor was there any point doing anything but heading back towards the Irish Sea. One afternoon, we stumbled across the warehouse. I knew there was something odd about it from the moment I saw it. The number of windows, the position of the ramp, and the layout of the loading bay were wrong. The place was an illegal fuel dump, the kind that sold agricultural diesel to people who wanted to avoid paying the duty for a commercial vehicle. It was all contained in these old tanks buried underground."

"You drove out of there?"

"Hardly. We spent the next day trying to find a clear route out by road, and we were spotted."

"By zombies?"

"Humans. It was a good thing I had Leon with me. Even so, we had a running battle through the suburbs, with the noise of gunfire drawing in the undead. It was… terrible. We were pinned down. Each time Leon fired, he hit someone. But he didn't fire that often, because they were in cover and being cautious. Me, that was the first time I'd fired a gun, and my hands were wavering so much there wouldn't have been any point aiming even if I knew how. I thought we'd die. Of course we weren't going to. Leon had it planned. He'd remembered that spot and picked it on purpose. I suppose he'd been in far worse situations than that. The gunfire attracted the undead, and They dealt with the bandits, leaving us to climb up a fire escape we'd not dared use when we were facing people with guns. We climbed up onto the roof and escaped.

"About ten minutes walk from there we found the car park, with its assortment of APCs, halftracks and tanks. They were lined up almost as if they were on sale. All they were missing was a price tag on the windscreen. Leon wouldn't let us take one. We didn't have enough fuel, and with just the two of us, there was no way we'd be able to secure the warehouse to get more. It turned out twenty people wasn't enough either. We found a car instead, and about five hours driving later, we found one of the safe houses. A couple of days after that we were out at sea and found that the redoubt in Ireland had been reduced to one small village. Half of Leon's men had died, and I don't think he's forgiven himself for not being there."

I tried to say nothing, to maintain a respectful silence, but curiosity got the better of me.

"And these safe houses—" I began.

"Ah now, let me stop you there. That's one thing the old man will definitely want to tell you about himself. They were his idea, you see. And what about you, though? How did you get manage to keep a baby alive out here for so long?"

"Well, to start with that was mostly Annette's doing…"

I kept the story as much as possible on Annette and Kim, and a little on Sholto, but skipped over Lenham Hill, and who I'd been. After what he'd said about politicians and the evacuation, I thought that was wise. As it turned out, that circumspection was utterly pointless.

About three hours later, when we'd long lapsed into silence we saw two figures heading towards us from the north. Sholto and Francois. Sholto went into the house, Francois into the barn. A few minutes after that, Francois and the old man came out. Carmen wasn't with them. And a few minutes after that, Francois climbed up to the roof through the skylight.

"She died," Francois said, simply. "She spent seven weeks in a motorway service station. Ten people were there to start with and she was the only one to walk out alive. I'll take over up here."

"I can stay," Donnie offered.

"No. There's no need. Anyway, you make too much noise." He held out his hand. I took it, and he helped me up. Then he kept hold of my hand and gave me a long calculating look, before nodding to himself. I followed Donnie back down through the skylight, leaving the French soldier to stand watch alone.

Down in the kitchen, a pot was bubbling away over the fire. The old man sat at the end of the table, Marcy next to him. Annette was curled up in a battered armchair, Daisy was in Kim's lap. I think she seemed happier. It was hard to tell.

"I told you there was a boat and a village in Ireland," Sholto said with a grin. He was stretched on a chair, his boots loose, looking supremely pleased with himself.

"Were there many undead out there?" I asked.

"Two or three. Seven if you're counting. Not many. There can't have been many people in these parts to start with." He rubbed at his arm where it had been burned during our exit from the tunnel.

"Let me see that," Marcy said, looking at the burn. "No, on second thought, first you need to wash, then I'll have a look it. There's a shower room, down by the back door."

"That way," the old man gestured with his thumb. "Showers don't work. You can boil some water on the stove if you want hot otherwise it's cold. Be frugal. We don't want to waste it, not if that boat's late."

"Who'd have thought the life of a living folk hero would be so mundane," my brother said, still grinning as he headed off down the hall.

"He's not really a folk hero is he?" I asked.

"A living legend might be closer to the truth," George said. "And not him, of course, but the idea of him. An American who knew about the end of the world and tried to stop it, then insisted on searching England for his brother. You have to admit, it's a good story. It was Sophia who came up with it. She's a captain of a fishing trawler. Has he told you about her?"

"A bit, yes."

"The story, or the idea of it, gave her crew and passengers the hope that amidst the death and horror there was still some humanity out there. Romantic nonsense if you ask me, just like the safe houses."

"But that was you," Annette said. "Marcy, you told me! You said he was the flag man."

"The flag man?" George asked.

"Down near the Abbey there was a house with flags," Annette explained. "Was that you?"

"That depends which Abbey you mean."

"Brazely, down in Hampshire," Kim elaborated.

"Hampshire? No, that wasn't me. Might have been Chester. Or Bran, of course. Not really sure where he goes or what he gets up to. I don't think that's his real name, just what he said I should call him, which is not the same thing at all. But everyone's entitled to rewrite their past." He glanced at me as he said that. "Could have been someone else, too. There's quite a few people working on my overground railway now."

"Railway?" Annette repeated, puzzled.

"It's what I call it. The network of safe houses, though that makes it sound grander than it is. Did you go inside this one that you saw?"

"No," she said, "but I know there were people in it, there was smoke coming from the chimney. Then I got lost looking for it. That's when I met Kim and Bill."

"Ah." He seemed to relax.

"We saw one, though," Kim said. "And went inside it. By the River Thames, near Windsor."

"You went inside?" George asked.

"Yes, but I think someone had emptied it of anything valuable. The cupboards were empty."

"Ah, well we always leave some food there," he said.

"And there was a map" Kim said.

"There was?"

"Well, no," she amended. "There had been a map, taped to the kitchen counter but that had been removed as well."

"Ah, yes. That sounds like Bran," he said, and only once it was gone did I notice the tension that had been in his voice. "Not taking the map and the food. I mean leaving it there in the first place."

"The map, was it directions to here?"

"Possibly, possibly," he said. "It's hard to say. Probably it just listed the other houses within a couple of days walk. No, these houses aren't anything grand, just a place that's empty, with a fireplace and, for preference, a flagpole out front. It's just somewhere we can leave some food, water, and firewood. And it all started by accident."

"It was an accident?" Annette asked.

"Completely," he stretched out. "When this all began I was in a home. A retirement home. I've not much to say about that place other than I've found a new lease on life since. The undead appeared a few days after the evacuation. I had to fight, I got bit, I found out I was immune. After the shock of that wore off, I realised our troubles had only just begun. You know what it was like in those first few days. We tried to get down to Cornwall. That was where we were meant to be evacuated to, but it took us a whole day to cover five miles and we were exhausted."

"Who's we?"

"Oh, me and the mayor. We thought if we got to the town we might find some police or Army, and they'd give us a lift. I mean, this was after the evacuation, but we didn't know, then, that the vaccine was poison. We just thought we'd been overlooked, that we'd been unlucky. We got to the hill overlooking the shopping centre. It was one of those out of town sorts, with the generic shops selling clothing that's more logo than thread. Anyway, we could make out these people, fighting. Except they weren't fighting zombies. They were fighting each other, just for a few meagre scraps that wouldn't last more than a couple days. I'd killed three zombies that morning, I knew there'd be more. I knew it was only a matter of time. And when you get to my age you get a real understanding of the value of time. We decided to turn around and head north."

"To here?"

"Not here, not this very house, no. But to one a bit like it, not that far away. I had a friend whose brother had a house here in Wales. That was the only place either of us could think of. So when I say we were heading north, it'd be more accurate to say we were just walking in that direction because it seemed better than any of the others. We met some people the next day, but they didn't want us to travel with them, not two oldies so close to death the undead probably didn't realise we were still breathing. Not that they said that out loud. They just said 'we'll see you further down the road'. And they were right. We did, and I had to finish Them off." He patted the spear at his side.

"Well," he went on, "we may be old, but we're not stupid. Being on foot just wasn't going to work, we needed a car and there were plenty of those. What we were lacking was petrol. Thanks to the rationing, there just wasn't very much left in any car. What I realised, and this is how the whole safe house business started, was that while there wasn't much in any one car, all together there'd be enough to get us wherever we wanted. We stopped early, picking this nice little cottage mostly because it had white roses trailing up around the door. That it had a flagpole in the front garden was what the mayor would call a fortuitous happenstance. We went around the houses, and the cars parked outside. By nightfall we'd enough food for a week and enough petrol to get us twenty miles. It wasn't enough, but it was too much to carry. So we decided to go and check the next village along. We took enough food for a day, and left the rest with the fuel, and made a note of the address. Then, and it's important that you remember this because no matter what anyone might tell you, this is the truth of it, we hung up a couple of flags. And we only did that in case we couldn't find the street. That was all. It was just a marker to help us find the place on our way back." He paused. "I think that water's boiled. You mind making some tea."

"Sure," I said, getting up.

"When you're young," the old man continued, "you think everything can be solved with action. One violent vigorous act and it's all settled. When you get a bit older, and a lot wiser, you realise that slow and methodical, that's the way. That's what we did, slow and steady. Perhaps those people we'd met had been right, because we didn't have that much trouble with the undead. Mind you, it did take us the entire morning to reach the next village and we were both exhausted. We picked a house, this time one with a flagpole, but again that was just so it'd be easier for us to find it later on. We found more food, we syphoned more petrol, and we avoided the undead. We worked out a bit of a routine. Distract Them, you know? Get Them heading off somewhere, because if you're clever about it, They won't realise that you've sneaked off and They're just following one another. That day our haul wasn't as good as the first, but it was still an extra ten miles or so of fuel. We reckoned that if we kept that up for a couple of weeks, we'd be set. But what we wanted and what the universe had planned for us was another thing entirely. We stumbled across this kid, Ronnie. He's about the same age as you," he added nodding to Annette. "Said he was heading up to Scotland to find his sister, except he'd been cycling west instead of north. He joined up with us. And that was one more mouth to feed, but it was also an extra pair of hands, and someone to go off scouting to check the roads ahead were clear. It was a lot quicker, and a lot safer, after that."

"Why didn't you all cycle?" Annette asked.

"The mayor can't."

"Everyone can learn to ride a bike," she said.

"I mean physically. She's in a wheelchair."

My eyebrows rose at that.

"A couple of days later we ran into a pair of girls, Finn and Ailya," George said. "They'd been hiking south in the hope that it'd turn out better than what they'd seen up north. They joined us, and that made five."

"And you didn't meet anyone else?"

"Oh we did. This was still the early days. That was one good thing about the evacuation, it cleared out the whole middle part of the country. No, we did meet other people, but five's enough to look dangerous, and we weren't carrying enough to make the risk worthwhile. I think, for most people, civilisation and all its trappings were still fresh enough in their memories that law and order still prevailed. Up until the morning of the tenth day." He paused again.

"What happened then," Annette asked eagerly.

"I'll tell you, just as soon as he finishes making that tea."

"Right, sorry." I filled half a dozen mugs, and handed him one.

"Thank you," he said, giving me that strange look again. "So on the tenth day, we were about forty miles northwest of that first... what did you call it? That first flag house. We'd covered a bit more than that, going in a sort of zig-zag and we'd decided we'd stockpiled enough. We were going to take a car, drive back, pick up all that petrol and food, and then drive west to that house in Wales I knew about. We were just working out whether to take one car or two when we heard this engine coming towards us. That was Bran. He'd found our stash, and had been driving around the countryside looking for more, collecting everything we'd left. Ronnie had been in charge of the flags, and he'd taken to putting them up as soon as

179

we picked a place. That was the reason Bran stopped. He thought he'd found another stash, and he wasn't alone. There were four of them in that car, and they saw the petrol and food as their property." He took a long sip from the mug.

"There are four types of people who didn't go on the evacuation," he said. "There's the ones like me who couldn't, the people too scared to believe the outbreak was real, the people who just didn't trust the government and…" He took another theatrical sip. "And of course, there's the people who knew, for one reason or another, that wherever law and order was, they wanted to be somewhere else."

"Criminals?" Annette asked.

"That's far too simplistic a word. But this is why the mayor is the mayor. They came looking for an easy haul. She persuaded them that we'd be better off working together. That if they took the food for themselves they'd stay alive for an extra day or two, but if we worked together we might all last out the year."

"And that was enough?" Annette sounded sceptical.

"Well she didn't say it like that. She's a better way with words than I have. But that was almost enough. One of them didn't want to go along with it. Don't know why. Bran dealt with him." He paused again, and this time, I noted he was watching Annette's reaction.

"Oh. Right." She just shrugged. "So what happened then?"

"Well," he said slowly, as if he was making a mental note of something, "there were eight of us, in a convoy heading north. And that engine attracted the undead, but it was also a siren for the survivors. By the end of the day we'd made a hundred miles and eight had grown to forty. When you take out the ones too old or too young, there were still thirty strong enough to wield a weapon. They needed to be, because we had to fight all night long, fending off the zombies that had followed us. But when dawn came, we were all still alive. That's when we decided to split up. With what we could scrounge from nearby and what we'd carried with us, we had enough fuel to get two cars to the Welsh coast. Bran and the mayor went on ahead with the young, the sick and the old. Me and the rest, we continued on foot."

180

"But you're old," Annette said. "Why didn't you go with them?"

"Because" he spluttered, more amused than indignant, "the mayor and I seemed to know where we were going, we weren't just wandering in the wilderness. You must have known it, the fear and despair that gripped everyone in those first days, and in the months since. Everyone else was ready to turn their faces to the wall, but we'd not given up. If two old folks at the end of their days could keep going then so could they. And we'd proved it. We'd fought a battle and we'd won. Or no one had died, and that's about the only kind of victory that matters. So while we led, they would follow, but only if we led from the front. That's why I stayed with that second group."

Annette seemed to weigh that up.

"Okay," she said eventually, "so what happened then?"

"Well," he said, "whenever we stopped, we hung out a flag, and we made sure to leave a little food for anyone coming after. A couple of days after we'd split up, we spotted a house with a flag already flying out front. Bran and the mayor had stopped there and they'd left some supplies for us. They'd also left an address of where they were going next. We followed and looked out for the flags. It wasn't easy but we got to the coast, met up with Mister Mills and crossed the Irish Sea to the village they'd turned into a redoubt. It's forty miles south of Dublin," he added, "or about seventy miles west of here. We had an election, and some people tried to carve out a life, others have stayed on their boats doing nothing but hiding from an indifferent world that suddenly turned cruel, but some of us." He nodded at the others sitting around the table, then gestured towards the barn. "We try to give others a chance. Bran and a few others went back out to set up the safe houses, some in Ireland, some over here. They put out the maps and left a route for people to follow. And us, well, we came back over here because we know that what we've got is not enough. We want to create something worthy of passing on to your generation." He nodded to Annette.

"How many?" Annette asked slowly. "I mean, how many people? Marcy said there were only two hundred."

"Oh there's a few more than that," the old man said, glancing at the doctor. "We've a policy of not knowing the exact number as it goes down as often as it goes up. The mayor keeps a record, of course, to keep track of supplies and the like. For the rest of us, we just focus on the idea that after the outbreak we were all on our own, and we're not anymore."

"And that's all that are left, out of the millions and millions?" Annette asked.

"Well," he said slowly, looking at me as he said it, "there are other places. Other communities. Places where if you walk down the path singing and shouting so they know you're not one of the undead, they'll as soon shoot you as they would greet you like a friend. And I'm sad to say that that's not the worst of it. But that shouldn't trouble you," he said, turning again to address Annette. "Tomorrow you'll be on a ship with nothing more to contend with than sea sickness and seagulls."

"Seagull stew. Once tasted, never forgotten," Donnie added brightly.

"Oh don't remind me," Marcy said with a rueful shake of her head. "We've fish now, lots of it. And wheat for bread and…"

They went on to describe, with genuine enthusiasm, the chicken coops, the nascent rabbit farm, the stable and its horses, and the rest of their menagerie. Annette was enthralled. I was more interested in the things that they were not saying. I listened for half an hour before getting to my feet.

"I'm just going to take a walk. Stretch the leg. It gets stiff if I sit too long."

"You're not going far?" the old man asked.

"Once around the house."

"I'll come with you," Kim said.

Conscious of Francois still sitting sentry on the roof, we waited until we were on the far side of the barn before either of us spoke.

"What did you get out of Marcy?" I asked. Kim summarised what she'd been told. It sounded very much like the story Donnie had told me.

"And what do you make of it?" I asked.

"It's not going to work, is it?" she said finally. "I mean, all those tankers? You'd need all the people who can drive. Machine-guns and armoured cars aren't going to help. Even if it works, too many will die, and the fuel will still eventually run out. It's a temporary solution that will create a lot more problems than it solves."

"It sounds desperate."

"It is. That's exactly the right word. It's as if they've reached this point and think there are no options left. Except I can see at least twenty that they haven't tried."

"We could disappear. Now," I said, and I was half considering it.

"No, don't get me wrong. I don't think they're dangerous to us, and we need that hospital. I just think that this airport plan is going to go disastrously wrong. And I think the only reason they're considering it is because otherwise they would definitely face disaster." She sighed. "We were so close. I thought we'd found safety, but we haven't. We'll go along with them for now, just until Daisy's better and then see if we can find a way across the Atlantic, or out to some small island or something. We can manage without electricity. Yes, that's what we'll do. Anyway, we have to go with them," she said, turning to look at me. "You'll need to know where to find us. Oh don't look at me like that. You're going off to find that scientist, aren't you?"

"Yes," I said.

"And you have to go now?"

"I think so. So we can settle down to a new life without the old one hanging over us."

"Okay," she said. I was surprised. I'd been expecting a fight. "But," she went on "Take your brother with you. I'd go, but one of us needs to stay with Daisy and Annette."

"True. And Sholto's not the maternal type."

"Nor am I. But if I go, Annette will follow and she won't leave Daisy behind. So you'll take him?"

"I'll speak to him in a moment."

"That wasn't a 'yes'."

"Yes. I'll ask him to come."

"Good. We'll arrange a time to come and collect you both. If Sophia was going to come here to collect him once, then she'll come back. We'll say the last day of the month, and if you're not here, then the last day of every month after that."

"No, it'll be a lot easier if we make our own way to Ireland. It won't take that long. Just a week, two at the outside. Don't worry. It'll be fine."

Had I known, I'd have come up with some better parting words.

Kim went back inside. I stood, looking at the fields for a time, lost in my own thoughts. When I finally went back into the house, Annette was asleep in an armchair, Sholto in one opposite, Daisy asleep on his chest. I'd just decided to let him sleep and talk to him in the morning when the old man came up and tapped me on the arm. He nodded towards the back door. I followed him outside.

"I just want to check the perimeter," he said. "And have a quick word while we're about it."

"Oh, yes?"

"Sholto, your brother, I never thought he'd actually make it here. Wasn't entirely sure he was real. He's certainly not what I expected. Nor are you."

"Oh?"

"Well, naturally, I assumed you'd be American."

"He's actually British," I said. "He's naturalised, you see."

"Yes. I sort of guessed that when I worked out who you were. I don't think I ever knew your name, but I remember the face, even now. Don't know that many people would, but I didn't have much to do except watch the telly. Yours was on it often enough. Might not have remembered it if it wasn't…" He trailed off. I stayed silent.

"So you were one of them," he said, eventually. "One of the politicians."

"Not exactly. I wrote speeches. That sort of thing."

"Nah, you were more than that," he said. "All that coverage, all those interviews. You were going to be someone. Always with Jennifer Masterton, weren't you? You'd grown up with her or something. I thought you were dating her."

"I wasn't. We did grow up together. Sort of. Her father adopted me.

Sort of."

"Huh," he grunted, then changed the subject. "So, Donnie told you of the plan. What do you think of it?"

"The tankers and the airport? Well, let's say it all works and you get this aviation fuel and rig up the boats, and the tractors and whatever else to burn it. What are you going to do when the fuel runs out?"

"Right, sooner or later we'll be out of fossil fuels, so we might as well accept that now. It's a good point." And then he seemed to change the conversation again. "You know Anglesey didn't get destroyed."

"I'm sorry?"

"The island of Anglesey. It wasn't nuked. It was evacuated. The RAF bases were cleared out, but it wasn't nuked."

"So does the nuclear power plant still work?" I asked.

"Technically, yes. The chief from the Vehement checked it out. It was switched off, or mothballed or whatever you want to call it. But they can get it running again."

"Well, surely that's an easier way of getting power than this whole Belfast airport business."

"And I thought you politicians were meant to be clever. There are two options for us, neither of which involves trying to get a fleet of boats to run on aviation fuel. Donnie doesn't know this. Leon does, and I don't know if he's told Francois. Gwen knows, but mostly because she's been my driver these last couple of months. The rest, and the ones who died, and the ones we left back at home, they think it's all about fuel. It's not. You know what else they have at airports? Planes. Enough planes to get us all out of here. Mister Mills took his boat south. Down beyond the equator, there's an island. Not a big one, not really anything more than a landing strip and some mango trees. There are no undead. None. The climate would be nice, too."

"You're thinking of leaving."

"That is one option. There are three planes more or less ready to go. Leon will take his men in and see to the refuelling. We'll load everyone else onto buses, and we'll use those APCs to clear the route. We'll get them onto the planes and fly south."

"Why not just turn on the power station?"

"That's plan number two, and the reason it's not our first option is that the Vehement isn't the only nuclear sub to have survived. There's another. That's what's preventing us from just flicking the switch and turning the lights back on. If we do, we stand a very real risk of being nuked."

"No one would do that, surely? Not now?" I said.

"Wouldn't you, if you were a captain who had already been damned by your actions when you launched your first missiles? What would another one matter?"

"You're not seriously telling me that there's a rogue captain out there who really would rather see the end of the species rather than some small group actually survive?"

"You see, you've forgotten. It's Mister Mills who went rogue. He was the one who mutinied. And it wouldn't be the end of the species. Like I said, there are other communities. It's difficult," he said, again seemingly changing the subject, "you know, being immune. Have you thought of what that means?"

"I have."

"Difficult, yes," he murmured. "Your brother came over here looking for the scientist who created the virus."

"Yes. I was leaving tomorrow morning to try to find him."

"You know where he is?" he asked.

"Well, we've an address of where he might have been."

"And where's that?"

"Here. Wales. Somewhere along the north coast," I said.

The old man nodded slowly. "He's not there," he said.

"What? How do you know?"

"Because I know exactly where he is. And that brings me back to this submarine and this other little community."

"And?" I asked.

"The scientist is there, with them. And that submarine that's not gone rogue, that's still following their orders. Orders from the British government. From the Prime Minister."

"Where?"

"Caulfield Hall."

My heart sank. "That's the Masterton's family home up in Northumberland."

"Spot on."

"And Jen's there?"

"She is," he said.

"And she's calling herself the PM?"

"Hardly. That honour goes to the right honourable Sir Michael Quigley."

"Quigley's alive? At Caulfield Hall. With the scientist? And Jen's there? And they have a nuclear submarine?"

"Yes to all of those questions," he said. "And we have the Vehement, and they know about us and we know about them. If we turn that power station back on, then they'll launch a missile and destroy us. Maybe they'll do that anyway. That's why we're thinking of flying out of here. We're not going to subjugate ourselves to the likes of Quigley."

"You've tried to talk to them?" I asked.

"Well, yes, of course. I went there myself. I suggested a merger, and they told us to surrender. Since we're with Mister Mills, and he's a traitor and all that, and since most of us aren't British, well, you see the problem?"

"Why don't they just destroy you anyway?"

"Because Mister Mills still does have his submarine. We know where they are, they know where we are. If they fire, so do we, and vice versa. Whoever fires first, we'll all die. Mutually Assured Destruction. It's the whole premise of nuclear war, isn't it? But maybe there's an alternative."

"You want me to go to Caulfield Hall?"

"What I want doesn't come into it. I'm too old to have wants and desires. This is a chance for those girls of yours to have a future. Think what it would be like without electricity. Oh sure, you can romanticise a life of candles and farming, but have you thought about what it would really be like? A third of the day in the fields, a third of the day on guard, and the other third asleep because you'll be working so hard that you won't be able to stay awake a moment longer. Have you thought about the decisions we'll have to make in the next few months? The crops we pick to grow, those will be the ones our descendants, or yours anyway, will have to eat. Forget chocolate, tea and coffee, pineapples, oranges, and bananas. There'll be no sugar because sugar beet takes up too much land and too much processing. Since there won't be any dentists, that's probably a blessing. We're not talking about glamorised Blitz-spirit wartime rationing. We're talking about a life of pre-famine Irish serfdom. Worse, since we've got no pigs. It'll be potatoes and eggs, and maybe a chicken at Christmas. Each year there'll be less food, but that won't matter because each year there'll be fewer people to eat it. Do you know how to make candles? Because when the batteries go that's all the light we'll have. Do you know how to spin wool? Because when the moths and mildew destroy what we're wearing you'll have to."

"There are the supplies on land," I said, "just waiting to be taken."

"They won't last for ever, and you know that. In a few years, I'll be dead. Donnie, he's funny, you know. Him and Ronnie, they talk all the time about what life will be like for them when they reach my age. I don't like to tell them that they probably never will. It's the same for your girls. Each year there will be fewer supplies from the old world left, and fewer people to go out and collect them. The zombies haven't stopped yet, so why should They ever? And you're not going to be the only people out trying to grab the scraps from the old world. Bitten, shot, or stabbed, from sickness and suicide and exhaustion, each year there will be more to do and fewer people to do it. The doctors will die, the medicines will run out, the tools will rust, the ammunition will be used up. With electricity, maybe it'll be different. Maybe we'll have a chance. Without it, then the only hope is somewhere a bit warmer with a better climate and a longer day. Otherwise our only legacy is going to be barbarism and despair."

"So," I asked again, "you want me to go to Caulfield Hall?"

"Alright, yes. I want you to go there."

"And do what? Burn it down?"

"Hardly. They must have some kind of signal to send out to their submarine, a way of each letting the other know they're still alive. If you destroy their radio set, the sub will assume they're dead and then they might launch their missiles."

"What is it you want then?"

"Just talk to Jennifer Masterton. If she'll listen to anyone, it's you. Tell her to talk to the sub and call it off, or stand it down, or whatever. We'll combine the two communities. We'll re-open the power station. There'll be no arrests, no trials, no punishments. We won't even bother with truth and reconciliation. She can even stand for election if she wants."

"And Quigley?"

"He won't listen. That's why you've got to speak to Masterton."

"You want me to kill him?"

"Someone should. But no, if I want anything, it's that submarine gone. Get it to stand down, and let us get on with our lives. And while you're there you can find this scientist, and see if you can find out what you need to know."

I ignored the obvious appeal to my own self-interest. "And if Jen won't help?" I asked.

"Then find the radio and try to talk to the sub yourself. Tell them it's just women and children. Tell them to go and look for themselves. They probably won't listen, but you can try. There's no time for half-measures now, it's all or nothing, every minute of every day, doing until we die. Maybe, just maybe, if enough of us do that, then in a hundred years, your descendants will have the luxury of leaving a dirty job for someone else to do. Here and now, that someone is you. So, will you try?"

I didn't bother to answer. I'd already made up my mind, and the old man knew it. I will go to Caulfield Hall. I'll find the scientist, and I'll try to stop Quigley, but I have to go alone. I'm sorry, Sholto, but Quigley might recognise you. Even if he didn't, he's bound to guess who you are. I can't risk it.

I'll leave this journal here. It's too dangerous to risk taking. Dawn's coming and I have to leave. I'm not going to write any parting words. That would be tempting fate. Instead I will just wish you good luck, and hope I see you somewhere down the road, soon.

189

Part 3:
Return, Reunion
& Retribution

Northern England
& Wales

5th - 8th August

Day 146
Somewhere over Northeast England

Dawn, 5th August

It's only been three days, so much has happened and I don't know whether anything has changed. Where shall I start? At the safe house, I suppose.

The Return

The old man led me down to where Gwen and Leon were keeping watch over the APCs. I took a beat up Jaguar from a nearby farmhouse, and enough diesel to get me to Northumberland and back twice over. Gwen gave me a map with two routes marked on it, one that I should take, and one to very definitely avoid. She also marked a safe house about thirty miles from Caulfield Hall.

"Stick to the route. Stay in the safe house," she said. "And don't try any of your own shortcuts."

Leon didn't say anything at all. He just handed me a pistol, a little snub-nosed thing he'd had hidden in an ankle holster. The bike went onto the roof and I drove off without a backward glance.

It took almost exactly twelve hours to get thirty miles from Caulfield. It would have been quicker but, particularly as I got closer, I did try a few of my own half remembered shortcuts. I got lost twice, and once found the road abruptly disappeared amidst the detritus of a horde's passage. I left the car five miles from the safe house, on a crest of a hill. I hoped that any undead that were attracted by the engine noise would have dispersed downhill by the time I returned.

I didn't stay in the safe house. Unlike the others, this one wasn't marked out by flags. It was just an anonymous house in a dilapidated housing development on the edge of a once prosperous mining town. I took one look at it and kept on for another hour until I was once again lost among the fields and hills.

The next morning, yesterday, I cycled the last twenty miles or so to Caulfield Hall. Usually my eyes stayed fixed to the road ahead, charting a route between the ubiquitous rubbish and occasional undead. The only time I glanced up was when a startled flock of birds suddenly erupted from a tree or hedge. I'd make a note of the place and decide whether I should stop and fight, take a detour, or just try to cycle past. That's why I didn't see the hot air balloon until long after its occupants must have spotted me. That red dot against the blue background was somehow more terrifying than that first sight of the horde. The old man hadn't mentioned it, and I'd not asked. I'd not asked him for any details about Caulfield. It was too late to do anything about it. Using the balloon as a marker, I cycled on.

The road I was on had two generous lanes with a grass verge on the left, and a three-foot-wide pedestrian footpath on the right. I remember when the footpath was put in. Ostensibly it was a safety measure to reduce the danger to hikers forced to walk on the road. In reality, the motivation behind it was to close down the paths that ran through nearby farmland, all of which belonged to the local party chairman. At the time, I'd honestly admired the way that local funds were diverted and a pedestrian thoroughfare, marked on the earliest of maps, was closed down. I saw the world as a game, one where no one knew the rules, but all was there to be won and lost just the same.

After half a mile on that road, I noticed a small but significant change. The few vehicles had all been pushed to the verge, leaving enough space for a vehicle far larger than a car to drive through. After a brief examination I realised that tyres, wires, cables, and anything else easily carried, had been removed.

I kept glancing up at the balloon, on the lookout for some flash of light. I assumed they'd be using a heliograph or something equally primitive. It was stupid, seeing as I knew they had a radio that could communicate with a submarine. I just wasn't thinking clearly. Everything I saw brought back a score of old memories, some good, some bad, all perilously distracting. That was why I almost missed the first field.

A chain was wrapped around the gate, a gleaming new padlock holding it closed. The key was attached to a piece of wire hanging from one of the gate's crossbars. The implications of that were disturbing enough. What I saw inside made it worse. A heavy lorry had gouged deep ruts into the field. Those ruts, the ground about them, and the inside of the hedge were coated in a thin layer of ash, blown from the pyre in the field's centre. The bones were unmistakably human. The foot high grass growing wild in the tracks left by the lorry suggested it had been done months ago.

The next field was the same, and the one after. In those, the cremation had been incomplete. An arm or leg stuck out here and there, and I could tell that these were zombies. But as for that first field, at that point, I could not say whether they were the bones of the living or the undead.

Then I came to the first barrier. It wasn't a particularly impressive affair. Four cars had been turned on their side, lined up in a V-shape across the road with two overturned skips adding their weight behind them. The skips themselves were filled with an odd mixture of metal and tyres, which, I realised, must have come from the cars I'd passed earlier. The hedgerows on either side had been reinforced with a mismatched assortment of barbed wire and wood. Some old, some new, some weather-proofed, some already beginning to rot.

The barricade looked like it would stop a pack of the undead. It didn't look like it would hold up against a horde. What I was immediately struck by was the question of how the people inside got out. Presumably there had to be another entrance, one where the barrier could be moved, but where was it? And why go to the trouble of clearing the road I'd just travelled along if there wasn't?

There were no bodies. No undead either. All was still and quiet save the cawing from a murder of crows. It was a grimly appropriate word for such an ill omen. I left the bike there and clambered up onto the barricade.

The fields beyond were full of wheat. Perhaps it was maize. Or oats. Unless it comes packaged in neatly labelled plastic, I can't tell the

193

difference. I think it was wheat, but there was something indefinably odd about it. While I tried to work out what, I realised why the barricades had been built on that road. The fields inside the barrier belonged to Caulfield Hall, were farmed by the tenants living at Grovely Cross, and watered by the irrigation system running under all the Masterton's land. State of the art when it was installed in the 1960s, there'd been talk of replacing it for as long as I can remember. Judging by the patchwork of wilted stalks and withered leaves dotted through the field, the system was finally falling apart.

I climbed down and, trying to work out what was wrong with the scene, headed towards Grovely Cross. The name suggests it should be a village. If you looked at it on the map you might even think it was. In a place with fewer historical pretentions, it would have been called Home Farm. Even that was too generous a description for the cluster of one-room flats, dormitories, and in recent years, mobile homes, bracketed by sheds, garages and barns, occupied by the legion of seasonal and temporary workers employed by the estate.

I didn't go inside or linger, not with that balloon watching my every move. I didn't want them to think I was a looter. I stayed just long enough to note the place was unoccupied, and the farming machinery was parked up neatly in the yard around the back of the sheds, before continuing up towards the hall.

It was that machinery that gave me the key to understanding what was wrong about the place. I'd not seen a single soul. I may not know much about farming, but I do know it's a lot of work, even more so now. Judging by the patches of withered crops and the weeds encroaching from the hedgerows, no one was tending the fields, and hadn't been for months.

Then I reached the second barricade. It was nothing like the first. I didn't think that outer barrier would withstand the undead. I could be certain about this inner one. It was made of two rows of double-linked chain fencing topped with razor wire, sunk into three feet high concrete supports. It certainly looked impressive, but it had looked impressive on the M4. That barrier had broken. So would this one. But it was sturdy enough to keep me out. I turned north and followed the fence along.

It had come from the same stockpile used to reinforce the motorway. Or, to put it another way, diverted from reinforcing some other evacuation route. At most there couldn't be more than a few miles of it ringing the Hall, but that's not the point. Nor is that any evacuees safely reaching a muster point would have been poisoned anyway. Whoever had stolen it couldn't have known that. And then I remembered who owned the land and wondered if, perhaps, they did.

Lost in that angry thought, I didn't hear the people behind me until a voice called out, "Alright mate. That's close enough. Most people see the walls and take a hint."

I turned around, slowly.

Reunion

Three men in Army uniform stood twenty feet away. To be clear, they weren't just wearing camouflage, they were in uniform, all matching, all relatively clean, with boots polished and not a strap out of place. The weapons were the only concession to the changed times. They carried rifles, all of which were pointed at me, but across their backs were slung felling axes. And again, the uniformity of that was disturbing.

"We don't give hand-outs. We don't provide shelter. We don't offer sanctuary. If you came here looking for that then you're out of luck." The soldier wore a sergeant's chevrons on his sleeve.

"I grew up here," I said.

"You a farmer, then?" the sergeant asked.

"No. I worked in London."

"That's a pity. For you. We might have made an exception for a farmer."

"But I grew up here. This is my home," I said.

"Not any more. It's ours now."

"No, you're not getting it. I don't mean I grew up on one of these farms. I mean I grew up there." I pointed up the hill towards the house. "I'm Bill Wright. I grew up in the Hall with Jennifer Masterton."

The sergeant's eyes turned wary for a moment. "You sure? We will check that out. If you're lying, you'd be better off leaving now."

From the way the guns were pointed at me, I doubted they would actually let me go.

"No, really. I grew up here. Just ask someone, they'll vouch for me. There are people from before the outbreak still here, aren't there?"

"Turn around, keep walking. We'll follow," he said, ignoring the question.

I didn't say anything as we walked. I couldn't think of anything I could ask that this sergeant might answer. The entrance was through a set of gates, made of that same prefabricated design, situated around an old track that led to the back of the estate.

We went through the gates and around the old stables and then, in front, lay the grounds and the Hall itself. The house was much the same, the old stone with its small windows, tall towers, wings, and conservatories, all tacked on by successive generations with no thought for architecture, just driven by a need to die leaving the house larger than when they'd inherited it. It was the grounds that had changed. The once manicured lawn that required a team of gardeners to keep clear of weeds was now covered in tents, washing lines, and men doing nothing more than lounging about. And they were all men. It wasn't a settlement. It wasn't even a redoubt. It was a military camp.

"Around to the front," the sergeant barked, loud enough that every head in the camp turned to watch.

As I walked down the path and around the house, I tried to take it all in, and work out what it all meant. Around the front, were parked, if that's the right word, two helicopters. Next to them, half on the gravel driveway, half with its tracks sunk deep into the grass, was a tank.

"Sir! Says he's Bill Wright. Friend of Jennifer Masterton, sir!" the sergeant barked. I turned around. He'd addressed a man wearing the insignia of a full general in the British Army. Before the outbreak, there were only a handful of men who held that rank. I'd been to enough dreary functions to recognise them all. I'd never seen this man before.

196

"Does he?" the general replied. "Wait here."

He went inside the house, leaving me to look over the camp. It was the right word. They'd been here for some time, going by how far that tank's tracks had sunk into the grass, but everything appeared temporary. That begged the question of where they thought they'd be going to next, and when. But those and all other thoughts were silenced by the next voice I heard.

"Bill?" Jen stood in the doorway, frozen. "Bill?" she asked again. My heart turned over at the sight of this far too familiar face. She hadn't changed. I mean that literally. Dressed in the sensible suit and impractical shoes, she looked ready for an appearance on the six o'clock news. By comparison, I was dressed in rags that were burned, singed, and encrusted with mud, yet were still more practical than the clothes she wore.

I don't know what emotions were churned up in her by my sudden appearance, what memories of childhood games, shared secrets, happy regrets, and wistful missed chances. When I looked at her, all I felt was an incomprehensible sadness. She hadn't changed, but I had. She'd returned home, but all in one moment I finally understood that it had never been a home to me.

"Bill? It is... is it?"

"Hi Jen. Sorry it took me so long." I tried to fill my voice with casual understatement. "The driver, the guy you sent to rescue me, he died. He was attacked before I could reach him. I didn't know his name."

"Driver?" she asked, and seemed genuinely confused.

"I was outside the flat then," I said, watching her reaction. "Couldn't get back in. Went from house to house, limping." I tapped my leg brace. "Just moving on when I ran out of food and water. I went to the river. Tried to find a boat. Couldn't. So I kept on, from one place to another, until I was strong enough to ride a bike. I tried to get down to the coast, but that didn't work out either. You know what it's like, with the undead." From the look of her I wasn't certain she did. "I ended up doing a tour of the Home Counties. I did find a boat near Windsor, but I couldn't get it past Teddington Lock. The last few weeks I've just been heading north. This was the only place I could think of. I hoped everyone would have survived, and thought at least someone would. Turns out I was right. It's good to see you."

"It really is you," she said, taking a step forward.

"It is me," I said, trying not to let my exasperation at her repetition show. "In the flesh. More or less," I added, waving my injured hand.

"My god, what happened to you?" she asked.

"Oh, well, you know about the leg of course. I lost the cast somewhere around Greenwich. I think it needed surgery. I've lost a few inches. That makes running a tad difficult."

"What about your hand?"

"Oh, that was the undead. One of those zombies took a bite… Whoah!" Suddenly the guns were all levelled, all pointing at my head.

"You were bitten?" the sergeant asked.

"Months ago," I said quickly. "Dozens of times. I'm immune."

"You're what?" the general barked, pushing Jen aside.

"Immune." I looked around at the soldiers. None of them knew. "You do realise that some people are immune, right?"

The gun barrels wavered slightly as heads all turned to look between me, Jen, and the general.

"Maybe it's just you. Maybe you're the only one," a young corporal said.

"No. There are others," I said slowly as I thought fast. "There was a house, down near the coast. A policeman, he'd been bitten. He locked himself into the house, waiting to die, except he didn't. He committed suicide in the end, but he left a note."

"A note? That's not proof," the soldier closest to me said as he stepped forward, the barrel of his rifle now only a few inches from my face. "If he was dead it doesn't count. I mean, you don't know he was telling the truth do you?"

What I said next was cruel, but it was necessary. I was starting to get a measure of this place, and it was dawning on me that I'd made a big mistake going there so unprepared.

"There was an old man and his grandaughter," I said. "This was down in Hampshire. They'd both been bitten. Both had survived. They were going round the country with their old address book, searching for their relatives."

"And you saw them?" another soldier asked.

"Yes," I lied.

"And talked to him?"

"Yes."

"And they were alive?"

"Both of them, when we went our separate ways, yes," I said.

"So, this immunity," the corporal asked, "you're saying it's inherited?" The barrel had lowered slightly.

"That's one possibility. I don't have any family, not blood relations, so I'd no one to come and look for except Jen. But I saw bodies, people who'd been attacked and trapped and who'd starved to death. I saw…" I stopped myself. "I'm not the only one," I finished, lamely.

"We have a strict policy," the general began. "A quarantine. It's how we keep safe. How we—"

"We should get the doctor, though," the corporal said. "And have him checked out. Didn't the doc say that he was looking for some kind of key, something to create a cure?"

"Immunity isn't the same as…" I began, but they weren't listening to me any more. The guns were still pointed at me, but their attention was on one another, as if each was prepared to back someone else's challenge to authority just as long as it wasn't them.

"Yes," Jen said, slowly. "We'll take him to the doctor and get this settled."

The Camp

But first I was escorted to a shower. It wasn't inside. Around the side of the house, where white tents had once been erected for the annual harvest supper festival, there was an improvised shower block. The water came from the same supply that fed the fields, pumped, I learned, by hand. The water went into a black painted tank, you then stood under the showerhead, turned a tap, and did the best you could under the slow drip.

Canvas and almost-opaque plastic sheeting offered the illusion of privacy. That didn't bother me. What did was the transparent way in which all of my possessions, including the weapons, were taken away 'for cleaning'. The pistol Leon had given me raised a few eyebrows. I made up some story about a dead body at a supermarket.

The water was tepid and far from refreshing, but it gave me time to think. The presence of the soldiers changed everything. I should have expected them, of course. Had they not been here, there was nothing stopping Leon and Francois storming the place. What that meant for me, I wasn't sure.

To replace my clothes, I was left an Army Combat Uniform of my own, still sealed in a plastic. And that explained why, despite the meagre water supply, their clothes were all so clean. I couldn't decide if that was a good sign or a bad one. I needed more information so, as I dressed, I tried striking up a conversation with the two soldiers watching over me.

"Those helicopters must be useful for getting supplies," I suggested.

"What? No," the taller and younger of the two said. "There's no fuel. Not since we got here."

"Oh. Right. There's an aerodrome, about twenty miles southwest of here. Did they not have any?" I asked.

"Dunno," he replied, and I noticed there was a distracted tone to his voice. "I mean, I don't think anyone went to check."

"They'd have checked," the other one said sharply. "The general would have made sure of it."

"Yes, I was wondering about him," I said. "I must have met him at a Whitehall function at some point, but for the life me, I can't remember his name."

"That's General Greely," the young man said, "but he was only—"

"He's Chief of the Defence Staff," the older man cut in.

"I see. Well, he's done a good job here," I said. "Supplies, walls, people. Water and food. Yes, a good set up."

Neither of them said anything. But it was a good set-up by the standards I'd had before I'd met Kim. When I'd been on my own, fleeing from London, all I'd wanted was a store of food, high walls and some other people to stand on them with me. Here it was, my dream made reality and in that realisation I saw how shabby a dream it was. They'd done well enough to make a place for surviving from one day to the next, but not a place for people to live, not somewhere anything new will ever be made. It was a model for stagnation and decay where the best hope is that death can be staved off until tomorrow.

"Yes," I said, slowly looking around again, "it's a good set up. How long until harvest? I mean I grew up here, but I grew up in politics, not farming."

"Not sure," the younger one said.

"I saw the wheat as I came in. Is it wheat? It looks like a good crop. Enough to get everyone through until spring. The farmers must be happy."

"Farmers?"

"I assumed that the people who'd farmed the land were still here," I said.

"They—" the younger one began.

"They left," the older one said tersely.

"The house—" the younger one began.

"Was deserted when we got here. It's just us," the older one interrupted again.

"Right. So it's only Jen then? Everyone else I knew, they're all dead?"

"Like everyone else on this planet," the older one said. He made no attempt at sounding sympathetic. He didn't even sound callous, he just seemed indifferent.

"Right." I sighed and was ready to give up trying to get anything out of these two.

"What's it like out there?" the younger one asked, perhaps sensing something in my tone.

"You've not been outside these walls?" I asked.

"Not since soon after we got here. Except to clear the undead. But only the ones within a couple of miles of the walls," he answered, winning a disapproving glare from the other man.

"And when was that?" I asked.

201

This time he'd barely opened his mouth when, presumably to stop him from answering, the older man asked, "So what *is* it like, then?"

"Well, London isn't too bad," I said. "There's no food or water and there are lots of the undead. But I managed to survive, and that was with a broken leg. Let me rephrase that, compared to everywhere else, London isn't too bad. North of the city, though, there are the hordes. Have you seen those?"

"When there's hundreds or thousands of zombies? That's why we've got the walls."

"No, I mean when there's more than a hundred thousand of Them. I hid in a tunnel for nearly a week as what must have been over a million went by overhead. Perhaps there's just one horde, but I think there are more. They roam the countryside, trampling villages, turning bricks to dust. I think the towns and cities are like break waters, too large for Them to destroy. But soon the cities will be all that's left, unless we do something about it."

"What d'you mean?"

"I mean, you're British Army, aren't you? Someone has to do something and you guys have the training. It's your job."

Neither took the bait on that particular hook. I sighed inwardly and sat down to lace my boots.

"This doctor, I take it he's more than an MD?" I asked, trying a different tack.

"He's a bio-science expert. He's been trying to recreate the vaccine."

"The vaccine?"

"Well, you must have realised. It was sabotaged. Terrorists, the Prime Minister says. It was part of a wider plot, the whole outbreak was."

"Really? I didn't hear any of that. I knew the evacuation didn't work, but didn't know about the terrorism."

"No, I suppose you wouldn't," the older one said. "We were attacked. You know about the nuclear bombs? It took out most of Scotland, the south coast, and a huge chunk of the country in between."

"What? No!" I tried to sound sincere.

"Oh, yes," the older soldier said, relishing being the bearer of sad tidings. "It's how most of the government was destroyed. They nuked the Isle of Wight, all of our nuclear power stations, took out some cities too. We thought they'd taken out London."

"Right. No. No, London was still there. How many bombs went off?"

"Dunno."

"Well, who did it?"

"Don't know that either. Terrorists, that's all we know."

"Not that it matters anymore," I said standing up. "We should go and see this doctor then, and find out if I'm the key to getting this vaccine working again. Where's the lab?"

"The old wine cellar."

"Ah. That seems strangely appropriate. Jen's grandfather used to keep a still down there. It was completely illegal, but since he'd been in the cabinet with Churchill, he felt that gave him licence to do whatever he liked. In the end that turned out to be nearly burning the house down."

There was a muted murmur from the two men. They weren't interested, but they seemed happier talking about the house and its history than in anything to do with the last few months. I tried to keep the conversation going and, eventually, learned that the generator was for the sole use of the doctor and for powering the radio. More importantly, I learned that their fuel supply was dwindling to nothing. They had food, but that too was a diminishing stock, mostly of rice and grain still in sacks stamped 'UN Food Aid'.

"There are rabbits," I said. "They make good eating."

"You've eaten meat? Recently?" the older man sounded shocked.

"The doctor says we're not to touch the animals," the younger man said. "We don't know what they've been eating, you see."

"The animals don't eat the undead. Even after I've killed Them, the birds will just circle a few times and fly off."

"And you watched that, did you?" the older one sounded disgusted. I'd said something wrong.

"What about your families, then? Where are they?" I tried, asking the first question that came to mind.

"They'll all be dead now. Everyone is."

With that, I gave up. We continued on in silence.

As I limped, and they walked a few steps behind, up the gravel drive towards the house I was reminded of the last day of the school holidays. There was always an hour after breakfast while I waited for the cars to be loaded and for Jen to say a tearful goodbye to her mother. I always spent that hour pacing the same gravel path, kicking the same stones, the same nervous trepidation growing within me as I wondered where the summer had gone. In my memory, those mornings were always brighter, the skies always clearer, the distant trees always filled with more promise of adventure. Even then I recognised it as a moment that could never last, in a day that would never be. The impossibility of the fantasy was what made the day's promise so glorious. I knew it when I was a child and I knew it again as I walked along that path.

Ignoring the guards' protests, I stopped and took one last look at the large oak at the edge of the estate. I'd spent as much time falling out of that tree as I had climbing up it. Good times, happy memories. I let myself dwell in the past for one last moment before banishing those thoughts, locking them away in the knowledge it would be years, if ever, before I would be able to recall them with fondness once more.

"Come on then," I said. "Let's get this over with."

The Doctor

It was called the wine cellar, but as far back as I can remember it was a dumping ground for the kind of junk that's fashionable one season and embarrassing the next. Furniture, suits of armour, a menagerie of stuffed heads and antiques old enough to be called exhibits in any museum, it had been all pushed into the corners and alcoves of the cavernous room to make space for the laboratory.

At first glance it looked just like a real lab should look. At first glance. A panoply of glassware filled racks above counters stacked with bafflingly intricate equipment. The oscillation of a centrifuge added its dull rattle to the whine of the electric motors powering a large, glass-fronted fridge. A doctor's couch, complete with a moveable light and surrounded by trays of gleaming steel tools, stood in the centre of the clean and empty space.

Everything about it, right down to the caution signs tacked onto every surface made it look believable. Until you looked a little closer. I might not have, if my suspicions hadn't already been aroused by their collective ignorance about the immune. I'd seen that video from New York. I'd seen the scientist bitten. The man Quigley had working in that dank basement should have known about immunity. So I looked more carefully at my surroundings.

The plastic sheeting that extended from floor to ceiling did not cover the ancient flagstones, nor seal in the top of this work area. It was nothing more than a transparent screen, held on by nails as much as by tape, offering no protection to anyone from anything inside. I'm certain that the couch, and the lights and tools around it, came from a dentist's surgery. As for all the equipment, that did nothing more than waste precious electricity. I doubted any of it came from anywhere more high tech than the local high school. There wasn't even an extractor fan. It was a lie, accepted only by those who wanted to believe.

Pushing his way through the sheeting, was…

"You're the doctor then?" I asked, extending my hand.

"I am," he said. "But you'll excuse me if I don't shake your hand. Not until we've given you a thorough check up."

He wore an all-in-one suit, with a mask that obscured most of the face that wasn't covered by the hood, but I knew, the moment he spoke, that this wasn't the man I'd seen in that video. This man's accent was one-hundred-percent Birmingham, not the cultured English with the trace of India of the real scientist responsible for the outbreak. As for his hand, he still had all of his fingers. The old man had been wrong. The scientist wasn't at Caulfield Hall.

"Well, I'll risk it," a familiar voice said from behind me. I turned. Sir Michael Quigley, dressed in a double-breasted suit, stood in the doorway, his hand outstretched.

"Sir Michael. You made it," I said, shaking his hand.

"And you too, Bill, thank God."

"It's a small world," I think I said. It was that or something equally trite.

"And getting smaller and bigger each day. What do you think of our set-up then?"

"Impressive. Better than anything I've seen so far," I said.

"You've seen many places where there are survivors, then?" he asked. I'd forgotten how sharp this man was.

"Not really. A few here, a few there. Five was the most in anyone place," I said, lying furiously.

"We must get you to a map. See where they are, send out a patrol to bring them here. It'll be safer for them. Our strength lies in numbers now, more than it ever did before."

"Oh, I agree with that," I said. "It's why I came here. Look, Sir Michael, I didn't ask Jen, but did Lord Masterton…. Is he…?"

"He didn't make it. When we arrived, the house was empty. Abandoned, along with the village. I assume he went on the evacuation, and that is a shame. Your plan had promise. It should have worked. It would have, if it wasn't for that terrorist cell."

"Yes, some of your soldiers said something about terrorists."

"And I'll tell you more about it at dinner. A proper meal. You must be famished."

"Well, yes, now you mention it." I wasn't hungry at all.

"Well first Dr Tooley needs some of your blood. Isn't that right?"

"Er, yes," the fake doctor said. "Just a small sample. Not much. Just to check whether I'm on the right track."

"He's recreating the vaccine, you see," Quigley said. "If you've got natural immunity, that will speed up the research, won't it doctor?"

"Oh, yes. Speed it up. Yes."

"We should have something in a matter of weeks, didn't you say."

"Weeks? Er, yes, two or three weeks. Yes."

"Maybe less. And with only a few hundred doses needed, we'll all be able to venture out with impunity before winter hits. We'll find these other survivors you mentioned and create a real sanctuary. A new England, eh Bill? All we've ever dreamed of, eh? Well, get to it, doctor."

"Yes, yes, er, yes," the doctor stammered. "If you'll come in here. Into the lab. I'll get the samples and then… then get back to work."

"Good. Good. And it really is good to see you, Bill," Quigley said, and left. The two soldiers stayed behind.

I followed the doctor through the plastic sheeting and sat on the edge of the couch.

"You're the man who created the vaccine?" I asked.

"Er, yes," he answered nervously.

"You must be pretty good."

"I was. Am. University at Oxford, masters at Imperial, doctorate at Cambridge, then two years at…" His voice relaxed as he listed his well-rehearsed CV. I just kept a track of the number of years he'd been working. If he'd been telling the truth, then he'd got his degree when he was seven. It was insulting, really.

At least the act of recitation relaxed the man, which was good since he was holding a needle. I've never liked needles. I don't have a problem with blood, just with needles. I turned away, my eyes idly scanning the prop-equipment. They fell on the glass-doored fridge. At the back, on every shelf, were bottles of wine. At the front, shielding the bottles from anyone more than a few feet away, were miscellaneous boxes, and racks of test tubes and vials. I almost smiled, until my eyes caught the writing on one of the racks. 'Lenham Hill'.

Sholto had said he'd destroyed them all. Or was it that he only thought he had? I tried to remember as I stared and puzzled and wondered if those vials were just a prop, or whether they did actually contain the virus.

Dinner

It was around six p.m. when I was escorted up to The Gallery. As the name suggests the walls were covered in paintings, all portraits of now deceased ancestors.

"Bill, all sorted then? Good," Quigley murmured as he ushered me to a chair. The general and Jen were already seated at a table that could fit ten but was set for four. "Come in. Sit down. Drink?" Quigley waved a hand dismissively at the pair of guards. They left the room.

"I expect this brings back some childhood memories. Dinner with the family, eh?" Quigley asked, jovially.

"Yes. Yes it does," I said, sharing a look with Jen as I sat down. Growing up, we'd always eaten in the kitchen, and we'd never eaten with her parents. That Jen hadn't told him this gave me some hope.

"There's some things you need to know, Bill," Jen began.

"They can wait, they can wait," Quigley said dismissively as he rang an absurd little bell.

It was a meal that made a mockery of the aristocratic splendour Quigley was trying to imitate. The food came from tins or packets, served on silver and antique china. I don't suppose it would have been too bad had it been cooked properly, but it was barely warmed through. I forced myself to eat. The wine was cold enough for condensation to bead around the glass, and that was a pleasingly unfamiliar sensation amidst the close air of the room. But knowing what had been stored with it in the fridge, I only took the most tentative of sips. I think some of the disappointment at the meagre repast showed on my face.

"Something wrong?" Quigley asked.

"Sorry, it's just, having seen all those fields, I thought… I suppose I was hoping for fresh bread."

"I know, I know. But there's the danger of cross-contamination. Until we can be certain it's safe, we can't risk eating any of the food growing in the ground."

I didn't comment.

"What happened to the rest of the cabinet?" I asked, when I decided I'd toyed with the food for a decently polite length of time.

"We split the government," Jen said. "Out of the eight in the emergency cabinet. Four went to the Isle of Wight, Sir Michael, myself, Nicole Upton, and Paul Haylett stayed in London." I sipped at the glass to hide my expression. "We'd built barricades either side of the river. We controlled a long strip of land, and we had the river itself. We thought we could hold onto that, keep it as our centre of government and supply it by river. But we were overrun. The undead, They got into the Tube."

"But you were still there, while I was still in the flat?" I pressed.

"I thought you were dead. Sir Michael, said—"

"I sent people to collect you," Quigley interrupted. "A couple of teams. One didn't come back, the others said you were dead. Mistaken identity I suppose."

I didn't want to catch him in a lie, not then. "Then you left London and came here?" I asked, instead.

"More or less," Jen said. "You know the Isle of Wight was destroyed?"

"By a nuclear attack of some kind? One of your soldiers mentioned it." The general frowned at that.

"After that we knew we had to move the government again," Quigley said. "I don't know why London wasn't destroyed, but we thought it could happen at any moment, and then what would have happened to our country? I checked a number of locations but this one seemed the best. The house was empty when we arrived. Deserted, but otherwise intact. I left some men to prepare the defences and returned to London. We needed someone up here, and I thought Jen was best for that role. If any of the locals did come back, seeing her friendly face would be far more reassuring than a group of soldiers."

"No one did, though. Return, I mean," Jen said sadly. "I do wonder what happened to them all."

"Yes," Quigley said. "So do I. It took a long time to get the rest of the survivors ready to leave. Before we did, the undead came up through the Tube. We ended up fighting our way out of the city. That was my fault. I take full responsibility. We lost Paul, Nicole, and hundreds of others on the way up here. Bandits. Near Oxford, if you can believe that."

I didn't. I was certain now that I had killed the undead Nicole Upton down by the River Thames. I decided to poke the hornet's nest a little.

"There's something I don't understand. The vaccine. Was it real? I mean, how do you make a vaccine for a virus you don't know exists?"

"Was it real?" Jen answered. "Yes and no. Yes, there was a vaccine, but we never had enough to distribute to the entire population. They were to be given a placebo at the muster points. But that would give us an

209

opportunity to examine everyone who arrived. We would have been able to weed out the infected. Then they would have a long train or bus journey to the coast. The worst that would happen was a train carriage would have to be sanitised. A few hundred uninfected people would die, but the majority would survive. In effect it was a mobile quarantine. And it would have worked."

"But the doctor, downstairs, he's working on recreating the vaccine. So does that mean there was one?" I asked.

"There was," Quigley said. "And it was going to be demonstrated to the leaders of the world. It wasn't a vaccine for this virus, but a vaccine for everything. All of the world's major diseases cured with one simple injection. There was enough for the demonstration, but not much more. The same terrorists who switched our placebo for the poison we distributed at the muster points, the ones who released this abominable virus onto the world, they destroyed the lab. Fortunately our doctor survived and now, thanks to your blood, we should have something that will work against this virus within a few months. It won't work against anything else, unfortunately, but it will give us a fighting chance."

It wasn't really an answer, but then, there wasn't much point asking him to elaborate since there would be no way of knowing if he was actually telling the truth.

"Who were these terrorists?" I asked instead. "I mean, this is so far beyond anything we've ever seen before."

"Well, we did have some warning something was going to happen," Jen said. "We just didn't know where or what. It's why we had the quarantine and martial law in place, but—"

"But we were betrayed." Quigley interrupted, "The nuclear bombs, the outbreak, switching that placebo for poison, that was their work. It was a cell that had its roots in our government, its branches in the corridors of power throughout the world. It's more than just a movement, it's an insidious international conspiracy that stretches back to the dark days of the Cold War. This organisation was behind it all, and it was all done with just one aim, to destroy western democracy and usher in a new world order. I tried to stop it. I failed, but I managed to mitigate its

210

effects. Our species is still alive and now we can focus on rebuilding."

I had no idea what to say. The man's gall was breathtaking, his lies so impassioned I wonder if he'd begun to believe them himself.

"They didn't succeed," the general said, breaking the increasingly uncomfortable silence. "We have a military, a Prime Minister and a monarch. England will rise again."

"A mon…" I stopped. I looked at Jen. "You're kidding?"

"It's only in name, Bill."

"You're the Queen?"

"Technically, just technically," she said hurriedly.

"She is eligible," the general added. I looked over at him and wondered what rank he'd held six months ago, or whether he'd held any rank at all.

"There were at least a few hundred people between her and Buckingham Palace," I said.

"And now they're all dead," Quigley said.

"It's all about continuity and legitimacy," Jen said. "Without a monarch, how could we have a Prime Minister?"

"Consensus?" I suggested.

"Then there would be no continuity," Quigley said, patiently. "We need to maintain the legitimate British government. Who has the right to order the military into action? What makes us different from some band of thieves? A Queen is what people are familiar with. Familiarity breeds loyalty. It brings comfort. And then there's the future, of course. Someone needs to consider the direction the nation will take over the next thousand years, and if not us, then who?"

"Yes, I suppose so." I tried to keep the disbelief out of my voice.

"It's not really important, Bill, not now, not yet," Jen said. "But in five years or ten, when we've got a proper country working again, we'll have something to fall back on. It will be democratic, of course. There's a constitutional conference planned just as soon as it's safe to hold one. There'll be a referendum. We'll give people the opportunity to vote for a republic, but honestly, do you think they will?"

211

There wasn't even any point answering that. "Then you're in contact with other groups, other communities?" I asked instead.

"We know where they are," the general said, which wasn't the same thing at all.

"It's not about power, Bill," Jen said. "It's not about ruling the world, but we've got to preserve democracy. After… what happened, after what was done to us. Someone has to, and it's only us left."

"We're looking at a period of consolidation," the general said. "We have a large military, but few civilians for it to protect. Our goal now is to bring together all the survivors scattered across the country."

I thought back to how I'd been greeted at the gate, how, if I'd not been who I was, I'd have been lucky to be turned away and more likely to have been shot. I thought about the people who must have been here when Quigley arrived. And I thought about all these soldiers, all these men, and what that meant.

"And you'll bring all these survivors here, will you?"

"Oh no," Quigley said, smiling. "We'll move to the coast. We need to be nearer to the fleet. Yes, we still have a fleet. The admiral has located a number of possible sites for the new capital. We'll relocate just as soon as the doctor is finished his work. Britannia still rules the waves and one day our Empire will stretch out its benevolent hand upon them."

I think he genuinely believed what he said.

After that, they spent the rest of the meal grilling me on what I'd seen and where I'd been. They masked the interrogation behind polite curiosity, but there was no question that Quigley and the general were only interested in where other survivors could be found. I named half a dozen places that had been abandoned when I arrived. The lies came easily, and I gave no thought to being found out. It didn't matter. I'd already decided to escape from the madhouse as soon as possible.

The Prison

There's an old saying, if you're going to find yourself imprisoned, then make sure it's in a cell you built yourself. My jail was the second best thing, my old childhood bedroom.

The room hadn't changed much since I'd last seen it, but that had been during the Easter Bank Holiday, two years ago. I'd never really stamped my identity on the room. The few childhood mementos I'd kept here, or more accurately forgotten to take with me back to school, had long since been packed up.

As a child, having a room to myself seemed a luxury compared with the shared dorm at boarding school. I took the simple, functional furnishings as a further sign of my acceptance as one of the family. Looking around the room, I saw it for what it was, the attic room of the unwanted child who couldn't be simply forgotten. I heard the key turn in the lock. That was an unfamiliar sound. All the bedrooms had keys, of course. That's a common feature of a house that historically hosted guests that didn't just dislike one another but were representatives of countries literally at war. It had come as quite a surprise, when I got to university, to discover that it wasn't the norm.

I listened by the door just long enough to be sure that the two guards who'd escorted me upstairs had gone away.

I walked over to the window, a long narrow one, painted shut decades before, and peered out. The sun was still a few hours from setting. Now I knew to look, I could make out the signs that Quigley and his private army were about to leave. I paced the room, trying to work out what to do. Then I realised that was the wrong question. I had to work out exactly what I would be able to do.

I'd have to leave that night. There were too many soldiers to leave during the daytime, and I'd foolishly told too many lies to survive any more questioning.

It was all a lunacy. A Queen, a Prime Minister, a general, a fake scientist, and a fake plot by a fake terrorist group, Quigley's story was the ultimate house of cards. His power, and I assume the general's, came from the soldiers. They followed because of this elaborate tale of terrorism, vaccines, and lost glory that they might, one day, regain. But I knew it was a lie. The barricades that ringed the house, the ones made of concrete and steel, must have been airlifted in. That had to have been done before the evacuation. In which case why would everyone have left Caulfield? They

213

wouldn't. Quigley had killed them, and he must have been certain he'd killed them all or he wouldn't have allowed Jen to come up here. They'd died because they would be more likely to follow her than him. He'd gone to Lenham Hill and killed everyone in that facility so his lies wouldn't be exposed. And he'd gone back to London and engineered the deaths of Nicole Upton and everyone else he couldn't trust.

Why he'd not just killed Jen was a bit of a puzzle. I assumed that perhaps he genuinely believed in the idea of a monarch and continuity. As for the doctor, Quigley knew he was fake, and there was no way that the man would be allowed to live long enough for that to be proven. Two weeks. That's all the doctor had left. As to what would happen to him then, that was obvious enough.

I paced the room, trying to work out, from the little contact I'd had with him, whether I could persuade the doctor to help me. I doubted it. There wasn't time. George Tull had said something about Quigley knowing where their community was. Taking that with what the general had said at dinner, it was clear that was the place that they were planning to invade. And that was where I'd just sent Kim and the girls.

None of which helped me very much. What could I do? There were two options, get out, get over to Ireland, warn the old man and let Mister Mills, and Leon, and those others with military experience deal with the forthcoming mess, while Kim, the girls, Sholto, and I went somewhere far, far away from the whole lot of them. Or I could try to stop Quigley.

The first option was clearly the easiest and the most likely to work, but there was Daisy to consider. That was the difficulty. If she did need medical attention, where else was she going to find it?

I turned back to the window. There was one other choice, built upon a slim chance. The old man's plan. Jen didn't know everything. If I could persuade her of the truth, perhaps she in turn could persuade enough of these soldiers to rebel or mutiny or whatever you'd like to call it. Then we'd contact the submarine.

It didn't seem likely, but it was worth a try. If she didn't think it would work, then we could at least burn the place down as we left. Perhaps the old man had been wrong about that as well. If there wasn't a radio signal, perhaps the submarine would just disappear. At the very least we'd destroy some supplies.

Decision made, all I needed to do was escape from a locked room.

Confrontation

The great thing about being locked in a room you spent much of your childhood in is that you've explored every inch of it. In a room like that one, it hadn't taken long. Other than the window and its meagre view, the only other thing with which a bored child might entertain himself was the lock.

As a child it took me weeks to realise that the nails in the back of the wardrobe were long and thin enough for the task. It took months to work them free, and months more before I'd learned how to pick the lock. As an adult, years later, it had taken about fifteen minutes to realise that modern locks were built to withstand such clumsy manipulations.

I listened at the door until I was absolutely certain the guards had gone. Then I listened for another ten minutes, just to be certain. Then I called out. There was no response. Twenty seconds after that, I had the door open.

My first task was to find Jen. Of course I didn't know what room she'd be in, but there was no reason for her not to be in the same room she'd used since she finished school. That was two floors below.

I crept along the corridor towards the main staircase. I stopped at the top of the stairs. I could hear voices below, and strained my ears to make out the words. It was something about a guard rota for the next day. I went back towards the servant's staircase at the corridor's other end.

There were no windows, no natural light at all, and without electricity to power the infrequently placed bulbs, the staircase was pitch black. Cautiously feeling for each step, my hands and elbows braced against the narrow sides of the steep stairwell, I went downstairs.

The corridor on which Jen's room was located was deserted. I tried her door. It was locked, but I had it open in a few seconds. I went inside. She was there, she was asleep, and she was alone. I put my hand over her

215

mouth. She woke, struggling.

"Jen, it's me. It's okay. You need to be quiet, okay?"

She subsided, slightly.

"Quigley is lying," I said quickly. "This super-vaccine he talks about, that was what caused the outbreak. He was there when it happened in New York. Him and a dozen other politicians from every corner of the world. That's how it spread, senior politicians got infected, flew home, and then turned. At the muster points, that was a poison, but it wasn't terrorists. It was Quigley."

"What?"

"Shh! Come on, you must have realised that doctor downstairs is a fake."

"I… fake?" she mumbled, confused and still half asleep.

"Exactly. Quigley was running the lab at Lenham Hill. You remember the place? When he left London, when he told you he was looking for somewhere to retreat to, he went there. He killed all the scientists. The doctor, the lab, recreating the vaccine, it's just smoke and mirrors."

"Smoke?"

"You must have noticed," I snapped, growing impatient. "Haven't you ever looked at it?"

"At what?"

"The lab! Quigley killed everyone, but not the scientist who created the virus in the first place. Look," I said, trying a different tack, "there are other people, hundreds of other people. We can go there now, you and me and however many of these soldiers you can trust."

"Trust?"

"Quigley's mad. You must have seen that. He's threatening to nuke anyone who won't submit to him." Words weren't working. Jen had never been much of a morning person. "Come downstairs. I'll show you. In the lab. I'll prove it to you. Please."

She hesitated, but then pulled on some clothes, and we went downstairs. There was a second way into the cellar, a narrow set of stairs from behind the kitchens, but they weren't empty. We had to wait an interminable five minutes for two soldiers to finish rifling through the cupboards before we could go in and down the stairs.

I'd not thought to find a torch. The cellar was dark, but the dim glow from the glass-doored fridge, and the display and standby lights, was enough to see by.

"Look," I said, pointing. "This isn't a lab. There's no extractor fan. It's not even a sealed environment. This stuff is just plastic sheeting. Look up there. It's nailed into the beams."

"That's just—"

I didn't let her finish. I didn't want her to think. I just wanted her to understand. "You see this?" I pointed at the fridge. "That's your virus. The stuff that causes the dead to walk." I pointed at the label. "See that? Lenham Hill. Quigley took this to New York and had his doctor, the real doctor, inject it into a bunch of people. Remember that night I spent at the Ministry of Defence? The interrogation? That's what they were doing. That's where that money was disappearing to. Then there was the bombing. We started that, too. Prometheus, that's what... what..." I trailed off. There wasn't much light, just enough to read the label, just enough to read her expression. "You knew about Lenham Hill. Of course you did."

"My father told me," she said. "When they took you in for questioning. It's why you were released. I had to promise you'd stop digging."

"You knew. You didn't tell me."

"I couldn't."

"Did you know what it really did, this virus, this super-vaccine?" I asked.

"I'd seen the test data. We all had."

"Test data? Who's *we*?"

"A cross-party committee," she said. "It was too important to be subject to petty politics. The test data showed it worked. It did work."

"And you believed it." It wasn't a question.

"Of course I did," she said. "My father started the work on it. Or his department did, decades ago."

"And Prometheus, did you know about that?" I asked.

"Grandfather told me about that. It was his idea originally. We knew that the government wasn't going to survive World War Three. Some people might, and all we could do was ensure that they had a chance, that our way of life might continue. Because of that, my father became involved in the vaccine project. And then so did I."

"And you supported it." Again, it wasn't a question.

"I wasn't the Prime Minister, what did it matter if I approved or not?"

"You could have said something. You could have announced it to the world."

"And? You think anyone would be surprised? Do you think anyone would care?"

"Mutually Assured Destruction. I thought we'd moved on from that," I muttered.

"The world turns, but it stays the same," she said.

"The muster points. The evacuees. Did—"

I didn't get to finish the sentence. The lights came on.

It was arrogance. It was complacency. It was spending a day under a familiar roof. I'd let my guard down. I'd stopped thinking about the threats hidden in every shadow. The bottles of wine in the fridge should have given it away. If not that, then the doctor's absence at dinner should have suggested it. Where else was he going to be, but sleeping down in the cellar with the electricity for comfort and the wine for company?

I didn't know how much he'd heard. He had a rifle in his hands, and from the way the barrel was wavering back and forth, he didn't know how to use it. That wasn't reassuring. He didn't even give me a chance to try to reason with him.

"Guards. Guards!" he bellowed.

I took a step back, keeping my eyes on his rifle, my hand searching for the tray with the medical equipment, looking for something sharp.

"Don't move. Don't!" he yelled, taking a couple of steps towards me. He'd found some courage from somewhere and the barrel was now pointing steadily at my face.

I stopped and raised my hands. It seemed like the only thing to do.

A few minutes later two more guards appeared at the stairs, then the general, then Quigley.

"What's going—" Quigley began. I didn't let him finish.

"That's the virus in there. In those vials," I said addressing everyone but him. "It was Quigley who created it. In a facility in Oxfordshire called Lenham Hill. He started it, but it's all over now. There's just a handful of survivors out there, with sixty million zombies at their backs. You can have a future, you can help us rebuild."

It wasn't the greatest of speeches, and I should know, I've written a few in my time. Certainly I've written enough and watched other people deliver them, my eyes glued to the audience while psychologists and body language experts spewed forth their opinions through an earpiece. No, this wasn't a great speech, but it wouldn't have mattered if it was. These soldiers didn't flinch. They didn't care. They knew.

Quigley hadn't killed all those people himself. He hadn't gone to Lenham Hill on his own. He'd had men with him, men he could trust, his praetorian guard. These men. They'd killed the scientists at Lenham. They'd killed the rest of the cabinet. They'd killed old Lord Masterton and everyone else who'd lived in or near the Hall.

"And he killed your father and everyone else in this house," I said to Jen. "All the farmers, all the locals who might prefer you ruling them. He had them killed, and burned the corpses out in the fields beyond the first barricade."

"Is that true?" Jen asked.

"What is truth?" Quigley replied, sarcastically. "This was all an act. I told you that, *your Majesty*. I told you in London, it was only a way of guaranteeing support for our rule. A way of making all the people we found certain we had the right to rule over them. Well, maybe I was a little disingenuous. I should have said my rule, but since the monarch has no power, it was your own fault for not realising."

"If this was just about power then you haven't done very well," I said. "Just you and a few hundred soldiers and how many of them can you really trust?"

"Power?" He shook his head derisively. "You've changed, at least. You're not the snivelling overweight pole-climber that I remember. You're still not very bright, though, but then, that's not something that can be acquired out in the wilds. I suppose you're friends with that old man. I thought we'd shot him."

I realised, that though he was looking at me, that last was addressed to the general.

"They outnumber you," I said.

"Really? They? Not we? So you know him, but you're not with him. Interesting. It doesn't matter. I have soldiers. They were the best-trained professionals in the world before, and now there is no one who can stop them. Set against old men and cripples, I think we'll manage."

"I won't allow it," Jen said.

"Oh, please, just stop!" Quigley snapped. "You really don't understand. He does. You've been coddled and protected your whole life. Picked for government because of your father, picked for the cabinet because I knew how to play you. Even your one petty rebellion, standing for the opposition, had little effect. The few principles you espoused early on, you abandoned the moment there was a chance at power."

"And so did you," I said.

"No!" And there was real anger in his voice now "This was never about power, mine or anyone else's. This was about a future for our entire species."

"Oh, so you're a true believer?" I asked.

"Hardly. I don't believe, I *know*. I know that at its worst, our country is better than the best anywhere else. Our island story spans thousands of years, and in a thousand more, this will be seen as our finest hour. I know England will prevail."

"It's the UK, or it was, but it was never just England. Not that…" I was about to start swearing at him, letting my tongue loose while I gauged which of the soldiers I might reach before being shot, but Jen interrupted me again.

"It's over. It's all over," she said. "I want this to stop. I'm ordering you to stop. No, I'm commanding you."

"Oh, for the love of… Commanding?" Quigley said. "You've served your purpose and served it poorly. You were meant to stop people from deserting, from running off into the wilderness. That was your one job. A figurehead, to make people think that though things were tough they had a future if they stayed with us. And you failed. You couldn't even get the women to stay. I should have picked someone else to be Queen. Maybe I will. So, let's see. Well yes, why not. Bill Wright is actually Bartholomew Sholto, brother of Thaddeus and joint architect of the whole plot. Yes, that does work rather well. Did you know that American contact of yours was actually your brother? He had some lunatic idea that he could stop me. It doesn't matter now."

He took a step forward.

"So, the brothers Sholto ran this terrorist group," Quigley continued. "We're still unclear what their motives were. With ideological terrorism that is often difficult to decipher. On discovering that there was one last refuge of peace and democracy in the world, he came here. Seeking to destroy the place. And then… And then…" He nodded at the general. The soldier began to walk slowly around the room.

"Let's see," Quigley went on. "I think you destroyed the lab. Ruining forever any chance at recreating the vaccine. Of course, we'd have to do that at some point, and the lab has served its purpose. It gave everyone something to cling to. Well, your sabotage will give them something different. A thirst for revenge. So you destroyed the lab. That just leaves the doctor." He turned and nodded to the general who was standing just a few paces away from the doctor.

"I'll take that," the general said in a kind, soothing tone as he took hold of the doctor's rifle with his left hand. "We don't want to wake up the people outside. Not with any accidental gunfire." And in his right hand was a knife. He plunged it deep into the doctor's throat, stepping smartly backwards away from the spray of blood.

"Now, where was I?" Quigley continued as the body collapsed to the floor. "Ah yes, after you killed the doctor, you destroyed the research. Or was there a struggle first? Yes, I think that would be best." He took another step forward and pulled down the plastic sheeting. He was two paces away.

"And then, there was an interrogation." He took another step and then hit me in the face. "I found out where you came from, where your base was. I'll have to come up with a story about how you brainwashed a lot of the civilians. The women, at least, not that I think any of my men will care." He hit me again. I could taste blood. "We'll have a trial of course. Then hang you. First thing in the morning, I suppose. That's when it's meant to be done. A war crimes trial, for the worst criminal in history. Yes, yes, I think that will work for the history books. The final thwarting of the terrorist. Justice and revenge, the seeds of the nation's rebirth. That leaves just one loose end. How you killed the Queen."

I was going to fight. I just needed Quigley to hit me one last time. I'd seen a pair of scissors on the floor. One more punch and I'd fall over, grab the scissors and stab him, while he was still gloating. Honestly, after what I've been through, what I've had to do to survive these last six months, I think I stood a fair chance. Jen did not.

Her leg shot out as she grabbed at his wrist. I think she was trying one of those judo moves they teach in self-defence classes. I don't know if she'd fought anyone over the past few months. I doubt it. And she'd certainly forgotten that before he'd become a politician, Quigley had worked in covert operations. He flinched, slightly, as her foot kicked his calf, and batted her hand away. Her other hand clawed at his eyes. He ducked, twisted, grabbed, and threw her across the room.

She slammed head first into the glass cabinet containing the vials of the virus. The glass door broke. So did the vials. She fell to the floor surrounded by glass and liquid and blood.

"Interesting," Quigley said, calmly. He wasn't even out of breath. "Hold him," he added. My arms were grabbed and pinned behind me. I hadn't even noticed the guards approach. My attention had been on the pinpricks of blood dripping down Jen's hands and face.

Quigley took another step back. "Well, you are a cruel man, aren't you?" he said. "Not satisfied with just killing her, you wanted to infect her, too. My, my, what a lot of hatred you do have. She turned, naturally, and was shot. It was self defence," he paused. "I said she was shot. One of you, please?"

"Wait," I said. "Don't."

"Why not?"

That was a good question. It was because she might be immune. I wasn't going to say that to Quigley. Instead, my imagination working on overtime, I said, "The blood. My blood. Maybe it has something in it, the same thing that protects me, maybe that can be passed on. If I injected those samples the doctor took, my blood into hers, then perhaps she'd live."

"I don't think viruses work like that," Quigley said.

"The small pox vaccine did, didn't it? Jenner, cowpox and all that. Perhaps it won't work, but what if it does? It's got to be worth trying. Imagine if a vaccine was just that simple. Do you realise what that would mean? How easy everything would be?"

He hesitated. "Okay," he said slowly. "Try it."

I doubted it would work, in fact I don't think I believed it at all as I scrabbled around the floor for a syringe. All I could hope was that a few more minutes of life gave me a few more minutes to come up with some plan. I grabbed the samples, still cold from the fridge, scrabbled about for a needle, and injected them into her.

"That it? You done?" Quigley barked.

"What? Yes," I said, not standing up. I was scanning the ground, looking for those scissors, but they'd been kicked out of sight.

"She doesn't seem to be getting any better."

"She's got a concussion," I said. She might have done. I bent over her. Her pulse was weak, she was barely conscious, and I had no idea how much of that might be the virus, and how much was due to her injuries.

"Help her up," Quigley said. "Take them up to her room. If it doesn't work then we'll say he broke in and infected her as she slept. That will fit the story. Even better if he dies in there, too. There's poetic justice in that. It'll make a good cautionary tale for our children."

I think that's when I understood the true depth of his madness, but it was too late. Awkwardly, I carried Jen back up stairs, the guards behind. They closed the door to her room behind us, and locked us in. This time, I could hear them waiting outside.

Endings

"Bill?' she mumbled as I carefully laid her down on the bed.

"It's all right. It's going to be all right," I murmured. I tried to pick out the fragments of glass. It was futile. There were too many and they were too small. I gave up, and knelt on the bed next to her, her head in my lap, stroking her hair as I felt her heartbeat flutter. I knew she was dying and there was nothing I could do.

"Bill?"

"Hey Jen."

"They made me promise not to tell you."

"Tell me what?"

"Your brother... I went to my father... He... I left you the book... I thought you'd get the... I'm sorry."

"Me too," I said.

Then she died.

My mouth was dry. I tried to let go of her. I knew what was going to happen. I knew what I had to do. I couldn't do it. But I had to. She would come back and I had to kill her. The idea was so repellent I pushed the body away and staggered to my feet. Perhaps it didn't have to be me that killed her.

"She's died," I called out. "It didn't work."

There was no answer.

"Didn't you hear me?" I yelled. "I said she's dead. She'll come back. She'll turn. You need to come in here and finish it."

I waited. I wasn't sure an answer would come.

"Then you do it," a voice finally said.

I didn't know if I could. To start with I'd need a weapon, something heavy. That was something I could do. Find a weapon. And not think about what I'd have to do after that.

There was an old Victorian washbasin and water jug on the dresser. It was delicate, fragile, and useless. I opened the drawers. They were filled with nothing but clothes. I tried the wardrobe. More clothes, all silks and satins fit for a Queen. I lifted the chair. It was heavy, but too cumbersome to be used as a bludgeon and too sturdy to break.

Fear growing, I bent down and looked under the bed. Nothing. Of course not. Quigley had it all planned. He knew he'd have to get rid of her one day and he wasn't going to make his own life difficult. I cursed. Her door had been locked, hadn't it? I'd not thought what that meant. She'd been as much a prisoner as she'd been anything else, though no doubt he'd told her it was for her own protection.

I half lifted, half dragged the body off the bed and onto the floor by the chest of drawers. I had a vague notion of lifting it up and letting the heavy oak fall down on her skull. I gripped and pushed and pulled and managed to lift it two inches.

Frantic panic now replacing the last vestiges of reason, I went back to the wardrobe. The dresses hung from a brass rail. It was flimsy but there was nothing else. I tugged. I pulled. There was a ragged gasp behind me. I stopped. I turned. Jen had rolled onto her side.

"Jen?" Maybe I was wrong. Maybe she hadn't died. What did I know about illness and heartbeats?

"Jen?" I asked again, taking a step forward. She was on her knees now, her back to me. Her hands grasping at the carpet, her lungs grasping for air. She was alive! Perhaps it had worked. Perhaps, by some crazy lucky chance, I'd been right and my blood was all that was needed. Perhaps this was the answer. A genuine vaccine, and it would work for us and for everyone else on the planet. We could save so many. We'd all be safe. We'd—

She turned her head and I saw her face and I knew she was as dead as all of the others. Her eyes were flecked with grey, her mouth opened and closed with a snarling snap of teeth. Her left hand swung out towards me, clawing through air. The movement unbalanced her, and she fell back onto her side again. Her feet kicked and her hands clawed. The motion twisted her round, and brought her back to her knees so that she was facing me once more.

And all that time I didn't move. I couldn't. I couldn't believe the person I'd known so well, the girl I'd grown up with, the woman I'd loved, in my own way, had become this.

225

She lunged again, the movement brought her first to her knees, then to her feet, and her hand snaked out, her nails gouging the flesh from my hand. I hadn't even realised I'd been holding it out to her.

The sudden pain brought me back from the edge of shock. I stepped back just as she sent her right hand swiping forward. I skipped backward again. My legs banged against the bed. She lunged. One hand gripped and grasped at my shoulder, nails biting deep, pulling me towards her and down onto one knee.

"Jen, please!" It came out as a whisper, drowned out by the guttural rasp of air as she jerked first back and then forward, her teeth snapping towards my neck.

I got my left arm up. My forearm connected with her windpipe with a sickening crunch. She didn't notice. Her teeth kept snapping, her hands kept clawing and I knew there was only one thing that would stop her. Only one thing that could finally bring her peace. It was the hardest thing I have ever done and I think it destroyed some small part of me.

Ignoring the pain from my shoulder I pushed myself back up to my feet. I punched, twisted, and shoved until her grip loosened and I could pull myself free. I grabbed her arms and, with all the strength I could muster, lifted her from her feet. She struggled. I couldn't hold her. Together we fell in a heap onto the floor. Her hands were everywhere, tearing and clawing as her teeth kept snapping down.

I pushed her down, raised my fist and brought it down onto her face. The blow knocked her back. Her skull hit the carpet. I hit her again. And again, and finally I was free.

I got back to my feet.

I stamped down on her head.

And again.

She stopped moving.

She was dead.

I don't know how long I stood there. It was long enough for the bloody gore to stop pooling around her body. An hour. Perhaps two. Perhaps less. I couldn't say except that it was still dark outside when the door opened.

There was a grunt as a powerful light was shone down on Jen's corpse.

"Right," a voice said. The light shone on my face. "The Prime Minister wants to see you."

I didn't move.

"Now."

Quigley was in The Gallery, in the same chair he'd sat in at dinner. He wasn't alone. Behind him stood the general. Opposite was my brother.

"Sorry Bill," Sholto said as I walked into the room. His eyes widened as I walked into the pool of candlelight and he saw me properly.

"Turns out you did have some use," Quigley said. "You two can leave us," he added, and the two soldiers left the room.

"She's dead. Jen's dead. I killed her. I had to kill her with my hands because you—"

"Yes, yes," Quigley interrupted. "The big boys are talking, so why don't you just be quiet."

"The old man tricked you, Bill," Sholto said, "or he didn't tell you the whole truth. As soon as I realised you'd gone, I got it out of him. Not that it took much to work it out. He asked you to radio the submarine, to get it to surrender or stand down or something?"

"No, to get Jen to… to persuade them it was over," I murmured.

"Which, if you'd taken the time to think about it, was not going to happen," Sholto said. "He just wanted the submarine to break radio silence so the Vehement could find and sink it."

"Oh." I didn't care. It didn't seem to matter.

"We're doing a trade," the general said. "Your life for their submarine."

"Two nuclear powers was always one too many," Sholto said. "It's too dangerous. So one has to go and it doesn't matter which. If the old man had told us the truth, and not sent you out here on your own, then it would have been his I'd have tried to save. But he did, so it's Quigley who'll win. For now. He reckons he'll rule the waves. I say he's wrong. In five years, ten at the most, that submarine will have broken down. It'll be useless. But he wants ten years and I want an end to all of this. So I'm going to give him the Vehement. That's our deal. He gets our submarine, and we get to disappear."

"Yes, yes," Quigley said impatiently, "and now that you've seen that he's alive, can we get to it?"

"Wait," I said.

"What now?" Quigley snapped.

There were so many questions.

"Why did Prometheus even exist?"

"What do you think the word Strategic in Strategic Nuclear Weapon means?" Quigley said. "Where do you think the word comes from? If you have a deterrent you have to have a strategy to use it."

"But everyone had the same plan. Russia, China—"

"Well of course! What's the point of a deterrent if the other side doesn't know about it? Carrot and stick, that was our approach. The vaccine and Prometheus. The new way forward for the new millennia."

"Join us or die?" I asked.

"When has it ever been different? For God's sake man, we were the good guys. We were trying to save the world. You're stuck in some idealised version of an Orwellian fantasy. If you're looking for a devil in all of this look to him." He pointed at Sholto. "The man who rigged elections, the man who blackmailed senators and planned assassinations. Now, please, can we get on?"

"I've one more question," I said. I didn't know what was going to happen next, but I knew there would be no other chance to ask. "Why did you kill the evacuees?"

"Because," he said scornfully, "there was never going to be enough food for everyone. We couldn't trust them to stay at home and starve to death. They would all have gone out looking for food, beating at our doors, forcing a way in and bringing the infection with them. Some had to die so others could live. Not that it mattered in the end. It all fell apart. But England will rise again. She always does."

"But does that mean you had that poison already waiting? Was it stockpiled somewhere?"

"Oh, come on! Does every trifling detail matter?" he asked, addressing my brother.

"No," Sholto said, "let's finish this." He stood up and took a phone out of his pocket. It was a smartphone, but with a host of wires and a small black box plugged somehow into the back.

"Take it," he said, holding it out in front of him. "I've set up a receiver outside your perimeter. That'll relay the signal up to a satellite I've had waiting."

"How did you get hold of a satellite?" the general asked, as he stood up and walked towards my brother.

"Money and influence. Like Quigley said, I used to own senators. Type the following, 2, 3, 8, 9, 7…"

The general snatched at the phone, but the moment his fingers tapped at the screen, the windows filled with light, then shattered as the house was rocked with an explosion. I staggered, half falling.

So, I thought, was my brother. But what I thought was a stagger, was a lunge. His hand plunged forward, straight at the general's face. The general stopped moving. I saw why. The hilt of one of the knives from the silver dinner service was embedded through the man's eye.

Quigley was off balance, his hand moving to a pocket. I scrabbled around looking for a weapon, looking for something to throw. I didn't need to.

Even as the general began to collapse Sholto had moved forward, grabbing the pistol from the man's belt. The gun came up, pointing at Quigley.

Quigley saw it. He froze.

Sholto fired.

Quigley jerked back, his hands moving to his chest.

He collapsed.

Escape

Sholto straightened.

"Right," he said. "Right," he said again. He looked down at the two bodies, and then fired again, once into the general and again into Quigley.

"Right," he said, paused, then aimed the gun down and fired twice into Quigley's head. "Just to be sure, you understand. Now, Bill, look—"

The door opened. The two soldiers who had escorted me down from Jen's room came in. Sholto's hand came up. He fired. Twice. They both died.

I wanted to ask him what he was doing there, but the words that came out were, "Who the hell are you?"

"Look in a mirror and ask yourself the same question," he replied. "Now come on, here." He ran over to one of the soldiers, picked up a rifle and threw it over to me.

"Grab a coat. In this chaos it might give us an extra few seconds."

I started dragging off the coats. That's when I noticed that he'd shot both of the soldiers between the eyes. Exactly between the eyes.

"That was all over in less than a minute. Less than a half a minute," I said.

"I told you I'd been planning to kill Quigley for years. What exactly did you think those preparations had been for?"

"But he died not knowing why."

"You think I should have said that this was for our mother and father, or your lost childhood? What's the point of speeches? What good have they ever done? Now grab that coat and let's find the radio. Any idea where it'll be?"

"The generator was to the southeast," I said, trying to think. "There were cables and wires running up from a window to the flagpole. It's probably in the library."

"Library? Good. We need to send the message, then we can get out of here."

"Then that part was true?" I asked.

"That there's only room for one submarine in the Atlantic? Yes, that's

230

what the old man is after. Personally I'd rather they'd all been sunk, but if it's a choice between one and the other I'll pick the one that's on my side."

"You'll use a satellite—" I began, trying to keep up.

"There is no satellite. That's the same thermal explosive we used in the tunnel, mixed with some C-4 I got from Leon. We need to hurry. Which way's the library?"

I pointed.

"Good," he said. "Stay three paces behind. You've got the rear. I've got the front and sides. Is there anyone in the house we need to rescue? You said Jen was dead. Anyone else?"

"No, Jen's dead."

"Yes, I know," he said patiently. "But is there anyone else?"

"No. No. Quigley killed them all."

"He did know how to do a job thoroughly. Three paces. No more. No less. Keep looking behind. If you see anyone, then shoot first, because there are no questions this lot can answer."

Even under the circumstances, I inwardly groaned at that line.

We made it to the library unseen, and just before half a dozen uniforms ran past.

"They'll look outside first," Sholto said. "We've got ourselves about ten minutes grace." He walked over to the radio.

It wasn't at all what I was expecting. I suppose, when I thought about military radios, I thought about old war films, not something that was more keyboard and computer than dials and knobs.

"Let's see." He bent over the keyboard and began typing.

"The scientist wasn't here," I said.

"Of course he wasn't. Quigley would have killed him if he knew where he was. He was a witness. The last witness."

"The old man knew that? Then is he holding Kim and the girls hostage?"

"Of course not. They're perfectly safe."

"Then why did he lie to me?"

"Because it wasn't about you," Sholto said. "None of this was, not really. If you'd managed to persuade Jen, if she did have any power, then fantastic, there would be no need for any bloodshed. But he knew Quigley. Or knew his type. He knew the man would have to die, and he knew you couldn't do it. I could. And the easiest way of getting me here was to get you to come here so that I would follow."

"He didn't know you'd come," I said.

Sholto paused, and looked up. "Of course he did. I crossed the ocean, didn't I?" He turned back to the keyboard, and continued talking as he typed. "About an hour after you left he woke me up and told me where you'd gone. I won't say I was happy about it, but I left Kim to do the shouting. He gave you the address of a safe house and a route to take. I followed that route and went to that safe house. You didn't turn up."

"I didn't like the area."

"Yeah, well it was the wrong time to get picky. The old man thought that if we were just a few miles away, we'd try to get into this place. It's not his fault. Hell, it's no one's fault. I found your car and then I found the bike. But then I had to wait until dark, until no one in the balloon could spot me. I set the explosives and here I am, and… hang on. There." He straightened.

"Is it done?"

"Just wait a moment. Right, there it is. That's the confirmation. They've received a set of co-ordinates. They'll go there looking for the Vehement, and it should be waiting ready to sink it. If it's not, then that's the old man's problem, not ours. The job's done. What are you doing?"

"The virus, they have some of it downstairs. Taken from Lenham Hill."

"Really? I thought I got it all."

"You didn't," I said. "It's how Jen got infected. There might be some more left."

"So you're going to start a fire?"

"Yep." I ripped the pages from another book. "You got a problem with that?"

"Hardly. I think you've enough though."

232

I looked down. I was ankle deep in torn paper.

"Here." He pulled out a lighter and handed it to me.

I kicked the loose pages up against one of the teak bookshelves, bent down and paused. "Do you have a plan for what's next?"

"You mean our daring escape? I saw two helicopters when I was setting the explosives. I figure that's our best bet."

"There's no fuel."

"Oh."

"Do you have a plan B?" I asked, as I flicked the lighter.

"Not exactly, but in about a minute there's going to be another explosion, and that's going to rip a hole through the barricade to the south. At about the same time, give or take, and if we're lucky, the last of those incendiaries is going blow a hole through the outer wall. Factor in time, distance, and lurching speed, and we want to be long gone in an hour."

"I didn't see many undead out there, not when I arrived this morning. Yesterday morning," I amended.

"Well, I had to do something while I was waiting for night. I lured in as many as I could find. I thought it would be good cover for us."

"How many?"

"A few hundred. Probably more by now. Call it a thousand."

"Right." I counted to three. "So there isn't a plan B, then?"

"Forget a plan, and just set the fire," he said slowly. "And do it now, because like I said, we really, really need to escape."

It's not the act of burning books that is a desecration, but the motives behind why they are burned. This fire wasn't just to destroy my past but was a final ending to all that had brought our species low. Nothing would ever rise from those ashes.

I bent down, flicked the lighter and held it to the first page. It was from Great Expectations. It wasn't the scene where the house burns down, but you can't have everything.

"We should go," My brother said, gently pulling at my arm.

"Yes." I didn't move.

"Kim's waiting," he said gently. "Annette's mad at you. Daisy, well, she missed you. Kept looking for you when she woke up. She was quite upset. Babies can be like that. They're all waiting just a few hundred miles away and now it's time to go to them."

"Yes. Yes, alright." I stopped him when we reached the door. "We should wait for the other explosion," I said.

"Seriously?" he gestured towards the flames, now trailing up the bookshelves to lick at the ceiling.

"We should."

"Alright, then head south, down the main road. We can try to reach that car you brought."

"No. I've a better idea. The old paddock, on the east side of the house. We go through the kitchens. Out here, turn left, then right, then straight on through the small door."

"And then?"

And then there was an explosion followed by another a moment later. The sound was muffled and, with flames between us and the window, we could see nothing, but it was loud enough to carry through the stone walls.

"Timer didn't work properly," Sholto muttered. "Ready?"

"Let's go." I pushed the library door open and limped out in front.

The house was filling with smoke. Every window let in an orange glow from outside. Shots were fired, and I think some were fired at us, and I know some were fired back by my brother. I pointed the rifle at an occasional shadow, but I didn't pull the trigger. The shooting stopped just before we reached the kitchen. Two soldiers, filling a rucksack with food, barely gave us a glance as we ran past and out into the cool air.

The noise. That's what I'll remember about our escape. The sound of distant fires being drowned out as the one I'd set in the library slowly turned into an inferno to consume the house. Wood cracked, metal split, and bullets flew. None were aimed at us. Or at least I don't think so. Wearing those camouflage jackets, carrying those rifles, our silhouettes must have looked like everyone else. Trying to escape, trying to shore up their defences, or just trying to find out what had happened, the soldiers ran right past us without a second glance. Then they were gone and we were alone and at the edge of the paddock.

"The balloon? Seriously?" Sholto said doubtfully. I was out of breath, exhausted and he sounded as fresh as if he'd just woken up.

"Quick question, your plan was to take a helicopter. Do you actually know how to fly one?"

"Fly, yes. Yes, I know how to fly one."

I'd worked in politics too long not to notice the equivocation. "How about starting the engine and taking off."

"Well, I figured we could work that out. And I suppose you know how to fly a balloon?"

"I don't need to. Hot air rises. Then it's down to the winds. It'll get us out of here."

"And the landing?"

"Let's let gravity work that one out. Come on, before anyone else gets the idea."

Three people already had, and had already begun inflating the balloon.

"Don't fire," I yelled, half to Sholto, half to them. Perhaps they heard me, perhaps they didn't. A bullet whined through the air a foot from my head. There was the crack of a single shot, and the soldier collapsed. Another shot, then another, and Sholto was running ahead of me, the gun raised, firing a single shot with every other step. Half-heartedly I raised my own rifle, but I couldn't make out a target. I lowered it again and continued my stumbling skip towards the balloon. I was a hundred yards away when the bullets stopped. Seventy when he reached the balloon. Fifty yards away, when he turned back towards me, and I saw him raise his gun again. He fired and a bullet whistled past my ear. I half turned. There were shadows following us. Three or four, I'm not sure exactly.

Not bothering to aim, I fired from the hip. The gun let loose a long staccato burst. At some point the selector switch had been flipped to automatic. I don't know if I hit anyone. I doubt it. The magazine was emptied in seconds, the barrel ending up pointing straight up in the sky.

"Come on!" Sholto called out. I don't know if he was yelling at me or the soldiers or at the universe in general. I slung the rifle and limped, as fast as I could, towards him.

I reached the balloon, just as an explosion ripped through the house. Perhaps that was their fuel dump or an ammunition store or perhaps it was something else. I fell into the wicker gondola, and that was more or less it.

The canopy had enough hot air to give us lift, and the moment we started rising, the gunfire stopped. I think those soldiers realised they'd need all their ammunition just to get out of there alive.

"It's over," Sholto said. About five minutes had passed. He'd spent it working out how the burner worked, fiddling with it until we'd risen up, high above the grounds. I'd spent it staring down at the burning building I'd known so well. The fire was spreading. Indistinct dots of flame moved erratically on their own towards the house. It took a moment to realise these were the undead. Their clothing and bodies were burning. They were flaming death stalking the land.

There was another explosion, smaller this time, and part of the roof collapsed. I wanted to remember it all. All that it had been, and all that it had become.

"It's not over," I finally replied, "not yet."

"No? Quigley's dead and you're alive," he said, quite cheerfully. "And we've earned ourselves a boat ride anywhere we want. I say the U.S. There's just something about this country. The food, the weather, I don't know what it is, but the longer I spend here the more I just want to get away. You, me, Kim and the girls. We'll be one big happy family. What do you say?"

"No. Not yet. There's still the scientist," I said.

"That doesn't matter anymore."

"It does. To me."

"Look," he said, "if this is about you being immune, then there's a load of easier ways to find out—"

"No, it's not that," I said, finally turning my back on the inferno and slumping down onto the bench. "You shouldn't have killed Quigley."

"What? Why not?"

"I mean, not then. Not yet. There was one more question I didn't ask. Whether the virus was part of Prometheus or not. Was it deliberate? Did he set out to end the world, or not?"

"Seriously. You think that matters?"

"More than anything. The wind's carrying us south. We need to get to the Irish Sea. We might as well do that by going through Wales. Do you remember the scientist's address?"

"You really want to go there?"

"If not us, then who?" I said.

"Kim will be furious if we don't go straight back. Furious with me, I mean. You, you can make it up to her with flowers and chocolate, and maybe a night at the ballet. But me, I'll be in the doghouse for months. I tell you, Thanksgiving is going to be real fractious this year."

"It's Britain. We don't do Thanksgiving."

"Yeah, well, I do." He fished in his pocket, and pulled out a notepad. "Here. Annette made me promise, and I don't want to get in her bad books as well. She said she wanted to know what happened. For the journal."

Day 147, 10 miles east of Chester, English-Welsh border

19:00, 6th August

"The houses of the dead, that's all I ever see these days. Nice homes once filled with hopes, now just death and decaying memories." I was in a bad mood.

"Don't be like that. This is a nice little place." My brother wasn't. He was jubilant, and has been since we left Caulfield Hall.

The hot air balloon wasn't comfortable, and it's hard to sleep when there are only a few inches of wicker between you and a thousand foot drop. We couldn't steer it. We couldn't do much but let it drift through the night, occasionally tinkering with the burner.

It took three hours before the inferno at Caulfield Hall was finally lost to the horizon. Then there was nothing but the stars and the moon, and even they disappeared behind the clouds every now and then. It was terrifying when that happened. There was no ground, no sky. All we could see was each other's faces, illuminated yellow by the flames from the burner. A stray bullet, during our escape, had smashed the altimeter. When we couldn't see the ground we'd no idea of our height. I kept thinking we were going to crash, that we were plummeting downwards and the ground was just feet away. But then the clouds would clear and, by moonlight, we'd see the ground was still a thousand feet below us.

Then the horizon began to glow, and dawn arrived. The feeling is difficult to describe. I saw the world anew. For the first time, I saw what it had really become, this new world where humanity no longer rules.

The reddish silver reflection of dawn's early light on the canals and reservoirs, and the occasional grey ribbon of road, the tall shadows cast by empty buildings, these were there, but they weren't the dominant colours. I could ignore these last traces of man, and see how the world will be in a few short years. Green was taking over, except for where the land was scarred red-brown from the passage of the horde.

We drifted south, through the night and into the dawn until, around nine o'clock, the day began to warm and we began to lose height. It wasn't a sudden drop, just a gradual descent in line with the laws of physics.

We came down in a field, some hundred and fifty miles south, and thirty miles east, of Caulfield Hall.

The landing was… interesting. There were two zombies in the field. They didn't notice us until the basket hit the ground. We fell out, at about the same time as They began lurching towards us. Then an errant wind and the sudden reduction of weight caused the balloon to take off again, bouncing across the field, the undead in pursuit, until it came to a halt, the canopy caught in the trees at the field's edge.

It took a couple of hours to find bicycles and water, and then we cycled until it was too dark to see. We slept for a couple of hours, and set off again before dawn. The balloon carried us nearly a hundred and fifty miles, the bikes not much less. I should be tired. I'm not.

"Yeah, a nice little place," Sholto said. "Small, but not too small. With a great view. You can see for miles and there's nothing to see but fields and trees. It'd be a great place to settle in when this is over."

"I thought you'd got your heart set on going back to the U.S.?"

"Oh sure, I didn't mean this house," he said. "I meant one like it."

"What about the hordes?"

"I also meant when the zombies die. They will, you know. One day. Whatever's animating Them will stop. Then the world will be ours once more. When it is, I want a place like this. Somewhere I can see people coming."

There had been five people in the house. Five zombies. They had turned recently enough that one of Them was recognisable as the woman in the photographs arranged neatly on the piano. Who the others were, whether they were friends or family or strangers seeking sanctuary, I don't know.

"We'll reach the doctor's house tomorrow," Sholto said, as he sorted through the few half filled packets in the kitchen, trying to find something we could eat.

"Yup. In the afternoon I guess." I was searching through a stack of board games looking for a chess set to take back to Annette.

"He may not be alone. If he's still there, then he probably won't be," he said.

"No. No I suppose not."

"They'll be armed," he said.

"So are we."

We have the two rifles and plenty of ammunition. Back at the paddock, while he was waiting for me to limp my way up the hill to the balloon, Sholto had stripped the soldiers he'd shot of all their ammo.

"Okay, little brother, just stop that for a moment and look at me. Right. They will be armed. We're not going to win in a fair fight, so we're not going to start one."

"No, and I don't feel like another battle," I said.

"But we may not be able to reason with him. He may be just like Quigley."

"I don't mean we leave him be. I mean we go across to Ireland, we get Francois and Leon and the crew of that submarine and everyone else who knows how to fire a gun, and we come back in force. Perhaps that's what we should have done to start with. It's what we're going to do now."

"And if they won't come back over here with you?" he asked.

"They will. This is important. I'll make them understand."

Day 148, at sea

7th August

It turns out that I don't have to. Finding the coastal hamlet in which the doctor had his house was hard. Finding his house was easy. It was the one with the flags flying out front. The house was empty. The doctor wasn't in.

It wasn't a laboratory. It was just a Welsh country home bought with a London salary and a city-dweller's dreams of a country retreat. Judging by the mismatched furniture, empty wardrobes and cracked glass in the empty greenhouse, those dreams never became reality.

Taped to the kitchen counter was a map with directions to a boathouse at the bottom of the cliffs. Underneath that was a note that read:

"You are not alone. There are other survivors. The mainland is dangerous. We have found sanctuary. There's food here, take what you need, but only what you need. Leave what you can't carry and, please, leave the place tidy. Follow this map, and come and join us, on Anglesey."

"Anglesey," Sholto said.

"Not the Irish coast."

"Could be a coincidence," Sholto said.

"No, I can see two houses from this window that would be better places to hold up than this one. It doesn't even have much furniture. They picked this house for a reason. The only reason can be that they knew who lived here. The old man wasn't just wrong about the scientist not being at Caulfield Hall. He knew where he was all along. He lied about the scientist and he lied about a village in Ireland. I knew he was hiding something. I thought—"

"But if you'd gone on that boat and went to Anglesey," Sholto said, "maybe you wouldn't have wanted to go to Caulfield Hall. Then I wouldn't either."

"He wanted someone to do his dirty work."

"Sounds about right," he said. "A folk hero. That's what he called me. The thing about folk heroes is they always die before the end of the tale."

"Well, that's an unpleasant thought. But it doesn't matter."

"It doesn't?"

"Kim and the girls are on that island. That's where we're going."

We followed the route on the map, along the coastal path and down the cliffs. Just where it was marked, we found three boats, their fuel tanks full.

We're about three miles out from the shore. The sea is calm, the sun is shining and in another hour we'll reach Anglesey.

Day 149, Anglesey

8th August

The lie was much bigger than we'd realised. Moored to the shore of the Welsh island were more boats than I'd ever seen before in my life.

"It's the flotilla," I said. "The refugees from Ireland, from the UK, from Europe, the U.S., and everywhere else. This must be all of them. At least a thousand boats, and how many more are on the other side of the island?"

"How many people do you think that is?" Sholto asked.

"More than a few hundred. More than can fit on a few planes," I replied.

"Well, it figures the old man would have lied about that too. You see that? A light." He pointed. I thought I could just make out a flash.

"They've seen us, then," I said.

A few minutes later, a motorboat far larger than our dingy came roaring across the waves towards us.

"Welcome to Anglesey," the woman at the boat's helm said, throwing a rope to us. "Visitors, immigrants, and tourists, all are welcome. Tie the rope off, and I'll give you a tow."

As we got closer to the shore I could make out people on each of the boats. Families, couples, groups, no one seemed to be alone and no one paid us any attention. I suppose, given the number of people, new arrivals must be a regular sight.

There were two people waiting at the jetty, but they weren't waiting for us.

"Hurry up ashore, then," the older of the two said. "We've got to get that boat back."

And that was it. Sholto and I were left on the quay while the motorboat, with its two new passengers, set off back the way we'd come.

"Some welcome," Sholto said, as we looked around.

It was unlike any town or city I had ever been to. There were few people on the streets, and all of them seemed to be moving with a purpose. And they were all armed.

None gave us more than a curt nod or second glance. Most people, and most of the life, was on the boats. Sitting on deck chairs, tending window boxes, reading or talking quietly, it could almost have been a scene from before. Except for the silence. There was no music, no singing, no loud voices, and no sounds of machinery.

"Where should we start?" I asked.

"I'm betting we'll find the scientist at the centre of government."

"And where do we find that?"

"I think that finds us." He pointed. Coming down the road towards us was a small group. In the front was an old woman in a wheelchair and the old man. About a hundred yards away the woman said something and the group stopped. The old woman, with the old man pushing the chair, came the rest of the way alone.

"You ready for this?" Sholto asked.

"For what?"

I'd no idea what 'this' was going to be and Sholto didn't get a chance to answer.

"The brothers return," the woman called out from ten yards away, loud enough that the group down the road could here. "Welcome. Welcome to Anglesey. We've been expecting you. You'll have to excuse me if I don't get up." She smiled. I didn't smile back.

"Where's Kim?" I asked. "Where are the girls?"

"Well," she said, her voice now low so it wouldn't carry more than a few feet. "Kim's on the firing range, I think she's working out her feelings for you there. I did send someone to fetch her. As for Annette, where would you expect to find a thirteen year old at this time of day?" She paused, waiting for a reply. When it didn't come, she continued, "She's in school."

"And Daisy?"

"The hospital. But don't worry," she added hurriedly "she's just under observation. Doctor's orders. No one who arrives here is healthy and we've so few infants it's hard to know what's normal."

"I want to see them," I said.

"It's a free country."

"Glad to hear it," Sholto said. "So, you're the mayor then?"

"That's right," the old woman said.

"What happened to the submarine?" Sholto asked.

"Theirs? The Vehement sunk it," George Tull said. "Took a hit though. Sophia's trying to tow it back. Not sure it's going to make it."

"Good," my brother said.

"And the power station, can't you start it up now?" I asked. "Or was that another lie too?"

"A lie?" The mayor glanced up at the old man. "The power station will come back on, but it's not as simple as flipping a switch. It'll take a few days."

"Oh."

"You're really the mayor?" Sholto asked.

"And this really is a democracy," she said. "We're holding elections again in November. We want to get them out of the way before Christmas. You can stand if you want. I don't know if I will. I was a compromise candidate. Not quite British, not quite not. Certainly not military, and equally certain not to live long enough to become a tyrant."

I said nothing. Neither did anyone else, and for a moment the silence stretched.

"You lied to us," I finally said.

"Sorry about that," the old man said, not sounding apologetic in the slightest. "Was there any lie in particular that's bothering you?"

"To start with, there are more than a few hundred people here."

"There's more than a few thousand," he said. "The moment I saw you, I knew who you were. I knew what you might be able to do for us. I didn't think it was wise to send you into the lion's den with all our secrets. Just in case."

"This isn't some Irish village," I said.

"No."

"And that plan you talked about? Belfast airport, that was a lie too?"

"Not exactly. There's no leaving here. There are too many of us, and nowhere left to go. This is where we stand. But we do want to get to that airport. We want the helicopters. Noisy beasts, we'll go over, fill up full and fly over here. We can just about make it. And then—"

"So Donnie knew?" For some reason I'd thought that the young man was innocent in all this.

"Of course," George said. "I told him to tell you the story. Essentially it's the same story we tell anyone we meet on the road that we're not sure of."

"And then, these helicopters? You're going to buzz the undead?" I guessed. "You'll lure Them all away somewhere?"

"And then burn Them all," the mayor said. "That's our grand plan."

"Quigley's dead," I said. "So is Jennifer Masterton." I looked down at my blood-stained clothes. I'd not even bothered looking for something to change into. "What would you have done if it hadn't worked? If we'd not come back?"

"Those APCs in that car park that Donnie told you about, we'd have driven them up to Northumberland," George said. "We'd have stormed Caulfield Hall and burned it to the ground. Mister Mills would have gone out looking for that submarine, and we would have just had to hope he found it."

"But instead you got to use us," Sholto said.

"Two lives instead of two hundred," the old man said. "It was a risk I thought worth taking. And I was right, wasn't I?"

I no longer cared.

"Where's the scientist? I've come this far. He's here. I know it. I want to see him."

"Okay," the mayor finally said. "You want to see Doctor Singh? This way, then."

It took five minutes.

"You keep him in a school?"

"*The* school," George said, "I was telling the truth there. Not many kids made it out. They've got a couple of classrooms, we use the rest to run the government.

"The school, the parliament, and the prison, all in one place. Efficient," I said.

"Who said it was a prison?" the mayor asked, as she was wheeled up the ramp. One of her assistants opened the door.

"After you," she said.

I stepped inside, and was stopped almost immediately by the long list of names pinned to the wall. The handwriting was small. The wall was long.

"We keep a note of everyone who makes it this far," she explained. "Over there," she pointed at a smaller list on the opposite wall. "They're the people who've left. Some go back to the mainland, some go further. They're the people with unfinished business. The people for whom guilt, love, or duty won't let them give up hope, no matter how small."

"And the maps?" Sholto asked. They were pinned next to that short list. One was a world map, on the wall next to it were pages from atlases, road maps, and some hand drawn sheets.

"Where we know, or think, other survivors are. Your Annette's added places from your journal to it."

And I didn't care about that, either.

"Where's the doctor?" I asked.

"Classes are to the left, the doctor is kept to the right. He's not dangerous, of course, but I don't want him upsetting the children."

I glanced to the left and saw that where the list ended, the corridor was covered in crayon and pencil drawings. It was a universe of yellow suns and two-dimensional houses amidst occasionally skilled watercolours. To the right, the corridors were bare.

I walked along the corridor, the others following behind, turned a corner and was confronted by a man at a desk covered in circuit boards. He looked vaguely familiar, though I couldn't quite place him.

"Hello Rahinder, how is he today?" the mayor asked.

"The same. Working," the man, Rahinder, replied, carefully putting down a soldering iron.

"These gentlemen would like to see him," George said.

"This is them, is it? The spin-doctor and his American brother?" he gave a searching look, his eyes lingering on the rifles. "You can leave those here."

246

I made no move to put the rifle down.

"Do I know you?" I asked him.

"I doubt it." He stood up and moved to the middle of the corridor, his arms crossed.

"Let them pass, Rahinder. They won't do any harm. He's up there. In one of those classrooms."

I moved past the almost familiar man, and along the corridor. There were classrooms either side, built back to back so that the doors to four of them were close together. These four classrooms all had bolts on the doors. I took another step closer and looked through the reinforced glass window. The desks, bookshelves, and all the other furniture had been removed. The floor was covered in the type of rubber mats used in gymnastics to cushion a fall. The windows had been painted over. Light came from ceiling lamps. Against the walls, and in front of the windows was a nearly continuous row of blackboards. Standing in front of one, almost directly opposite us, was a man wearing nothing but a pair of blue shorts. He held a piece of chalk in a hand missing two fingers.

"Do you have any idea how hard it is to find chalk?" It was Rahinder, I'd not realised he'd followed us. "Actually," he added, his voice soft and low, "the hardest part was finding the blackboards. We can't give him pens. Or pencils. Or paper. You can't cut yourself on chalk. But we needed enough for four classrooms. He doesn't sleep, you see. He just writes. All day and all night. Every day and every night. When he finishes, I take him to the next room, then I photograph what he's done."

All of the blackboards to the left of the doctor were full of an illegible scrawl. The ones to the right were blank.

"What's he writing?" Sholto asked.

"We don't know. Maybe it means something, maybe it doesn't. I don't know how much of him is left. I take the photographs and other people look through them."

"Not you?"

"I'm not a biologist or a chemist. I repaired televisions and washing machines and all those other little household marvels for a living. My brother was the one with the brains."

247

"Your brother?" Then I realised where I thought I'd seen Rahinder before. He looked almost identical to the man I'd seen in that video of Lenham Hill. Though he bore almost no resemblance to the clean but unkempt man in his padded classroom-cell.

"I found him in his house a few days after the evacuation," Rahinder Singh went on. "My wife and I decided not to go, not to trust the government, but went to his house in Wales instead. We brought some friends with us, but… It was a hard journey. I arrived alone. I found him there. If I hadn't, I don't know if I would have had a reason to go on. He wasn't like this then. He talked. He talked all the time. About New York, about the laboratory, about the experiments and the trials. He talked about Quigley and the secret orders, and about New York and that final trial that went wrong."

"He talked? Then can he answer questions?"

"Not now. I think it's the lack of sleep. I think it's killing him. Now, when he speaks, it is only in equations and formula, and I don't think they make sense."

"But he told you about the trials? About the virus?" I asked.

"About the vaccine? Yes."

"Was it real? Did it actually work?"

"Oh yes, it was real. And it almost worked. There is one unfortunate side effect to it, though."

"The undead?"

"Exactly."

I realised that I'd asked the wrong question.

"Did he know that?" I asked. "When Quigley took him to New York, did they know what would happen?"

"I almost wished they did, that would be far better than the truth," Rahinder said sadly. "From what he said when he was lucid, the project had money but most of it was spent on security. He was the only real scientist working there. The only one good enough to actually make this fantasy of curing the world's ills real. He'd taken the dead-end work of two generations of scientists and made it work. He ran trials. They were successful. But they were only on animals. You've seen animals out there?

This contagion, it doesn't affect them. Then there were the human trials. Five of them. Five people, not five sets of trials, you understand. Disappearing even five people in Britain is hard enough. None of those five suffered any adverse effects."

"Were they cured?"

"They had chronic conditions. They didn't seem to get any worse, and there wasn't time to find out if they would get any better because Quigley saw the report and took it to mean that this super-vaccine worked. He couldn't risk waiting until after another election when it might be someone else who got the credit. He set up the demonstration in New York. My brother still wasn't satisfied. He wasn't sure it was safe. So he injected himself. And that made six. Six people. All of them were immune. What are the odds? I suspect they are about the same as picking a group of patients for the trial in New York and finding that they all turned into the undead. Luck. That's what brought about the end of the world. Bad luck, and decades of hubris and petty jealously projected onto the international stage by people who rated the pursuit of power above their own humanity. That is what caused all of this. What he did has driven my brother mad. And that knowledge, one day soon, will kill him. I know why you've come. Why you are here. You are not the first. Now you've seen him, do you still want your revenge?"

"He's no different to me. Or you," I said to Sholto. My brother just shrugged. He had a thoughtful expression I'd not seen him wear before.

"Tell me one thing," I said to Rahinder. "Your brother, and everyone else who is immune. Are we carriers?"

"No. From what we can tell it doesn't work that way. He didn't know that. We had to work that one out for ourselves. It was an interesting experiment. We've whole families here where someone was bitten and infected and then locked up or chained down because no one was able to do the merciful thing. Mercy, ha! How meanings change. Do you want your revenge then?" he asked again.

"What would be the point?" I looked over at my brother.

"Let's get out of here," he said, "and find somewhere we can call home."

Epilogue

Anglesey

12th August

Day 153

Happy endings only happen in fairy tales and this world is certainly not one of those.

Daisy is still in the hospital. We don't know what, if anything, is wrong with her. We just have to hope she'll recover.

Annette is finally confronting all the horrors that she encountered out there. She can't sleep inside the house, but only up on a shelter we built her on the roof. When she does sleep, she screams. We just have to hope that will pass, too.

We have a house, but it's not a home, at least not a permanent one. There are too many people on this small island, and soon there are going to be more. A radio signal was received yesterday from the USS Harpers Ferry. It's a hospital ship, dead in the water down in the South Atlantic. The plan to collect the helicopters has been put on hold as all efforts go into rescuing the crew, patients, and passengers.

That has delayed Thaddeus's departure, at least for now. He still wants to return to America. He lasted twelve hours before he became restless again, and he spent six of those asleep. He's taken with the idea of extending the safe house network across the Atlantic. But he can't, not until the Santa Maria returns from its rescue mission. So, for now, we are all together.

As for Kim and I, perhaps we'll get a happy ending and perhaps we won't. I'm looking forward to finding out.

I started writing this back when I thought my story was important, when I thought I was important. I was wrong. If there is a hero in all of this, then it was my brother and by his own admission he failed.

Back in that room in London, when I was a different person, I thought that this journal might become the first chapter in a new history. Now it is finished, if it becomes anything, then it will be as a footnote in the last chapter of the tale of our old world. That's fitting, because I was never more than a pawn, my path dictated by the unseen plans of others. But that is over, my life is now truly my own.

Something new is beginning here on this small island. Perhaps it will be better, perhaps it won't, but for this journal, this is definitely the end.

Printed in Great Britain
by Amazon